THE ICED COFFEE COMETH

My driveway was empty of all but my Escape. It was also late enough that all the lights in the neighborhood were off, including Caitlin's, so it wasn't her playing her guitar that had woken me.

I was about to step back into the house when I noticed a single sheet of paper fluttering against my front door.

A wooden-handled knife was holding it into place.

I blinked at it incomprehensively at first, not quite sure what I was looking at. My brain supplied an inane "How did that get here?" and then my heart started racing. Someone had been to my house. Someone with a knife.

Without thinking, I snatched the page off the door, leaving a chunk stuck to the knife, which was still jammed into the wood. I scuttled back into the house and slammed the door closed, locking it in one swift motion.

I didn't need to read the words on the page to know it was a threat, but read it I did.

If you know what's good for you, you'll stop interfering. This is your first and only warning . . .

Books by Alex Erickson

Published by Kensington Publishing Corp.

Death By Iced Coffee

ALEX ERICKSON

Kensington Publishing Corp.
www.kensingtonbooks.com

KENSINGTON BOOKS are published by

Kensington Publishing Corp.
119 West 40th Street
New York, NY 10018

All Kensington titles, imprints, and distributed lines are available at special quantity discounts for bulk purchases for sales promotion, premiums, fund-raising, educational, or institutional use.

Special book excerpts or customized printings can also be created to fit specific needs. For details, write or phone the office of the Kensington Sales Manager: Attn.: Sales Department. Kensington Publishing Corp., 119 West 40th Street, New York, NY 10018. Phone: 1-800-221-2647.

The K and Teapot logo is a trademark of Kensington Publishing Corp.

First Printing: May 2023
ISBN: 978-1-4967-3667-3

ISBN: 978-1-4967-3668-0 (ebook)

10 9 8 7 6 5 4 3 2 1

Printed in the United States of America

1

Sweat dripped from my face as though I'd just walked through a rainstorm. The sun beat down upon me with a relentless heat that sucked the air straight from my lungs. All I wanted to do was go inside and find a tub of ice to curl up in, but I couldn't. I'd made a promise, and despite how miserable I was feeling, I intended to keep it.

The inaugural Pine Hills marathon had yet to begin, but people were already dropping like flies. When I'd first arrived, there had to have been at least a hundred people here, ready to run. Now, after only fifteen minutes, we were down to maybe sixty, and from many of the expressions and complaints, I expected we'd lose a dozen more before we started.

"We can do this."

Another runner stood next to me, looking as miserable as I felt. She was Black, extremely pretty, and nearly a foot shorter than me, which was saying something, considering my less than stellar height.

"Cassie Wise." She stuck out a hand.

I shook. "Krissy Hancock. I hope you're right. This heat is something else."

Cassie glanced toward the sky. "When I woke up this morning, I felt so good, I was pretty sure I'd make it through today, no problem. Now I'm worried."

"Me too." Though, since I wasn't much of a runner in the first place, I wouldn't be too disappointed if the marathon were to be canceled. If it weren't for the fact that it was for a good cause—and for my promise—I would have dropped out already.

"How are you feeling, Krissy?" I turned to find my current boyfriend and town's police officer, Paul Dalton, watching me with concern. He was in full uniform as he was working security for the marathon. He nodded a greeting to Cassie as he approached.

"Very nice," she whispered before taking a couple steps away to give Paul and me privacy.

I had a feeling I was going to like her.

"I'll be fine." I held up my water bottle, which was already lukewarm, despite all of the ice I'd put in it. "I'm going to keep hydrated."

"Rita would understand if you dropped out. It's too hot for this." Paul took off his hat and fanned himself, though it didn't appear to help. Considering I felt overdressed in shorts and a T-shirt with the sleeves rolled up and a number 138 pinned to my chest, he had to be downright miserable in his long pants and stiff uniform shirt.

"Where is Rita, by the way?" I asked, glancing around. My friend, Rita Jablonski, wasn't running, but she had promised to be here to show support since I was taking part at her behest.

"I'm not sure." Paul wiped his arm across his forehead with a glance toward the sky. "I'll keep an eye out and let her know you're looking for her."

"Thanks." If Rita had stayed home in the heat, I was *so* not going to be happy.

"I'd best make the rounds. This heat is sure to shorten some fuses."

"Good luck."

Paul waved and then melted into the crowd. Half the Pine Hills police force was here, not because they expected any sort of major trouble, but Paul was right; with heat like this, tempers often flared. Already, I'd seen one near scuffle between two women fighting over a sliver of shade.

I turned back to find Cassie, but she was talking to another woman who looked ready to pass out, and I didn't want to intrude. Instead, I wandered over to a small tent that had been set up for runners and rooted around in my bag for sunscreen. I'd already applied it once, but I was sweating so much, I was certain most of it had come off by now.

"Have you even seen the route?"

The angry tone caught my attention as I squirted a glob of white sunscreen into my palm. The man was red in the face, and it wasn't solely from the heat. He might have been good-looking, but it was hard to tell for sure with his face twisted in rage.

"It'll be fine, Glen," said a tall man with thick legs, thin arms, and a potbelly tucked into a threadbare tank.

"Fine?" The angry man, Glen, scoffed. "Do *you* want to run up those hills, Calvin? I sure as hell don't. You don't route a marathon through hills."

"This *is* Pine Hills," a Black man with a near-gray beard and bald head replied in a tone of voice that suggested he was used to Glen flying off the handle.

"And there are perfectly flat roads between and around these hills." Glen gestured toward our starting point, which, while not entirely flat, wasn't hilly either. "I swear, Trevor, you of all people should be throwing a fit. You'll never make it through this thing with your knees."

Trevor flexed said knees, which were encased in a pair of braces. "They haven't let me down yet," he said, though he did shoot a nervous glance toward the starting line.

"I should give Maxwell a piece of my mind." Glen turned his angry red glare toward a small gathering of people I assumed contained Rod Maxwell, one of the organizers of the marathon, though I couldn't see the short man among the group from where I stood. "He knows better than to run a marathon in the middle of a heat wave."

A jangle of music had Calvin jumping nearly out of his skin before he snatched a phone from the bag next to him. "I've got to take this." He hurried away before anyone could stop him.

"This marathon is going to be the death of all of us," Glen said, continuing his rant. "They should have postponed it, altered the route. *Something*."

I had to admit, I was kind of with Glen on this one. When I'd first seen the marathon route, which started near the hilly portion of town but not actually on the hills, I considered dropping out right then and there. The marathon would send us past my bookstore café, Death by Coffee, all through downtown, and then back through the hilly residential segment of Pine Hills. Just over twenty-six miles was already asking a lot. Sending us up and down hills in the middle of summer was downright cruel.

Trevor's face went serious, and he started to say something to Glen, but before he could, Glen shouted at someone else and marched away, leaving Trevor standing there alone. He stared after his friend with a frown, and then he walked off in the other direction.

I realized I was still holding my dollop of sunscreen and quickly ran it over my arms before it could melt away. I noted hugs and concerned expressions among the runners and their loved ones. I was starting to feel like we were in *The Running Man* and only one of us would survive to the finish.

Maybe Paul is right and I should drop out. No one would accuse Krissy Hancock of being in running shape. I didn't exercise, despite promising myself I would start nearly every other day. Something more interesting, and less exhausting, always came up.

I was shoving the sunscreen bottle back into my bag when I noticed movement near where the trees met a pair of storage sheds.

The woman I didn't know, nor could I get a good look at her since she vanished behind the sheds almost as soon as I saw her. I'd caught a glimpse of blond hair, dark clothing, and then she was gone. The man, however, I recognized.

Johan? I frowned. Johan Morrison was Rita's boyfriend, though that was most definitely not Rita he was with now. Johan ducked his head as he followed after the woman, and in seconds of me noticing him, he too was gone.

"What are you up to?" I muttered. I'd never taken to Johan, despite how happy he seemed to make Rita. There was just something about the man that bothered me. The way he stared vacantly ahead. The small, almost knowing smile he always gave me.

And now, here he was, sneaking off with some other woman.

There's probably a perfectly good explanation for it. Just because I didn't like Johan didn't mean he was doing anything untoward.

"Oh, my Lordy Lou, it's hot." I jumped about a foot in the air and turned to find Rita standing next to me in a dress that hid much of her shape. She wasn't looking toward where Johan had gone, so I could only assume she hadn't seen him. "Can you believe this?" She was holding a handheld electric fan that was making an awful buzzing sound, as if it was seconds from short-circuiting. "I'm glad I don't have to run in this."

I gave Rita a flat look, which she completely missed—or ignored.

"It's not the turnout I expected," she went on, glancing around the rapidly dwindling number of runners in the tent. "But I suppose it can't be helped. And to think there are still people out there who insist there's no such thing as global warming. Look at this! It's hotter than I can rightly remember, and we're not even into the worst months yet."

"Maybe we should talk to the organizers and get it called off," I said.

Rita looked stricken. "Over a little heat?" She waved off my concern. "I'm sure you and the rest of the marathoners will be fine. I talked to Rodney, and he assured me there are drink stations set up throughout. He won't let anything happen to anyone. I even saw a few doctors milling about, so if someone does pass out, they'll be taken care of right away."

That didn't reassure me, but there was no sense in pressing the point. If Rod Maxwell and the other two organizers—women I didn't know—wanted to hold the marathon, they were going to do it, no matter what I had to say.

But there was one thing I would be remiss if I didn't mention.

"Hey, Rita," I swallowed, nervous about bringing up Johan, but needing to do it. "Just before you came over, I thought I—"

Before I could finish, alarmed shouts erupted behind me as a scuffle broke out. I turned, like everyone else, to see what was going on.

It wasn't hard to figure out. Glen had Rod Maxwell pressed against one of the tent's supports, shirt balled up in his fist. Trevor was trying to pull Glen off the smaller man, but to no avail.

"You're trying to kill us!" Glen shouted, spittle flying from his mouth. "To kill me!"

Rod pressed a hand to the side of Glen's head and pushed, but the other man refused to relent.

"Oh, dear," Rita said, hand fluttering to her chest, all while watching the fight with rapt fascination. I had a feeling she'd be on the phone with her gossip buddies as soon as the fight ended.

"Admit it!" Glen pressed his face close to Rod's own. "You thought you were being so sneaky, but I know what you're trying to pull. I won't cave, not to you, not to them, not to anyone."

"Come on, let him go, man," Trevor said, still vainly trying to pry his friend away from Rod. "The cops are coming."

Trevor was right; Paul was working his way through the gathering crowd, toward where Glen had Rod pinned.

Glen snarled and then stepped back, releasing Rod's shirt as he did.

"It's all right," Rod said, making a "calm down" gesture with his hands as soon as he was back on his own two feet. "The heat is just getting to everyone. We all just need to cool off a little bit."

"You know it's more than that," Glen spat, jabbing a finger toward Rod. "And I'll tell everyone about it if you don't take me seriously."

"Come on." Trevor's grip was tight as he led Glen away. "That's enough."

Rod watched them go with a worried expression that vanished the moment Paul approached him. "I'm fine," he said. "We're all fine. Mr. Moreau and Mr. Conway and I were just talking." He managed to smile, though I could tell he was shaken by the encounter. "How about we get this thing started?"

"Good luck, dear," Rita said, touching my arm and then hurrying away, toward a covered area set aside for those who wished to watch the start of the marathon. Like the drink stations, there were many such areas set up throughout the route. It would allow spectators to keep an eye on their loved ones while standing in the shade.

The runners who decided to tough it out—me included, though I was already regretting it—headed for the starting line. There was no set order to the start, so most of us just milled about under the heat while we waited for Rod and the other organizers to get things started.

Cassie stepped up next to me and gave me a smile that hinted at the misery to come. "Here goes nothing, I suppose."

"Good luck," I told her. I had a feeling both of us would need it.

A moment later, Rod stepped up to face us at the front of the line.

"Welcome, everyone, to the first-ever Pine Hills marathon," he said, raising his hands above his head. "I want to personally thank everyone for coming—runners, workers, and spectators all. We're here for a good cause. I lost my mother to cancer. I hope that soon, with all of our help and donations, we will lose no one else."

A smattering of applause met that. Rod clapped along with it, eyes darting over us, never landing on any one person for more than a heartbeat. I got the distinct impression he was searching for someone before he continued.

"I know it's hot and we're all anxious to get this thing started." He paused, arms raised once more, and then he shouted, "So, let's do this thing!"

A half-hearted cheer went up as Rod stepped aside. Someone handed him a flare gun, which he aimed at the sky. A beat passed, and then he pulled the trigger.

We moved as if we were made of molasses. I caught a glimpse of Paul out of the corner of my eye and shot him a wave as I slumped ahead with the rest of the overheating runners. He waved back, and then I turned my focus to the road ahead.

The first leg of the marathon wasn't as bad as I expected it to be. I kept my mind focused on putting one foot in front of the other, on breathing in and out. The steady *pat-pat-pat* of feet on pavement had a rhythm to it that was easy to get lost in. I didn't try to press, knowing that winning meant little. Just finishing was winning in my book, and I was determined to make it to the end, even if I had to crawl the last mile on hands and knees.

Cassie remained at my side, keeping pace with me, though I was pretty sure she could have gone faster without winding herself. I would have talked to her if I dared speak, but I feared that I would trip over my own two feet if I so much as opened my mouth. Cassie seemed likewise focused, though I did get a wink from her.

And then everything narrowed.

The only thing that mattered was the road in front of me. Some runners drifted ahead, while others fell behind. I didn't fall to the back, as I expected, but managed to hover somewhere near the middle of the pack. My ears were ringing, and breathing was becoming difficult. Time passed, but I had no idea how much. Minutes. Hours. It was all the same to me.

Just breathe.

I was vaguely aware of people slowing and stopping around me. One skeletally thin man fell to his knees, muttering, "I can't do this" over and over again. I considered stopping to see if he needed assistance, but before I could, Paige Lipmon, my doctor, stepped from a golf cart keeping pace with the main pack and made straight for him.

By the time we reached Death by Coffee, at least a dozen runners had dropped out, if not twice that. My hair was plastered to my face, and my shirt felt as if it weighed a hundred pounds. Even my shoes felt squishy with sweat, but I refused to quit.

A faint cheer made me look up as we passed the store. My friend, and the co-owner of the bookstore café, Vicki Lawyer, stood outside with her husband, Mason, waving. I was too exhausted to return the wave, but I did manage a nod of appreciation. I could just make out a handful of customers inside the blessedly cool air-conditioning of Death by Coffee and longed to be among them.

I fell back into my zone, pausing only when we passed a drink station so I could take a sip of some sort of unmarked energy drink. I didn't drink too much, knowing I'd make myself sick from it sloshing around in my stomach, but I did need to keep hydrated.

Waves of heat rose from the pavement, and I found myself fascinated with the way everything seemed to vibrate. It was either a by-product of the heat or I was about to pass out. At that point, either one was just as likely as the other.

This was a bad idea. My head started pounding, and my mouth and throat were dry. My next drink didn't want to go down, and I feared I might be sick all over myself, but I somehow managed to swallow it before I continued on, around a curve, and toward the path that would lead us into the hills, which were shaded by hundreds of trees.

Just make it there, and I'll be fine. The shade will make it easier. The hills would be another story, but I'd deal with them when I came to them.

Cassie was panting next to me, sweat coating her entire body.

Dizzy, and with legs burning with a heat that threatened to eat me from the inside, I pressed on. My shoulder started aching in a deep-bone way that made me realize it wasn't fully healed from an encounter I'd had a few months back with a crazy killer who'd tried to take me out in my own home. Every step caused it to jar, and each time I moved my arm, spikes of dull pain shot through my shoulder.

I slowed, unable to keep up the pace. Cassie glanced back but didn't slow down. I had a feeling that if she did, she'd come to a stop, and the race would be over for the both of us.

The crowd of runners had thinned considerably, and I didn't remember losing most of them. I felt half-delirious, unable to tell exactly where I was. It took me a moment to realize I'd come to a near stop. I blinked, confused. I barely remembered slowing. When I tried to resume a quicker pace, my legs refused to obey. I thought someone called my name, but the ringing in my ears drowned nearly everything out.

"Somebody help!"

Now, that caught my attention.

My head jerked upright, and a wave of nausea washed through me as the world snapped back into focus. The shout had come from ahead, inside the bend of trees where the blessed shade awaited.

"Please! Help!"

I started running.

Okay, it was more of a shamble as I made for the source of the shout. I had enough wits about me to realize that the person who shouted was male, and that his voice had come not from the marked path ahead, but slightly off to the left. I veered off, toward a bike path that wound through the woods, not quite parallel to the marathon route, and came to an abrupt halt when I saw what awaited me.

A small crowd had gathered, maybe four, five people, though my vision was swimming enough that it looked closer to ten. They were all looking down, just off the bike path, toward where a pair of running shoes stuck out from the brush. It took my brain a moment to realize those shoes were currently being worn by someone lying half on, half off the path.

And kneeling down next to the shoes, eyes wild with panic, was Trevor and his knee braces.

"Is someone here a doctor?" he asked, voice cracking. "It's my friend. I . . . I think he's dead."

2

My head was pounding with such an intensity, I wanted to throw up. This wasn't a normal, everyday headache. The sun, the exercise . . . it was all too much for my poor, out-of-shape body to handle. I was almost thankful when the police sent those of us hovering around the scene away while they, along with the doctors on site, tried to figure out what had happened to Glen Moreau, the owner of the shoes that had been sticking out of the brush.

With how I was feeling, and how red in the face Glen was, even before we'd started to run, I had a pretty good idea what might have done him in.

I was sitting in Death by Coffee, an untouched iced coffee on the table in front of me. As soon as I'd come in, Eugene, a lanky new hire who was still in the trying-too-hard stage of his employment, had delivered the coffee to where I'd collapsed. I was parched, but I feared the coffee might interact poorly with my already dehydrated system. I wanted a water in the worst way but was too far away to get it myself.

At least, that's what my jelly-filled legs were telling me.

"You look terrible." Vicki sat down across from me, materializing from the black void growing around my vision like a specter. She slid a cup across the table with the tips of her fingers. A peek inside told me she'd read my mind.

"I feel terrible." I gulped a mouthful of blessedly cold water, which instantly wanted to come right back up. I clenched my teeth, refusing to let it.

Vicki leaned across the table and put her wrist against my forehead, much like my mom used to do when I was a kid. Up close, her features were distorted, as if I was looking at her through cellophane. She was still gorgeous, with her movie-star looks and perfect hair, though she did appear a bit fuzzy around the edges.

"You're burning up."

"I feel cooked."

"No, it's more than that." She sat back with a frown. "You really should go home and lie down. Or, better yet, see a doctor."

"I'm fine." Though I felt a long way from fine. I raised the cup of water and pressed it against my forehead. I expected it to steam, but all it did was make my headache worse, so I lowered it again. "I'll feel better after I sit here for a little bit."

"Can Paul drive you home?" Vicki asked. "Or should I?"

"It's not necessary. Besides, Paul's kind of busy right now." I blinked, and my eyes wanted to stay shut. They felt both dry and gummy, and I had strain to open them again. "Someone died."

Vicki sat back, eyes going briefly wide. "At the marathon?"

My nod was slow, so as not to make my headache worse. "I think he passed out from the heat. He wasn't on the marked path, which was probably why no one got to him in time."

"That's terrible." Vicki glanced out the large plate-glass window. The flags that served as route markers were still in place, hanging limp, but there was no one on the road. "Did you know him?"

"Not really." I thought back to the angry man, how he'd snapped at nearly everyone he talked to, and felt nothing but sad. I should have known then that the heat was too much to run in. The organizers should have stepped in and stopped it. "I saw him before the marathon started, but not after. He must have gotten lost."

Delirium could do that. I know I'd been feeling pretty rough by the time I'd reached the point where Glen had been found.

I was actually kind of surprised that word hadn't spread about his death, but then again, the bookstore café was pretty quiet. Nearly everyone in town had been involved in the marathon in some capacity. They were either running, watching, or had helped set everything up. Even those who worked had come out to watch us when we'd run through downtown before heading back to their jobs.

I looked toward where Eugene stood behind the counter, eyes half-closed. He always appeared as if he was seconds from falling asleep, even when he was wide awake. He saw me looking and jumped into action, wiping down the counter, which I assumed was already spotless.

"How's Eugene doing?" I asked, looking to change the subject. I wanted to think about anything but the dead man and how I felt like I was a sunray from joining him.

"Good," Vicki said with a smile that slipped away almost as soon as it formed. "Better than Pooky, actually."

Pooky, real name Claire Cooper. I didn't know why she insisted on being called Pooky, but she wouldn't so much as look at you if you called her by her given name.

"Oh no," I said. "What happened?"

"Nothing really happened." Vicki reached out and started playing with my iced coffee, which was now just lukewarm, watered-down coffee. "But something is up with her. She comes in when she's supposed to, yet she's never really here, if you know what I mean?"

"Distracted."

"Exactly. She's messed up a few orders, forgotten to check the oven. She didn't start out like this."

No, she hadn't. Despite her odd choice in name, Pooky had been an ideal employee. She'd demonstrated an acute attention to detail, to the point where every coffee was filled to the exact same height, every cookie was evenly baked, every customer treated as if they were a king or a queen. I'd worked with her a lot at first, but over the last couple of weeks, our paths hadn't crossed much.

"What do you think is wrong?" I asked.

"I wish I knew." Vicki spread her hands as she sat back. "I'm worried that if it keeps up, we're going to have to move on. I like her and all, but there's a point where customers start to complain, and if she's not careful, someone could get hurt."

I didn't like the idea of firing her, but what could we do? If she forgot a batch of cookies in the oven or, worse, put something in there that shouldn't be, she could start a fire. Then we'd all be out of a job—and my livelihood.

"Could someone be harassing her? A customer, I mean." Pine Hills was a pretty laid-back place, but there are always people who are unhappy, especially in this heat.

"Not that I'm aware. And she seems to get along with everyone here fine." Meaning our employees. "I think it might have something to do with her homelife, but I can't tell you what that is like. She doesn't talk about it. And I've tried."

I took another drink from my water. The cold burned all the way down, but at least I didn't want to throw it back up right away.

"I'll talk to her," I said, setting the cup aside. "Maybe I can figure out what's bothering her. It's one of the things I'm good at."

Vicki considered it before standing. "That might

be a good idea. I don't like prying, but I don't want to lose her if there's something we can do to help."

"Well, as you know, prying is practically my middle name."

"You mean, it's your title." She framed her hand in the air, capturing my sunburned face in the middle. "Prying Krissy Hancock. Need to know someone's deepest, darkest, secret? Look no further."

"Har, har." Though I did smile. It *was* kind of catchy. And accurate.

"I'd best check on Mason. He's been in the back for a while now. The last time I checked on him, he had his head under the sink faucet." She rolled her eyes. "It gets hot back there, but come on."

I laughed, though it was short-lived, thanks to how it made my head hurt all the more. "You do that. I think I'm feeling good enough to head home." Theoretically. I'd see how that panned out once I stood up and tried walking in a straight line.

Vicki headed behind the counter and through the door that led to the backroom. Before it closed, I heard her say, "Mason! What are you doing?" There was laughter in her voice.

I considered my water and iced coffee, and decided it might be best if I didn't take the chance and drink them. All I wanted to do was to go home and lie down in a tub of ice. My skin felt hot all over and was so sensitive, it felt like my shirt was peeling me raw.

As I made to stand, the bell over the door jangled, and Rita Jablonski walked in. I immediately dropped back down into my chair, knowing she wasn't here for a cup of coffee. Her eyes found me right away, and she hurried over.

"Lordy Lou, can you believe what happened?" she said, flinging herself into the chair across from me. "It's a travesty. Horrible. I mean, a murder on such an important day. A good cause ruined, is what it is. Are you going to drink that?" She motioned toward my iced coffee.

My mind wasn't running as quickly as it usually did, so I'd already shaken my head by the time Rita's words fully registered.

"Wait. Did you say 'murder?'"

"You haven't heard?" Rita's eyes gleamed as she took a sip through the straw. She made a face and set the iced coffee aside. "Really, dear, you shouldn't let your drinks sit so long. Bacteria can build up, and in a public place like this . . ." She tsked. "It's simply not healthy."

I ignored her complaint to focus on the bombshell she'd dropped. "Are you saying Glen was murdered?"

"Of course he was. He was found dead, if you recall." She said it like it was impossible to die any other way.

I understood what she was saying, yet somehow it just didn't want to compute. "But the heat. Didn't he die from that?"

Rita waved a hand as if shooing away a fly. "That's ridiculous. Who dies from the heat?"

With how I was feeling, I thought I was pretty darn close to it myself, but telling her that wouldn't help anything. Or get to the meat of the conversation.

"Tell me what happened," I said. "I left soon after he was found." Like everyone else had. Or so I'd thought.

Rita made another tsking sound. "You shouldn't have done that, dear. I stuck around because I needed to know what happened so I could be forewarned."

You mean, you needed to file it away so you could tell your friends. I didn't say that out loud, of course. Not only would it have offended her, but it was also petty and rude and a product of my overheated brain. I nodded for her to go on.

"The police tried to get me to leave, but I had a right to be there. He was found in a public space, and I wasn't stepping on their crime scene, so they had no reason to send me, or anyone else, away."

Other than having people get in the way and spread rumors, but once again, I kept that to myself.

"Anyway, your man spent quite a long time with poor Glen Moreau, let me tell you." My man being Officer Paul Dalton. "I mean, the place was swarming with cops, not just Officer Dalton. And that includes our resident detective."

Detective John Buchannan. If my life was a television show, he would have been my nemesis. Or would that be my foil? Either way, he was always looking at me like I had something to hide.

In most cases, he was often kind of right.

"Hence why you think it's a murder," I said.

Rita shook her head. "I know it's a murder because they said it was. I heard Doctor Lipmon say as much. She was there, you know. So were the other local doctors, so they had multiple opinions. It did make me wonder what would happen if someone got sick and needed to see one of them. I heard there was a new doctor in town, but I can't imagine they left her alone at the clinic. I suppose they might have if she is worth half her salt, but still . . ."

I hadn't heard about a new doctor in Pine Hills, but it was always possible. I almost asked about what Rita knew about her, but if I did that, Rita would go off on one of her tangents and I'd never get her back on track.

"What did Doctor Lipmon say?"

"That he was dead. And that someone strangled him." She gave me a meaningful look that was lost on me in my current state. "They took that friend of his aside and started questioning him like they thought he was involved."

"Who?" I asked. "Trevor?"

Rita shrugged. "If that's his name. I didn't know the man myself. And I only knew Glen by reputation and rumor."

Rumor. Her specialty. "What did you hear about him? Glen, I mean."

She leaned forward, that gleam coming into her eye that spoke of how much she loved to gossip. "The way I heard it, Glen Moreau was into financial schemes that bordered on criminal activity."

"You think someone killed him over money?"

"He owed people some serious cash, or that's the rumor, anyway." Rita reached for the iced coffee and took another sip, making the same disgusted face as she had the first time. "I don't know what exactly he did or how it came back on him like that, but I'm telling you now: Glen Moreau was no angel."

I filed the information away for when I next talked to Paul. Knowing Rita, she'd tell the entire town about the rumors but would fail to go to the police with her information.

Then again, rumor wasn't fact. It would take a little digging to find out if Glen really was involved in criminal activity or if these financial crimes amounted to much more than skipping out on his bill at the Banyon Tree.

I also had a hard time imagining that someone involved in financial crimes would strangle Glen, rather than just shoot him, but hey, what did I know? Strangulation *was* quieter.

And far more personal.

Speaking of something personal . . .

"Hey, where's Johan?" I asked, glancing past her, as if I expected to see him standing behind her, that odd, empty smile of his on his face. "I figured he'd be with you."

"Johan? Why, he's out of town today." Rita patted at her hair like he might walk through the door at any moment and she wanted to look her best. "He should be back tomorrow, but sometimes these things drag out and he's gone for a few days longer. I won't know until he comes knocking at my door."

"Out of town?" My heart plummeted straight through the floor. "Are you sure?"

"Of course, I'm sure, dear." She rolled her eyes at me. "Do you think I'd actually misplace him?"

No, but I do know he's lied to you.

My brain wasn't working at its best, and I'd been pretty distracted at the marathon, but I *did* remember seeing Johan. He hadn't been dressed for running.

But could I tell her that without knowing more? She was practically glowing as she talked about him. If I told her that I thought Johan might be cheating on her, I could ruin not just her relationship with the first man she'd dated in years, but our friendship as well.

I swallowed with some difficulty and grabbed my water and downed half of it in one go.

Better composed, I pressed her further. "Do you know where he went today?" I asked as casually as I could manage, while avoiding her eyes entirely.

"Work, I assume," Rita said. "You know how he is. Always busy." She got a faraway look in her eyes that only made me feel worse. She was in love. And the man she was in love with had been lurking around the woods with another woman, at a marathon not long before a man was murdered.

I prayed it was all one big coincidence, because if it wasn't, I wasn't sure how I could ever break the news to Rita.

"Well, I should get going, dear." Rita rose, taking the now warm iced coffee with her. "You should get some rest. You're looking rather cooked."

"I will." I somehow managed a smile, which made my face hurt. "I'll talk to you soon, okay?"

"Of course, dear." Rita took a sip, made a face, and shook her head, yet she carried the coffee out of Death by Coffee with her.

I watched her go with a feeling of dread. Rita was my friend, and here I was, thinking her boyfriend might be cheating on her.

Or worse, that he might have had something to do with a murder.

3

I shivered as I lay on the couch, a cold compress on my forehead. My eyes were burning, so I kept them shut. Every movement hurt. My muscles, my joints, my very skin—all screamed at me, but I didn't know what to do to ease my discomfort.

I'd left Death by Coffee over an hour ago and had come straight home, where I'd collapsed onto the couch. My fluffy orange cat, Misfit, had tried to lie on me once, but I couldn't stand his weight. He hadn't even put out his claws, yet it felt like he'd been trying to tear me apart.

I've probably gotten heatstroke. Or was it the exercise that had done me in? Probably a combination of both. I should have known that running in the marathon was a bad idea.

It was a lot worse for Glen Moreau.

There was a ping in the back of my mind, a niggling of a memory that kept trying to surface. If

I'd felt halfway decent, I would have figured it out by now. As it was, every time I tried to pinpoint what was bothering me, I found my mind wandering or, in one worrisome moment, blacking out entirely.

Johan.

Could that be it? Rita claimed he was out of town, yet I was positive I'd seen him at the marathon with another woman. Well, close to the marathon anyway. And I was pretty sure it was Johan, not just a man of similar build. Even that memory was starting to get hazy.

But no matter who it was, he'd most definitely snuck off with another woman, into the same forest where Glen Moreau had been murdered. I prayed it was a coincidence, but what possible reason could Johan have to go into those woods?

And no, I refused to go there. Just because he'd slipped behind those sheds with a woman didn't mean he was doing something indecent.

I groaned as I shifted positions on the couch. I didn't want to think Johan could be capable of cheating, let alone murder, yet he'd always rubbed me the wrong way. I'd once had Paul look into him, and while it was only a surface background check, it had revealed nothing—as in, he barely existed online, which was awfully suspicious, especially now.

What about Cassie? She *had* run ahead of me moments before Glen's body was found. I didn't know much of anything about her, other than she seemed nice and I would have liked to get to know her better. If nothing else, maybe she'd seen something that would help identify Glen's murderer.

Blindly, I reached out and felt around on the floor next to the couch. I'd set my water bottle there, rather than on the coffee table, because I'd spent a good chunk of the last hour on my side, and it was easier to reach down with my dead-feeling arms than straight out. Of course, trying to lift said water bottle to my lips took a heroic effort that was more trouble than it was worth.

But right then, my lips were dry and cracking, and I felt parched. My hand bumped against the bottle, and I managed to get my fingers to wrap around the cool plastic without dropping it. I was forced to sit upright to twist the cap off and take a drink, and a good swallow's worth of water spilled down my chin when I tipped the bottle too early.

It felt oddly good, and I was considering emptying the entire thing over my head when there was a knock at the door.

"It's open," I croaked. The knock came again, and I realized that there was no chance I was going to be able to raise my voice loud enough to be heard in my current state, so I groaned my way to my feet and staggered across the room toward the door. The floor tried to dance out from under me all the way there, but somehow, I made it without ending up flat on my face.

The door opened to reveal my neighbors, Jules Phan and Lance Darby, standing arm in arm. They each held a plastic container filled with a pale yellow liquid, and they were both grinning from ear to ear.

"Krissy!" Jules said, his smile faltering even before he'd finished my name. "What happened to you?"

I said something that was supposed to be, "I'm fine," but it came out a gummy, muddy mess. I was so far from fine, I was actually starting to get a bit worried. It was obvious that both Jules and Lance felt the same way because their expressions turned serious.

"Come on, let's sit you down," Jules handed his container to Lance before he took me by the arm and led me across the room to my table, where he eased me down into a chair. "Pour her a lemonade, Lance. The cups are in that cupboard over there." I assumed he pointed to the correct cupboard, but by then, my head was drooping and my eyes were closed.

"I just need some sleep." I spoke slowly, carefully, and this time, the words came out sounding like actual words. "I overdid it today."

"I can tell." Jules gently lifted my chin and looked into my eyes when I opened them a crack. "You shouldn't have run that marathon today. Lance and I were there at the beginning, but it was too hot to stick around, and we went home and made lemonade for the neighborhood instead."

"Fresh squeezed," Lance said, setting lemonade down in front of me. A pair of ice cubes clinked against a glass already dripping with condensation.

"Thank you." I started with a sip that turned into a gulp that turned into downing the entire contents of the glass—other than the ice cubes, of course—in one go. Lance immediately refilled it from one of the containers he and Jules had brought with them.

"It's good," I said, managing a smile.

"That's nice to hear." Jules was still watching me

with concern. I noted he'd recently gotten a hair-cut. His dark hair was cut closer to the scalp than I remembered him having it and wondered if it had something to do with the heat or if he was simply trying something new. "I heard about what hap-pened. The murder."

I nodded, wrapping my hands around the lemon-ade glass. I planned to take my time with this one. The first glassful had felt cool going down, but now it sat like a lump in my stomach.

"I didn't know the man that died all that well," I said. "I know his name was Glen, but that's about it."

"Glen Moreau," Lance said. Like Jules, his blond hair was cut shorter than his usual. But that didn't detract from his looks in the slightest. He was well built and was serious eye candy for anyone with an interest in men. Most people agreed that Jules was a very lucky man. "I knew him."

"Really?" Jules turned to his significant other, eyebrows climbing. "I didn't know that."

"It was a long time ago." Lance got a faraway look in his eye. "A lifetime ago, really. We're talk-ing high school."

"Were you friends?" I asked, taking a sip of lemonade. The stuff must have had magical prop-erties because I felt a million times better. My eye-lids still felt like sandpaper, and my stomach was roiling, but I could now think straight, which was a vast improvement.

"Friends? No. I can't even say we were acquain-tances. We didn't run in the same circles." Lance laid a hand on Jules's wrist, as if reassuring him. "But I did know of him."

"You know everyone." Jules smiled and nudged his partner. "Mr. Popular."

"What was Glen like back then?" I asked. A part of me hoped that something he'd say would dislodge whatever memory was stuck in the back of my mind, though I found it unlikely since we were talking about over twenty years ago, not the marathon. Still, it would be nice to know more about the victim.

"What was Glen like?" Lance made a face, like the memory wasn't a good one. "He wasn't popular, but he wasn't a nobody either, if that makes sense?" He went on when I nodded. "He . . . well, he's kind of hard to explain."

"He was angry when I saw him," I said. "One of his friends had to hold him back from one of the marathon organizers."

"I'm not surprised," Lance said. "Glen was known to have a hot temper back in school. He'd get into a few fights, but it was never anything that got him expelled or in trouble with the police. I always figured it was all for show. You know, tough guy stuff, like he needed to keep up his image or else he'd lose what respect he'd earned. He used it to his advantage, that's for sure."

"How's that?"

"It feels almost sexist to say it, but a lot of the girls loved him. He was the guy your parents didn't want you seeing because they knew he was after one thing and one thing only."

Lance didn't have to spell it out for me to get it. I'd known a few guys like that in my time. I sipped more lemonade and tried not to think about them.

"I think he went through about a half dozen girlfriends during his senior year alone. He was a year above me, and I know for a fact that he dated at least four girls from my grade. Probably the same number in his own, so my estimate is on the conservative side."

"Geez." I shook my head. "I can't imagine falling for someone like that."

"Me either," Jules said. "Loyalty and trust are important parts of any relationship."

"I think most of the girls knew what they were getting into with Glen," Lance said. "It was a badge of honor for some, I guess. The cheerleaders, especially. I think they had a competition to see who could hold his interest the longest. I remember hearing a few of them talk at the football games. I'm not sure why it stuck with me, but it did."

I thought back to the red-faced man I'd seen and couldn't fathom lusting after him like that. Such anger and resentment didn't make for an attractive man. "He must have been a different person back then."

"I'll admit, he *was* good-looking, just not my type." Lance winked at Jules, who laughed. "And Pine Hills isn't a big town, so there are only so many options out there. Glen made himself stand out, which was something a lot of us didn't aspire to. He didn't want to fit in. It didn't make him popular, just well-known. He wanted to live a rock-star life, get all the women, never settle."

And yet here he was, still in Pine Hills. I wondered if he resented that he never got out, or if something good had come into his life, something that kept him in such a small town. I asked Lance as much.

"Oh, something happened all right. Namely, Melanie Johnson."

I had a feeling I knew where this was going. With a history like Glen's, it was almost inevitable. "She got pregnant, didn't she?"

Lance shot a finger gun at me. "Right before he graduated. She was a year older than him, was already out of high school, and was content staying right here in Pine Hills. Glen wanted out, but he, much to everyone's surprise, decided to do the right thing. He proposed to her the very day she told him about the baby."

"Wow." I imagined there were a lot of guys out there who would have run in the opposite direction, especially guys with a history of using and losing women. "Did they get married?"

"They did," Lance said. "And as far as I was aware, Glen cleaned his act up for a while. They seemed happy enough, though you could tell he wasn't entirely thrilled about being stuck here."

"Didn't they divorce a few years ago?" Jules asked. "I didn't know Glen, but I know Melanie a little from the store." Jules owned and operated a local candy store, Phantastic Candies. "From what little she said on the matter, I gathered it wasn't an amicable split."

"It wasn't." Lance looked troubled. "I don't know exactly what happened. I knew Glen was still around Pine Hills, but I wasn't friends with him or his wife. I did get the impression that he'd started sleeping around again, but I have nothing but rumor to base that on."

"It's a shame," Jules said. "Melanie seems like a nice enough woman."

I couldn't tell if Lance's nod was in agreement about Melanie's character, or if he likewise considered what had happened a shame.

What I did know was that this was all stuff that the police needed to hear. If Glen had cheated on his wife, that was a strong motive for murder. And while the divorce had happened years ago, that kind of anger and resentment didn't just magically go away.

"Do you know anything about Glen's friends?" I asked, thinking back to the marathon. "Trevor Conway and Calvin . . ." I frowned. "I don't know his last name."

Jules and Lance shared a look before they both shook their heads. It was Lance who answered. "Sorry. I vaguely remember the name Calvin from school, but not a face or last name."

"That's all right." I wasn't sure if the two men mattered anyway. If anything, they'd been trying to keep Glen from getting himself into trouble at the marathon, not kill him.

"We should get going," Jules said, rising. He paused halfway up. "Unless you want one of us to stay with you for a little bit?"

"No, I'll be fine." And to prove it, I stood. I only wobbled a little. "You two go ahead and get on with your day."

Lance picked up one of the two containers. "Want me to put this in the fridge? We brought one for you, and the other is for Caitlin." Caitlin Blevins was my other immediate neighbor.

"I'll get it," I said. "Get that to Caitlin before the ice melts."

Jules and Lance shared a worried look, but they headed for the door anyway. I could almost feel the heat radiating from the other side of it and dreaded having to go outside again. Maybe I'd wait to leave until tomorrow, or sometime late at night, when the sun was down.

"I'll stop by and check on you later," Jules said, pausing at the door. "You really should lie down and get some rest."

"I will," I promised him as I opened the door. I leaned on it, hoping Jules didn't notice how my knees trembled like they wanted to give out. "Thanks again for the lemonade."

"If you want more, feel free to drop by the house," Lance said. "I made enough for the entire town, so there's plenty."

"I swear he bought every last lemon in Pine Hills. Maybe even the entire state."

"When it's hot, I like lemonade." Lance grinned. "You can't fault me for wanting to share that love."

"No, I guess I can't." Jules put an arm around Lance and squeezed. "Just as long as that's the only love you're sharing."

With laughter that echoed throughout the neighborhood, the two of them left to deliver the lemonade to Caitlin. I watched them cross the yard but closed the door before they reached her house. I was feeling light-headed again and desperately wanted to lie down. I considered calling Paul to let him know what Lance and Jules had told me about Glen but decided it could wait. It was all I could do to cross the room to put the lemonade in the fridge and make it over to the couch before I collapsed. Finding the energy to make a phone call was definitely beyond me.

I leaned back, closed my burning eyes, and instantly fell asleep.

4

Thump! Thump! Thump!

The world spun around me as I jerked upright. My feet were on the floor, but for an instant, I felt as if I were falling and grabbed at the couch cushions to keep from plummeting. Even then, my vision spiraled out of control, causing my empty stomach to do its own uncomfortable flips.

Thump! Thump! Thump!

The spinning room finally locked into place, though I still felt light-headed. I ran my tongue over my lips, which was like running a piece of cotton over barbed wire. Misfit was nowhere to be seen, which I supposed was to be expected, considering the incessant pounding I wasn't entirely sure wasn't coming from my head.

"I'm coming," I mumbled as the knock came again and I realized it was indeed the door. When I stood, the floor tried to jump away from me, causing me to fall into a half crouch before it settled once again.

"Ms. Hancock? I know you're there."

I groaned. I recognized that voice, and I really didn't want to have to deal with its owner just after waking up from a heat-induced nap. My stomach growled, and I considered ignoring Detective John Buchannan's knocking to grab something to eat. I wasn't so sure I could deal with him on an empty stomach.

"I'll break down the door if I have to."

"Fine." I didn't say it loud enough for him to hear. I didn't think he'd actually knock down my door, but with Buchannan, I didn't want to chance it.

My bare feet dragged as I crossed the room. This wasn't what I'd hoped to wake up to. In fact, I hadn't wanted to wake up at all—not yet, anyway. I put on by best annoyed expression and opened the door.

"I was asleep," I said before Buchannan could speak. He was in full uniform, which I found odd considering he was now a detective. Then again, what did I know about proper police attire? On TV, detectives were always in suits, but here in Pine Hills?

If Buchannan felt guilty for waking me, he didn't show it. "You look awful," he said, glancing past me, into the house. "Are you alone?"

"I am. Unless you count my cat. And I just ran a marathon. In the heat. I think I'm allowed to look this way."

"The marathon is why I'm here." Buchannan

cleared his throat and straightened his back, putting on a formal expression. "May I come in?"

My initial reaction was to tell him that no, he couldn't, but the heat was beating down on us, and the longer I kept the door open, the hotter it would get.

"Sure." I stepped aside.

"Thank you." He ducked his head as he entered, as if he expected the doorframe to clunk him upside the head. Buchannan was tall, but not *that* tall. He paused just inside the door, taking in the disheveled state of my house, before he moved to stand beside my island counter.

"Can I get you some lemonade?" I asked. I might not get along with John Buchannan, but that didn't mean I had to be a bad host. "It's fresh-squeezed. Jules and Lance made it."

"Lemonade would be great." He very nearly smiled.

Feeling much more grounded now that I'd been awake for a few minutes, I grabbed two glasses, filled them with ice, and then poured us each some lemonade. I considered snacking on an apple but decided to hold off until Buchannan had left. I had a feeling that whatever he had to say would leave me with an upset tummy.

"Thank you," he said as I handed him the glass. That was two thank-yous in as many minutes. Maybe this wouldn't be as awful as usual. He took a sip of lemonade, made an appreciative face, and then set the glass aside. "I assume you know why I'm here."

"Because of the marathon." I refrained from pointing out that he'd already said as much. "And

Glen Moreau's death." I motioned toward a stool and sat down in the one opposite. Buchannan took the proffered seat. I felt far more relaxed with us sitting around the counter like old friends, rather than having him loom over me.

"What can you tell me about it?" he asked once he was settled.

"Not a lot, actually. I saw Glen with a couple of his friends before the marathon started. He wasn't happy about the conditions of the race, and he confronted one of the organizers about it."

"Which one?"

I held my lemonade glass to my forehead as I thought back. I couldn't tell if I had a fever or was just sunburned, but I did feel a bit warm. "Rodney Maxwell. I don't recall if the other two organizers were with him, not that I know who they are. I just heard that he'd organized the event with two women."

Buchannan nodded but that didn't tell me if he knew who those women were or if he was simply urging me on.

I took it as the latter. "It was really hot out, and Glen wasn't happy about the route. He complained that marathons don't normally run over hills or in the middle of a heat wave. He made it sound like he thought Rod was trying to kill him, but I don't really think he meant it literally."

Of course, now that the man was dead, I was beginning to wonder if I should reassess my opinion.

"Did Glen speak to anyone else? An argument perhaps?"

I tried to remember, but my memory of the whole event was still hazy. "I don't recall."

Buchannan narrowed his eyes at me.

"Really," I said. "As I said, it was hot, and tempers were running high for a lot of people. Many of us were complaining about running in the heat, and quite a few people dropped out early because they felt like they were going to pass out."

"But you didn't."

Something in the way he said it felt accusatory. "No, I didn't. I promised Rita that I'd run the race, and I intended to keep that promise."

I waited to see if Buchannan would accuse me of something, but he merely sipped his lemonade.

"I probably should have dropped out," I finally admitted. "I wasn't feeling too good by the time we got going. Once the marathon was underway, I focused on running, not what Glen Moreau was doing."

"Did you see him once you got started?" He leaned forward. "I need you to remember if you saw anything at all that leaped out at you as strange."

Johan Morrison. I bit my tongue before I could say his name. Rita would never forgive me if I accused her boyfriend of something without getting the full story first.

"I'm not sure," I hedged, not meeting Buchannan's eye.

"Ms. Hancock, I need you to be honest here."

"I am," I said. "I keep thinking I saw something, but I can't remember what it was."

"You can't remember." Flat. Disbelieving.

"I wish I could." And I did. That old niggling in the back of my mind started up again, yet I couldn't pinpoint what it was. "I do know there are some rumors going around about Glen. Maybe one of those rumors could be the reason he was killed."

Buchannan scowled into his lemonade glass, which was nearing empty. "Rumors. Really?"

"It's the best I've got."

He sighed. "Tell me."

I explained what Rita had told me about Glen and a possible connection to financial crimes. I didn't have details, which only made Buchannan scowl all the harder, but it was all I had.

"And I guess he cheated on his wife. They're divorced now, but maybe she still resented him for it."

"I see." Buchannan didn't look happy. "That's all you know?"

"It is. Sorry."

Another sigh, this one more of a huff. Buchannan shoved his glass aside and stood. "I'd better be going then. Thank you for the lemonade."

I rose with him. "I hope something I said helps you get to the bottom of this. Glen didn't seem like a nice man, but no one deserves to be murdered."

Buchannan walked to the door and opened it. He paused there, not looking at me, but not leaving either. A couple of seconds passed before he gave a curt nod. "I hope so too."

And then he was gone.

I went to the window and watched as he got into his car. There, he rubbed at his face, as if the stress was already getting to him. That, or the heat. His shoulders slumped, and he just sat there, looking down. He seemed to feel me watching, and he looked up to stare back at me. After a few seconds of that, he put his car in reverse and backed out of my driveway.

I felt guilty for not telling him about Johan, but I couldn't betray Rita's trust. Maybe he had a perfectly good reason to be out there with another woman without Rita's knowledge.

Right. And I'm a world-class bodybuilder.

I let the curtain drop back into place and went into my bedroom, where I'd left my laptop last night. I carried it back to the island counter and poured myself another glass of lemonade. It *was* really good. I'd have to ask Jules if I could get another container of it.

But that could wait. I opened up my browser and brought up the Facebook page for the marathon. Neither Rod nor the other organizers had sprung for a full-on website, just the free Facebook page. I'd visited it a couple of times before the marathon but had never really *looked* at it before.

The first thing I did was to check for the organizers. Rod Maxwell, Alleah Trotter, and Jen Vousden. I jotted their names down on the back of a nearby envelope before clicking over to each of their profiles but found little since all three had their profiles set to private.

I went back to the marathon site and scrolled through the posts there.

Runners and contributors had been added as members to the page, and many had posted photos before and during the run. There were tons of comments as well, with many lamenting that the death had cut the marathon short and tarnished an event that was supposed to be for a good cause.

Kind of harsh, isn't it? I thought as I read through some of the worst comments. Sure, a few people were sad about Glen's death, but not as many as I would have thought. He wasn't all that well-liked, which would make finding his killer that much harder.

I scrolled back up and skimmed through some of the photos, but I struggled to put names to faces, let alone focus on any one person. One photo did show me looking like I was about to have a stroke, running next to Cassie, who, while tired, didn't look all that bad. I made a mental note to contact her here on Facebook, since I didn't think to get her number before the race. And after . . . well, there was a good reason why we didn't stick around to socialize afterward.

My stomach growled and complained so much, it sounded like it was having a conversation with itself. If I didn't eat soon, I was going to pass out.

I closed my laptop lid and was about to grab that apple I'd considered earlier, when another car pulled into my driveway. I immediately thought of Buchannan and that last look he'd given me. If he'd come back to drag me down to the police station, I was going to have some serious words with not just him, but his boss—and my boyfriend's mother—Chief Patricia Dalton, as well.

I stomped my way to the door, already convinced that Buchannan was going to attempt to do just that. I jerked the door open, lips parted to say something particularly snarky, when I realized it wasn't Buchannan's car in my driveway.

It was Paul's.

My heart gave a little flutter that found its way to my complaining stomach as he stepped out of his car. He wasn't smiling, which wasn't a surprise considering the murder, but it was disappointing nonetheless. He was still dressed in his uniform and looked as if he'd just come from the scene of the crime. His cheeks and the tip of his nose were red from the unrelenting sun.

"Krissy," he said, pulling off his hat long enough to wipe his forearm across his forehead, before replacing it. "You don't look so good."

"People keep telling me that." I tried to make it light, but it came out sounding exhausted. "You've gotten a bit of sun yourself." I resisted the urge to touch the tip of his nose, but the thought did make me smile.

He squinted up toward the cloudless sky. "Too much sun, if you ask me." He approached, and I stepped aside, letting him in.

"I'm glad you're here. Buchannan already stopped by to ask me some questions."

Once inside, Paul removed his hat again and ran his fingers through his hair with a grimace. He was sweaty and looked miserable—kind of like how I felt.

"I'm not surprised," he said. "John said he wanted to talk to you. He was shocked you didn't hang around to mess up his crime scene."

"I didn't do anything." I scowled. "And I wouldn't have messed up his scene. I'm smarter than that." Though I did tend to stick my nose where it didn't belong. That didn't mean I'd intentionally sabotage the investigation.

Yeah? What about not telling him about Johan?

"You are. But you also tend to ask questions and notice things that some people would overlook." Paul finally smiled. "Consider it a compliment."

"I guess." My stomach chose that moment to growl loud enough that my neighbors could have heard it. A wave of dizziness hit me at the same time, and I staggered back a step, catching myself on the wall before I fell.

"Are you sure you're okay?" Paul asked, taking me by the arm to steady me. I would have leaned into him but was afraid I'd miss. The world was doing that loop-de-loop thing again.

"I'm fine." I managed a smile. "I'm just really hungry." It wasn't quite the full truth, but I had a feeling that if I got some solid food in me, I'd feel a thousand times better.

Paul studied me a moment, clearly not convinced. "I've got an hour before I'm due back," he said. "How about I take you out for something to eat?"

A date? In the middle of the day? Count me in. "That sounds great."

"It'll have to be the Banyon Tree."

Less great, but food is food. "I'll try not to get myself thrown out."

I expected Paul to laugh. We both knew how Judith Banyon felt about me. It seemed that every time I went there, she found a reason to chase me out. I'm surprised she hadn't tried to get a restraining order to keep me from setting foot in her diner.

Instead of laughing, however, Paul guided me over to the table, where I'd left my purse. I picked it up, careful not to lose contact with him because, one, his hand felt good on me and, two, I feared I would fall if he didn't keep me upright.

Misfit came in from the bedroom, sensing I was leaving. He glanced at his nearly full food dish, and I could feel his displeasure.

"I'll get you a cool treat on the way back home," I told him, which earned me a tail flip as he turned to go back into the bedroom.

"Tough customer," Paul noted, some of his good humor returning.

"You don't know the half of it." I shouldered my purse with a wince. Apparently, my shoulder was as burned as the rest of me. "I'm ready if you are."

He looked down at my feet.

My *bare* feet.

"Oh." My running shoes were sitting beside the couch, but the thought of pulling them on and tying them was too much for me at the moment. My flip-flops were next to the door and were far more convenient, though not as fashionable.

I tugged off the number 138, which I was still wearing, tossed it on the couch, and then slipped my feet into the flip-flops. "Now I'm ready."

Paul took my arm, and, together, we went.

5

I entered J&E's Banyon Tree like a criminal looking to remove evidence from a crime scene while
the police were there. Rockabilly music played over
the speakers, and the smell of greasy food per-
meated the air as I walked through the doors,
shoulders hunched, head lowered, with my hand
concealing my face. The diner wasn't a bad place
to eat, but it was one of the places in town where I
wasn't welcome.

"Don't worry yourself, Krissy," Paul said, guid-
ing me across the room to a table. "They know me
here. And Judith is an understanding woman
when you get to know her."

I almost laughed. If I hadn't been so hungry
and light-headed, I very well might have.

"Besides," he went on, "I don't think she's here."

So far, he appeared to be right on that account.
Other employees, most of whom I only knew by
sight, ran from table to table, filling orders. A

harried-looking woman who couldn't have been more than eighteen saw us, and her face burst into a wide grin before she made her way over to where we sat.

"Hi, Paul," she said, beaming at him without giving me the slightest glance. "Do you want your usual?"

His smile was just as radiant as the teen's. "Not today, Constance. I think I'll take a grilled cheese and a Sprite and call it good."

"Coming right up." Constance paused as she finally seemed to notice me sitting with Paul. She didn't exactly frown, but her smile did dim. "And for you?"

I didn't have the energy to look through the menu, nor did I want to spend any more time in the Banyon Tree than I had to. Who knew when Judith would pop up like a jack-in-the-box and run me out of the place?

"I'll have the same."

Constance nodded once, beamed again at Paul, and then hurried to the back.

I raised my eyebrows at Paul in question.

"She has something of a crush on me," he said, clearly embarrassed, but not so much that he didn't smile. "It's flattering, of course, but nothing will ever come of it." He reached across the table to take my hand. "I have you."

And she's young enough to be your daughter. I stomped down on the jealous voice in the back of my mind.

"You seem to have cast a spell on a few of the women here, I've noticed." I said it playfully, though I did glance around to see if his ex, Shannon, was around. I didn't see her, which I supposed was no wonder. She was very pregnant at this point and working as a waitress had to be hard on her.

"Perhaps. But only one woman has cast her spell on me."

The line was so cheesy, it actually worked. Maybe it was the heat and my hunger that did it, but quite suddenly the temperature in the room rose about ten degrees. I melted into my chair, a dopey grin on my face.

Paul checked his watch and glanced toward the door like he expected someone to come bursting in at any moment. It took me a moment to realize that he was likely anxious to get back to work. You know, there had been a murder and all. And here I was, keeping him from it, all because I'd gotten a little too much sun.

"If you need to go, I won't be upset," I told him. "You've got more important things to do than babysit me."

"No." He turned back to face me. "I don't mind the break. Besides, I was told to take this hour and get something to eat and to clear my head. We don't expect to get much free time at the station for a few days, so this hour might be it."

Which meant this could be our last meal together until the culprit was caught. "I can't believe Glen was murdered in the middle of a marathon being run by what? Fifty people? More? You'd think someone would have seen something."

You know, like me.

"It happens," Paul said. He was still holding my hand, and he squeezed it. "We shouldn't talk about it. John is on the case, and the rest of the department will back him up while I'm away. We've got more than enough people working it."

The implied *So you don't have to* was left unsaid.

Guilt made my guts churn. I tried to make myself believe it was just my stomach complaining some more, but it wasn't. I'd held off on telling Buchannan about Johan and the other woman, but I couldn't do the same with Paul.

And, for the first time, I realized that even if Johan was innocent of the murder, he might be a witness. I didn't have to mention the woman—not until I knew for sure why he was with her—but if Johan had seen something—like someone strangling Glen Moreau—the police needed to know about it. And if he mentioned the woman and it got back to Rita, well then, that was on him.

"I was thinking about what I might have seen before the marathon started, and—" Before I could finish the thought, Paul's phone went off.

He snatched it out of his pocket, took one look at the screen, and frowned. "I've got to take this," he said, rising. "Work." He brought the phone to his ear and hurried out of the Banyon Tree to talk.

Maybe it's a sign, I thought. If Johan was innocent, I could be doing harm to his relationship with Rita by casting suspicion on him. Could I do that to my friend without bringing it up to her first? I mean, if Johan had seen a murder, he would have reported it.

Right?

Constance returned with a pair of Sprites. She looked disappointed when she didn't see Paul in his seat. She set the glasses down on the table and didn't pay me any mind when I thanked her. She caught sight of Paul out the diner window and kept her eyes on him as she walked away. She nearly bumped into a couple of chairs before she made it to the back.

"I guess I'm invisible today," I muttered. That wouldn't be such a bad thing if I decided to poke my nose where it didn't belong, but for now, it was inconvenient.

With little else to do but sip my Sprite, I glanced around the diner at the customers. When I'd looked around before, I'd been checking for Judith and Shannon specifically, which meant I'd only looked at the employees.

Pine Hills wasn't a big town. While I didn't know everybody, I'd seen quite a lot of faces around, mostly because they'd stopped in at Death by Coffee at one time or another. And since J&E's was one of the few places you could go to sit down and eat in town, that meant a lot of people came here when they didn't feel like cooking.

And that included people involved in the marathon.

I just about choked on my Sprite when I saw them sitting at a table across the room. The woman I knew from my earlier perusal of the marathon's Facebook page: Alleah Trotter. She was blond and looked like a runner, with legs that rippled with muscles whenever she moved. Her shorts were just this side of too short, and her matching black-and-pink top was just as tight and revealing. She was leaning across the table, talking in low voices with a man sitting across from her.

A man I recognized.

Rod Maxwell.

Now, it shouldn't have surprised me to see them together, considering they were two of the organizers of the marathon, but something in the way they were talking seemed awfully suspicious. Rod looked anxious. He kept glancing around, as if afraid someone might overhear their conversation. Alleah looked intense, her eyes blazing holes straight through Rod as she spoke.

I glanced toward Paul. He was still outside, talking on the phone and pacing back and forth. Another look around the diner reinforced the idea that Judith wasn't there. I didn't even see her husband, Eddie Banyon, which meant chances were good I could move around without being noticed.

Be good, Krissy. Let Paul handle it.

But what was there to handle? Two people talking? He'd think I was crazy if I told him that I found the conversation suspicious.

Or at least he would if I didn't have something else to give him.

Just a few words, that's all I need to hear. I rose from my seat and made for the bathrooms, which would take me right past the table at which Alleah and Rod were sitting. There was nothing strange in that. I was invisible, remember? Just a woman in need of washing her hands.

Neither Alleah or Rod noticed me as I approached their table.

"He *knew*," Rod was saying at a whispered hiss. "What are we going to do?"

Oh? That sounded interesting. I needed to hear more, so I feigned tying my shoe, only to remember a second after I'd dropped to one knee that I was wearing flip-flops.

"Nothing," Alleah said. Her voice was commanding. "It's done. We can't change what's already happened. We can only adapt."

"But what if he told someone? One of his friends? You know how word spreads in this town."

"He didn't. I made sure of it."

I couldn't stop my gasp. I jerked upright, thinking they'd heard me. But even if they hadn't heard the gasp, they surely heard my still-sore shoulder as I whacked it on the underside of the empty table next to them.

Alleah's head snapped up, and Rodney spun in his chair to stare at me. They weren't the only ones either. It seemed like everyone in the entire diner paused to stare as I rubbed at my shoulder, my face taking on a deep shade of crimson.

"Sorry," I said, loud enough for everyone to hear. "I had something in my flip-flop. It's gone now."

Most everyone turned away, including Rodney. Alleah, however, continued to glare, as if she'd seen straight through the lie. Admittedly, it wasn't a very good one, and I felt the need to apologize some more.

"I'm really sorry. Really."

Alleah finally looked away, though she didn't look appeased.

I scurried back to my table without stopping in the bathroom. I could feel eyes on me, and knew, just *knew*, that this little incident would get back to Judith.

Even if it did and Judith banned me from her diner for life, I thought it was worth it.

They were talking about Glen. There was no question in my mind about that. I'd seen Glen assault Rod before the marathon had begun, had heard him accuse him of . . . what? Trying to kill him, for one. But why?

I tried to remember the exact words he'd used, but like my take on much of the day, it was hazy. But just because I didn't remember didn't mean others wouldn't.

I need to talk to Cassie.

I was about to reach for my phone to look her up when Paul returned. Constance arrived with our grilled cheeses at the same moment, as if she'd been waiting for him to reappear before approaching.

"We've got to take these to go," Paul said to Constance as she set the plates on the table. He turned to me. "I'm sorry. They need me back at the station. Something's come up."

I really wanted to ask him what that something was but decided to be a good girl and not pry. Yet. "I understand," I said instead. And before Constance could walk away, I added to her, "If you have some vanilla ice cream, can I get a small scoop to go?" When Paul gave me a curious look, I told him, "It's for Misfit."

While Constance went to the back to get the boxes—and Misfit's ice cream—I chowed down on my grilled cheese. There was no sense in letting it get cold, especially as hungry as I was. By the time Constance returned with two boxes and my ice cream, my grilled cheese was a distant memory. She gave me a look as though I'd just devoured an entire cow on my own and then boxed Paul's meal up for him. He handed her a twenty and a ten, told her to keep the change, and then we were out the door and on the way back to my house.

"I'm sorry about this," Paul said, clearly distracted by whatever he'd been told over the phone. "I thought I had more time."

"Don't worry about it. Your job is important."

"So are you. I . . ." He shook his head, though it was clear he had something else he wanted to say.

He pulled into my driveway soon after, and I started to get out, but he stopped me with a hand on my wrist.

"I'll make this up to you," he said, looking deep into my eyes. "There are some things I'd like to say, but . . ." Another shake of his head, and another moment in which he dropped whatever he'd intended to tell me. "Get some rest. I don't want you making yourself sick. Stay out of the sun, all right?"

"Good thing it goes down soon." Already, the sky was changing colors, though I doubted the temperature would drop all that much.

"I'm serious, Krissy. I don't want anything to happen to you."

There was a strange tone to his voice that made me nervous. He acted like he was afraid we didn't have much time left.

Is he sick? Dying? My heart leaped into my throat before I swallowed it back with a firm thought: *He'd tell me if something was wrong.*

Wouldn't he?

"I'll be good," I said, and then, for good measure, I leaned across the seat and kissed him on the cheek before slipping out of his car.

Paul sat there a moment, almost as if he were

stunned by the kiss, before he backed out of my driveway. He honked once, and then sped away, though I noted he didn't turn on his lights. Whatever he'd been called in for, it wasn't that sort of an emergency.

I was about to head inside when I noticed a note taped to my door. It was from Jules.

Just came by to check on you, but you're not in. If you need more lemonade, just stop by!

I carried the note inside, a faint smile on my lips. I'd need to do something to repay Jules and Lance, but what? I wasn't much of a cook, so I'd have to come up with something else.

I gave Misfit his treat as my mind drifted back to what I'd overheard at the Banyon Tree.

What had Rod and Alleah been talking about? Could it have something to do with Glen's murder? I mean, it almost had to, didn't it?

I grabbed my laptop and brought up the marathon's Facebook page intending to find Cassie Wise and send her a message. More posts had been added, as had more photos, and I found myself being drawn to them. It was odd that many of the posts didn't even reference Glen's death, as if these people had already moved past it, but I guess we all handle tragedy differently.

I scrolled through the photos, this time looking for specific faces. Glen Moreau was one, of course. But I also was hoping to spot Johan, Alleah, and Rod. Had their paths crossed more than what I'd seen or remembered?

It was like playing *Where's Waldo*. There were too many wide shots, focused more on the runners than the crowd. Too many blurry photos in which details were too indistinct to tell one person from the next.

I'm not sure how long I scoured the photos. It was long enough that the sun had gone down and the only light glowing in the house was from the screen of my laptop. My head was spinning, and my eyes felt like someone had superglued them in place. Moving them hurt. Staring at the screen wasn't making it any better.

And I still hadn't found whatever it was I was looking for.

Maybe Paul was right and I needed to rest. I could always come back to the photos later, when my head was clear, and I didn't feel like I'd been awake for a month.

I was about to close the page—and my laptop— when I caught sight of a post halfway down the page, sandwiched between a photo of a leggy brunette and a group of middle-aged men.

I'm going to make sure Rod Maxwell gets what's coming to him.

The author of that post?

None other than Glen Moreau.

And it had been written after the marathon had begun.

6

When I woke in the morning, my brain was mush. I had a vague inkling that I'd planned to do . . . well, stuff. Cassie's name floated through my head and then vanished like mist. Others followed suit: Rod, Alleah, Glen, Johan. None of them stuck around long enough to tell me why I was thinking of them.

I peeled myself out of bed, barely able to open my eyes, and limped my way to the shower. Everything hurt. My head, my muscles, my skin. I felt as if I'd been left under a heat lamp overnight to crispy-fry, and when I turned on the shower and stepped under the spray, I knew I had been.

Misfit was sitting by the toilet when the first stream of lukewarm water hit my sunburned flesh. The scream that followed caused him to teleport from the bathroom, leaving behind a floating tuft of fur.

I stood to the far back of the shower, where the

spray could only reach the tops of my feet, which were blessedly pale white, unlike my legs, which were a splotchy white and red.

"What in the . . . ?" Carefully, I stepped out of the shower and looked at myself in the mirror. My nose was a pulsating red, as were the tips of my ears and cheeks. There was also a line across my forehead where I must have missed with the sunscreen. The same went for my shoulders, all the way down to my thighs, where I noted a half-formed white handprint where I'd started to apply the sunscreen and must have gotten distracted before rubbing it in only in that one spot since it was surrounded by red-hot, unprotected flesh.

I licked cracked lips and winced. If I was going to be home all day, I'd have skipped the shower entirely, but I was due at Death by Coffee in an hour. Since I was co-owner, I could stay home any time I wanted, and I trusted my employees to handle the morning rush with ease, so it wasn't like I had to be there.

"No, I can do this." I eyed the shower distrustfully and then reached in to turn the heat all the way down. The spray turned into an icy blast that still hurt my charred skin but didn't make it feel as if I were standing under lava straight from the volcano.

My shower was quick, and I hardly used my loofah-turned-torture-device, but I managed to get through it. Shivering, in a sort of pain that was almost surreal, I stepped out of the shower, thankful the ordeal was nearly over. Drying off was a chore; my fluffy blue towel felt like it was made from steel wool when I passed it over my skin, which glowed a vibrant red that would stop traffic. I looked—and felt—radioactive.

Misfit watched me with the same distrust I showed the shower as I got dressed and went into the kitchen to feed him. He wasn't used to sudden, loud sounds. He overcame his worry that I might scream again as soon as his food hit the bowl, and he just about knocked me over to get to it.

"Glad I could be of service," I told him, unwilling to bend over to pet him, as was my custom.

I somehow managed to get through breakfast without whimpering too much, though Misfit watched me with concern once he was done with his own meal. I was a total wimp when it came to pain, a fact that had been made abundantly obvious over the years. I gathered my purse, making the mistake of pulling it up onto my shoulder for a half second before yelping and choosing to carry it instead. This was going to be a fun day.

Outside, the heat-lamp feeling intensified as the early-morning sun beat down on me. It was just as hot as it had been the day before and, with my burned skin, felt ten times as horrible. I scurried to my orange Escape and leaped for the shade inside like a vampire chased by the sun. I turned the AC on full blast and sat back with my eyes closed.

A knock on the window startled yet another scream from me. I jerked upright to find my neighbor Caitlin Blevins standing outside my vehicle, a chagrined smile on her face. She'd recently moved into the house of my late neighbor, Eleanor Winthrow, and while our relationship had started out rocky, we'd become something akin to friends.

I rolled down the window, managing my own weak smile as I did.

"Hi, Caitlin," I said. Caitlin was short and stocky, with shoulder-length brown hair that was pulled up off her neck. She was dressed in shorts that went to her knees and a tank top that sagged on her frame. Her feet were bare, and I noted definition in her arms that I could only dream of. I guess playing guitar served as a pretty good upper-body workout.

"Hey, Krissy." She wiped a hand across her forehead, which immediately beaded with sweat again. "I'm not going to keep you. I just wanted to warn you about tonight."

Uh-oh. "What's going on tonight?"

Caitlin glanced back toward her house, but no one else was there. She lived alone, and as far as I was aware, she didn't have a boyfriend or girlfriend. "It might get loud."

"You don't have to tell me when you want to play your game," I said, relieved that it wasn't something worse—or deadly. Caitlin played a video game, which required a real guitar, at a volume that was often just this side of deafening. "It's what the guitar is for."

She ducked her head, as if embarrassed at the mention of the guitar I'd bought for her as both a peace offering and a thank-you for saving me from a murderer. "I'm not playing *Rocksmith* tonight," she said. "But I am having some friends over."

"That shouldn't be a problem," I said, wondering why this was such a big deal. Then again, I hadn't met her friends yet and was kind of curious. Caitlin had kept mostly to herself since moving in. I knew some of her reticence was because of an old friend who used to stalk her, and I hoped she was starting to come out of her shell a bit more.

"We're playing." Another embarrassed head bob. "Practicing."

I almost asked her, "For what?" before I finally understood. "You're in a band?" I made it a question, though I was pretty sure that had to be it. Why else would she need to warn me about the volume?

She nodded, red climbing up her neck to color her cheeks. "Yeah. We've just started out, so we're not that good yet. We normally practice at Teek's place, but his mom is visiting."

And I assumed his mom wasn't a big fan of rock music. "It shouldn't be a problem," I said, wondering how true that was. As I noted before, Misfit didn't like loud sounds, though he'd get over it eventually. "You guys can practice all you want."

"Thanks. We won't play late." Caitlin stepped back. "I'll let you go." A mischievous smirk found her face. "I'll keep the guys in line. They won't bother you, other than the noise."

"I'm sure you'll be fine." I hoped.

Caitlin finally relaxed. She waved before she returned home, a skip in her step. I watched until she was inside her house, wondering if I'd just made a huge mistake, and then deciding that no, if she was happy, I was happy. I could put up with loud music, just as long it wasn't a nightly event.

Feeling as if the day was starting to look up, I backed out of my driveway and headed for work.

Death by Coffee was already open by the time I

arrived, and most of the seats were taken by customers nursing cold cappuccinos, iced coffees, and, in some cases, ice water. There were a few hot drinks being consumed, but not as many as usual, thanks to the oppressive heat.

Beth Milner was working the counter downstairs, while a new hire, Eugene Dohmer—pronounced *Dough-mer*, not *Dauh-mer*, as I'd made the mistake of saying—was upstairs with the books. I slid in behind the counter and immediately began helping Beth fill orders, albeit slowly, and with much wincing.

Within an hour of my arrival, the rush died down enough that Beth and I could lean against the counter for a breather. Sweat made my shirt heavy and sticky, despite the air-conditioning, which was running overtime.

"This is brutal," Beth said, retying her hair, which had come loose during the rush. "I heard it's not supposed to cool down for another two weeks."

"We'll get through it," I said, hoping I was right. I wasn't even sure I was going to make it through today, let alone another two weeks of this.

Beth must have thought the same thing because she glanced at me askance. "You're looking pretty rough. And I don't mean that as an insult."

"I *am* feeling pretty crummy right now," I admitted. "Too much sun, not enough water." Just the thought of water made my dry mouth drier. I filled a cup with some from the tap.

"I'd ask how the marathon went, but . . ." Beth frowned. "I can't believe he's dead."

I downed half of my water and felt marginally better for it. "You knew Glen?"

She made a seesaw motion with her hand. "Kind of, I guess. He used to come in a lot while I was working, mostly when you and Vicki weren't here. He used to be pretty flirty with me, and I'd started to wonder if he was only showing up because of me."

That jibed with what Lance told me about Glen Moreau and his past. "I heard he thought himself a ladies' man."

"Well, if he was, his charms didn't work on me," Beth said, making a face. "I found him kind of creepy. He eventually got the message and didn't come around quite as much as he used to. When he did show up, he barely looked at me, like he was giving me the cold shoulder, which was fine by me. Not to be rude, but I wasn't interested."

"When was the last time Glen was here?" I asked.

"Three or four days ago." A customer came in, and Beth filled her coffee order before continuing. "He ordered two iced coffees, which surprised me because he always got just the one and he always got it hot. It's why I remember it." She pointed toward a corner table well away from the windows. "He took them over there, to where a blond woman sat. I figured at first that she was the reason he'd given up on me."

I perked up at mention of the woman. "Did you recognize her?"

"I didn't get a good look at her," Beth said. "Her back was to me, and honestly, I wasn't paying them much mind. I had a lot going on that day. I just know that at one point, Glen said something the woman didn't like. She raised her voice, stood, and then hurried out of Death by Coffee. Glen typed something into his phone and then followed her out. They both left their drinks on the table."

My mind raced over the possibilities. Jules and Lance had said Glen and his ex-wife had split on bad terms. Could they have met here, in Death by Coffee, to attempt to work through those troubles? Could it have been the woman he'd supposedly cheated on her with? Someone else? Like someone involved in the alleged financial crimes?

Someone involved with the marathon?

Thinking back to what I'd seen at the Banyon Tree, I wondered. Rod was worried Glen would talk about something, something that Alleah Trotter also knew about. Could she have been the woman Glen met with, and could that meeting have somehow led to his death? She *was* blond, but so were a lot of women.

And wasn't the woman Johan snuck off with blond as well?

I know a man died, but I couldn't help but feel that whatever Johan was up to was more important. Rita had a lot to do with that. And if it turned out he had something to do with the murder . . .

The door opened. and two women came in, saving me from having to finish that thought. Beth said something else, but I completely missed it in my surprise at seeing them together.

"Trisha?" I asked. "Shannon? I didn't know you two knew each other."

"Hi, Krissy," Shannon Pardue said, smiling as she rested a hand upon her bulging belly. I'd only learned her last name by chance a few months ago, which I was kind of ashamed about. We'd known each other a lot longer. "We didn't until recently."

Trisha Dunhill, who was resting her own hand upon her own belly, nodded. "But when you are pregnant at the same time, it's almost impossible not to bump into one another."

"Literally."

They both laughed.

I'd found out that both Trisha and Shannon were pregnant nearly at the same time. Trisha was married to my ex-boyfriend, Robert Dunhill, and Shannon had once dated my current boyfriend, Paul Dalton. Thankfully, the child wasn't his. I wasn't sure how I'd have navigated *that* if it had been.

Either way, it was strange seeing the two women together. They were connected to me thanks to the men I'd dated. And while our relationships with one another hadn't always been smooth, I was on good terms with each of them now.

"Well, I'm glad to see both of you," I said, and I meant it. "Is there something I can get you?"

"A pair of iced coffees, I think," Shannon said, glancing at Trisha, who nodded. "I'd normally go for something chocolatey, but oddly, I haven't wanted chocolate since I've gotten pregnant."

"I can't get enough of it," Trisha said. "I'm trying to wean myself off the sweets or else I'll end up a bigger balloon than I already am."

Both women looked fantastic to me, although they looked like they wanted to be off their feet. Trisha kept shifting her weight, while Shannon winced every time she leaned one way or the other. "The coffees are on me," I said. "You two should go ahead and sit down. I'll bring your drinks out to you."

"Thank you," Trisha said, relief in her voice. They waddled over to the nearest table and eased down, making sure not to knock into anything with their bellies as they did.

A strange sensation fluttered though me as I watched them. I'd never wanted kids all that much, yet looking at how uncomfortable Shannon and Trisha were now, I wondered if I was missing out on something special. It was a strange thought, but it wasn't one I could shake as I put their orders together and carried them out to the table.

"I can't imagine what she's going through," Shannon was saying as I set the coffees down. "They might have gotten a divorce, but you can't just pretend you didn't have a history."

I really should have walked away and left them to their conversation, but I couldn't help myself.

"Who are you talking about?" I asked, pretty sure I already knew.

Trisha bit her lower lip and looked away. It was Shannon who answered.

"Melanie Johnson," she said. "Her ex-husband just died."

"He was murdered," Trisha said. "You've probably heard about it."

"Glen Moreau." Both women nodded.

"Melanie runs a sort of new-age group from her home," Shannon said. "She helps women get through tough times, including pregnancy, which can be mentally rough. And it's really helped with some of the stuff I've been going through with my family."

Shannon's family didn't approve of her boyfriend choices, and they most definitely didn't approve of her getting pregnant by a guy who didn't stick around afterward.

"She's helped me quite a lot," Trisha said. "I have my own issues to navigate through. Melanie's group is how we met, actually."

They shared a fond smile that made me feel left out. Quite suddenly, I wanted to be a part of their group, to hang out with these two women and help them through these tough times.

But that was something that had to happen naturally. I couldn't just butt my way into their lives and start following them around.

"Did Melanie talk about Glen much?" I asked.

Trisha and Shannon glanced at one another. Something passed between them, a silent communication that once again made me feel as if I was being left out, before Trisha answered.

"Not really. She mentioned him from time to time, mostly when she was trying to explain how to get through certain mental traumas. I guess things got bad between them near the end of their marriage, and she was in a dark place for a while. She got through it, though. It's what inspired her to start her group."

"She's strong, but I do worry about her," Shannon said. "Divorced is one thing. Having someone you loved enough to have a child with end up murdered is a whole other animal."

She looked up at me, and I swear I caught a

flare of something in her eye. I had no doubts that she still cared about Paul, but she'd promised she had no interest in trying to get him back, and I believed her.

Still, the history was there. It wasn't something I could—or would want to—erase. And that history could someday either bond us or cause friction that would ruin any chance of a friendship between us.

"What's the name of her business?" I asked. "Maybe she could help me with a few things." Like my burning desire to know what happened at the marathon where her ex-husband had died.

And if she knows something about Johan, all the better.

I had no evidence that she even knew who he was, but I was finding it hard to believe that Johan just happened to show up at a marathon he wasn't running in not long before a man was killed.

"A Woman's Place," Trisha said.

"It's a play on the dated idea that a woman's place is in the kitchen. She has a story about how Glen told her that once and how he ended up spending the night on the couch with a spatula-shaped welt across his cheek." Shannon smiled, but it faded quickly. "And now he's gone."

"Hey, if you are thinking of going, maybe you can come with the two of us," Trisha said. "You don't have to be pregnant to join the group. There's a lot of self-reflection, meditation, and stuff like that going on. Everyone is welcome, and I find it's better to have someone you know there with you. It makes opening up a little easier." She reached across the table to clasp Shannon's hand.

I didn't want them to know the real reason I wanted to talk to Melanie Johnson, though I was flattered that Trisha wanted me to go with them. Maybe she'd noticed how I'd felt excluded and was trying to make up for it. Or maybe she genuinely wanted me around.

Either way, it made me feel bad rejecting the offer, but if I wanted to ask Melanie about Glen or Johan, I couldn't have Shannon and Trisha there.

"For my first time, I kind of want to go alone to meet Melanie," I said. "You know, get a feel for what she does and decide if it's for me?"

"Oh." Trisha looked crestfallen.

"But if you want to get together and do something else, I'd love to get to know you better." I turned to Shannon. "Both of you."

"That'd be great." Trisha pulled out her phone. "I could always call you sometime, and we could set it up." She sounded genuinely excited by the prospect. Hormones? Or a real desire to get to know her husband's ex?

I took her phone and typed in my number. I then took Shannon's device when she offered it and did the same thing. Considering how our relationships had started, this felt almost surreal, like I was still in bed, hallucinating. With how I'd felt earlier, I'd put the odds at fifty-fifty.

I handed the phones back. Both women immediately sent me a text so I'd have their numbers. My phone buzzed in my pocket twice to let me know I'd gotten them.

"I'd better get back to work," I said, suppressing tears. I was touched that they actually cared enough to reach out. I didn't make friends easily, thanks to my blunt, nosy-but-semi-introverted nature. "Enjoy your coffees."

"I'll get hold of you soon," Trisha promised me.

I left them to their coffees, returning behind the counter, where I spent the next five minutes trying not to cry.

Who knew making friends could be so emotional?

7

A Woman's Place was located in a gathering of tiny homes scattered around one of the smaller hills that Pine Hills was named for. A few mobile homes lined the winding street, and a camper sat surrounded by a circle of fledgling trees that made it look like an overlarge fairy ring.

But just because the houses were small didn't mean they were unsightly or rundown. The mobile homes had gardens and flower beds, and looked to be well cared for by their owners. Even the camper appeared as if it had grown roots and become a permanent dwelling. No trash littered the yards. No grouchy smokers sat outside with beer cans in hand, screaming obscenities to anyone who passed.

It was the perfect location for women who simply wanted to escape the bustle of their lives, even if only briefly.

I wound my way around the bend until I came

upon the address I'd found for A Woman's Place. The house, like those around it, was small, but tidy. There was no marquee out front, no OPEN sign or any indication that it was anything more than someone's home. A mailbox sat beside a gravel driveway that looked to have recently been replenished with fresh gravel. The stones had that almost white, dusty appearance to them, and they made a loud crunching sound as I pulled in behind a shiny PT Cruiser.

I'd changed from the clothes I'd worn at work, but despite having the Escape's air-conditioning on full blast, my shirt was already plastered to my back, and my face felt as if I'd shoved it into a large bowl of butter. I glanced at myself in the rearview mirror and tried to do something with my limp hair, but in these conditions, it was impossible to do much more than pull it into a ponytail and hope it didn't look *too* bad. My makeup was a disaster that would have to do since it would just melt off again if I tried to fix it.

A curtain swished in the small house, telling me I'd been noticed. With nothing else I could do to make myself semi-presentable, I climbed out of my vehicle.

The door to the house opened before I'd reached the front stoop. A woman in jeans and a plain black T-shirt stood in the doorway with her muscular arms crossed. She stood a head taller than me and wore her blond hair in a way that was reminiscent of Joan Jett in her heyday. Minus the black, of course.

"Melanie Johnson?" I asked, somewhat wary. When Shannon and Trisha had told me about the place, I'd envisioned a barefoot, ring-laden spiritual woman wearing a flower-print dress, not someone who looked like they could handle themselves in a bar fight.

"I am." The corners of her mouth quirked, as if she was amused by my trepidation.

"I'm Krissy Hancock." I stopped in front of her, unsure if I should offer my hand to shake or if I was expected to bow. I opted for neither. "Is this A Woman's Place?"

"It is." Some of the tension around her eyes eased, and her smile became far more relaxed. "Come on in." She stepped aside.

"Thank you. It's miserable out here." I entered the house with a sigh of relief as cool air blasted me.

There wasn't much to the place that screamed business. Immediately to the right was the kitchen, which was small, but efficient. To my left was a short hallway with two closed doors I assumed led to Melanie's bedroom and bathroom. The only other room in the place was set up to be comfortable, with chairs facing one another, rather than toward the TV hanging on the wall.

I definitely didn't get a new-age vibe, though I suppose I wasn't exactly sure what the term meant.

"How'd you hear about me, if you don't mind me asking?" Melanie asked. "Can I get you a tea? Coffee?"

"A water would be great," I said.

She nodded and went to the fridge for the water.

"Trisha Dunhill and Shannon Pardue told me," I said when she'd returned with the water bottle. It was cold and tasted like heaven. "They only had good things to say about you and what you do here."

Melanie's eyes crinkled at the corners when she smiled. She had one of those faces that normally looked young, but when she made certain expressions, you could discern her real age in the wrinkles. I could see what Glen would have seen in her.

"I'm glad to hear it. I've taken to both those women a great deal." She paused, looking me up and down. "You said your name was Krissy, right?"

"I did."

Melanie gestured for me to sit. When I was settled, she took the seat across from me. "Both Trisha and Shannon have spoken of you."

"Good things, I hope."

There was enough hesitation in her response that I knew that wasn't the case. "Mostly," she said with a laugh that was on the husky side. "Your history with them is complicated, so some conflicted emotions are natural."

I felt a moment of shame for causing any sort of distress for Shannon or Trisha, but considering our pasts, I should have expected it. I mean, I've confronted our history face-to-face a few times and had worried about it myself over the years, so it's not like it should have come as a surprise to hear that it still might be an issue for them.

"So . . ." I glanced around the room. There were no crystals or incense burners or anything like that around. No tarot cards either. "What exactly do you do here?"

Melanie considered the question before sitting back and resting her ankle on her knee. "We talk. This isn't a business where I make money, so don't worry about that. I'm here for you. To listen. To give advice. To support you in areas of your life that you don't feel strong enough or capable enough to handle on your own."

"Like a therapist?" I asked.

"In a way, I suppose," Melanie said. "But I'm not licensed, and like I said, I don't take payment. I wanted to create a place where women could go to get away for a little while. Where they could talk about things that are bothering them without judgment, where they can find the support they need when no one else is willing to listen."

I wondered if both Shannon and Trisha were feeling that way. It made me want to call them and apologize for whatever frustrations I'd caused them and offer an ear for them to vent those frustrations.

"We all have things that trouble us," Melanie went on. "Sometimes it's our love life. Sometimes it's family. And sometimes it's simply life in general." She leaned forward, placing both feet back on the ground. "What is it that's bothering you, Krissy?"

I hesitated, unsure what to say. I wasn't there for myself, not really. I wanted to know why Johan was sneaking off with another woman, and why Glen was murdered. And whether or not those two things intersected.

Yet something about Melanie's demeanor made me want to talk, to relieve some of the stresses that have lurked just underneath the surface for years.

"I guess I feel bad," I said, lowering my head. "I feel like I make people's lives worse by being a part of them."

"What makes you think that?"

I shrugged. I felt like a little kid again. "I'm nosy. I sometimes act before I think. And because I do, I hurt people's feelings." I thought back to all the times I'd said or done something that upset someone in town. The shame made my face burn worse than the sun had.

"We all say and do things we regret," Melanie said, reaching out to tap my knee with her finger. "Hey, look at me."

I raised my chin, though it was a struggle to meet her eye.

"We all make mistakes. We're human. It's a cliché, but that doesn't make it any less valid. What's important is that you stay true to yourself, that you don't give up on what makes you *you* because someone doesn't like it. Trying to live for someone else is no way to live."

I started to drop my eyes again, but her firm stare held me in place.

"Now, I don't mean that you shouldn't strive to make yourself a better person. We all could use a little self-improvement every now and again. But never, ever give up yourself for someone else. If they don't like the way you are, the way you live, then that person isn't right for you. Do you understand what I'm saying?"

I nodded. "Be me."

She jabbed a finger at me as she sat back. "Exactly. If you like taking bubble baths with a horde of little green army figures while listening to Celine Dion's greatest hits played at full volume, then do it."

That sounded awfully specific, and I wondered

if that was the sort of thing Melanie, or one of the women who came to talk to her, was into.

"What made you get into this sort of thing?" I asked, hoping I could steer the conversation onto something less about me and more about her and her ex-husband.

"People need a place where they can let their frustrations free," she said. "Where they won't be judged for who they are."

"I know, but I mean, was there something specific that caused you to become interested in helping other women?" And then, to goad her in the direction I wanted, "I heard you were married to Glen Moreau."

Her face clouded over, and her lips pressed together, causing lines to form around her mouth. "I was. And, yes, he was a driving factor in why I do what I do."

"I don't know if you've heard, but—"

"He's dead." It came out flat, almost emotionless. "I know. My phone just about rang off the hook when it happened."

"Were you two still close?"

She laughed. "Hardly. I hadn't talked to Glen since we divorced. Not in any meaningful way, anyway. Our split wasn't amicable."

"So, you didn't meet him at Death by Coffee?" I'd noted her blond hair and had instantly made the connection to what Beth had told me.

She made a face. "No, I didn't. I wouldn't have met with him, even if he'd asked. We'd already said what we had to say to one another long ago, and there was no sense rehashing it or allowing the arguments our being in the same place at the same time spawned."

"You fought?"

"All of the time, especially near the end. Honestly, we shouldn't have gotten married in the first place. We were kids. We were stupid. I got pregnant with Jase, and I suppose Glen wanted to do the right thing by proposing."

"Jase is your son." Obvious, but I wanted to keep her talking.

"He is." She said it with the same lack of emotion as she had when she'd commented on Glen's death. "I think our constant fighting affected Jase far more than we realized at the time." She sighed. "And I suppose I did love Glen. I knew what kind of man he was when we started dating, and honestly, I wasn't intending to marry him, let alone get pregnant."

"But things happen."

Her smile returned, albeit barely. "That they do. Glen was always getting new girlfriends, having one-night stands. It had been his life since he discovered women existed, and I suppose I thought it was kind of exciting being with a guy everyone wanted. Then, when we got married, he seemed to settle down, but I could tell he wasn't happy."

"He couldn't be him," I said, thinking back to what Melanie had said about me.

"No, he couldn't. Until he was."

"He cheated."

Her nod was more thoughtful than angry. "I don't know exactly when it started. I'm sure he was doing it before I found out about it." This time, her laugh was bitter. "But then I caught him red-handed, and the arguments began in earnest. We'd been having trouble long before that, but after I saw him with that woman . . ." She shook her head. "It was bad."

I could only imagine. "I had a boyfriend cheat on me once before." I considered whether or not to reveal who that boyfriend was, and then decided Melanie wouldn't use it in a bad way. In fact, it might help her understand Trisha better. "It was Robert Dunhill, actually. Trisha's husband. This was long before they'd met."

"Really? He cheated on *you*?" Some of the tension bled from her as she considered that. "That explains some of Trisha's anxiety . . ." She trailed off as if she said more than she'd meant to. "Anyway, it's not fun having someone you care about look for love elsewhere. I mean, I get that sometimes people feel the need to explore, to break routine, but that wasn't what Glen was doing."

"He planned on leaving you?"

"I think so. The relationship that broke us was a full-on romance sort of thing. Flowers, dates, and so on. Not just a fling. Not just a side piece he planned on discarding once it became inconvenient or stale. I was upset, of course. But when Jase found out . . ."

"He was angry with his father."

"Angry?" She laughed. "He exploded. I swear, I thought he was going to kill him. Jase has always had a problem keeping his anger in check. To live in a house so full of unhappiness, it's no wonder." She closed her eyes, and I could see the pain flash across her face as she thought about her part in that.

"I'm sure it wasn't your fault."

"Yeah, well, tell that to Jase. He blamed Glen for cheating, of course, but he also accused me of not doing enough to keep my husband happy. As soon as he turned eighteen, he was out of the house, and I haven't seen him since." She blinked rapidly, and then a mask fell into place. "Anyway, that's why I do what I do. We all need to get stuff like that out so it can breathe. No one should let such emotions fester."

All the talk about cheating made me think of Johan and the blonde he'd slunk off with. I didn't want to think about how hard it would be for Rita if he was indeed cheating.

But while I wanted to ask if Melanie knew anything about Johan Morrison, I also wasn't done asking about her husband.

"I heard a rumor that Glen was involved in some sort of financial crime. Do you know anything about that?"

"No, I don't. I wouldn't put it past him, honestly, but if he was involved in anything of the sort, he did so after we'd separated."

There was a tentative knock at the door. "Melanie? It's Cora Lynn. I really need to talk to you."

"One moment," Melanie called before looking at me. "This should take only a minute or two." She rose and started toward the door.

"Actually, I should get going," I said, rising. I hadn't asked her about Johan, but I was feeling more and more like I should talk to Rita about him first, just in case. "Thank you for your time and for talking to me about Glen. It couldn't have been easy."

"No, but things like that rarely are. It was my pleasure to listen. Please, come back anytime." She rested a hand on my bicep and squeezed.

"Thank you. I might do that." And I found that I meant it.

We both turned toward the door, but before she opened it to Cora, Melanie hesitated. Something passed over her face, an emotion that was both conflicted and determined.

"You know, if you want to know more about what Glen was up to before his death, you should talk to Ivy Hammer." Her face hardened, and I saw genuine anger simmering behind her eyes. "She's the woman he cheated on me with, and I'm pretty sure he was with her the night before he died."

8

Misfit purred from his spot next to me on the couch. Every so often, one of his massive paws would reach out, claws extended, and then would pull back into the ball of his orange fur without grabbing anything. My best guess was that he was having a pleasant kitty dream in which he was kneading a blanket. I made sure to keep my toes well away from his grasp lest he catch hold by accident.

I was seated cross-legged, laptop in my lap, and a mug of once-hot tea sitting on the coffee table in front of me. I was feeling more myself, though my skin still felt a smidge too tight, a little too crispy. It appeared I had mostly recovered from my over-cooked state and was now in the itchy healing stage.

But my body's recovery didn't mean I was having any luck coming up with Glen Moreau's killer. Or remembering whatever it was I felt I was forgetting about that day. If anything, the suspect list was growing, though I was glad it consisted of more names than Johan Morrison, who I still wasn't sure what to do about. Rita was my friend, and I felt a responsibility to let her know that her boyfriend might not be who he says he is.

Unless he was out for a stroll with a coworker before they both left town on business. I could be making a big deal out of nothing, though I still had no idea what it was Johan did for a living or if he even had coworkers.

No, it was more likely that my first assumption was closer to the mark and he was cheating on my friend.

I sighed and clicked over to the marathon's Facebook page in the hopes of spotting a clue. More posts. More photos. And, like before, nothing jumped out at me.

"Someone had to have seen something," I said, causing Misfit to raise his head briefly before going back to sleep. Hundreds of people had shown up for the event. Between the runners, the organizers, and the people who'd come to support us, there were eyes everywhere.

There was no way I was going to be able to talk to everyone who might have seen something that would explain Johan's presence or Glen's murder. I wasn't even sure the police could pull off questioning everyone. Even with the posted photos as a guide to who was there, it would be nearly impossible to identify all of the spectators.

So, where did that leave me?

Stuck. That's where.

Unsure what else to do, I decided to be proactive and send out some feelers. I sent messages to all three of the organizers—Rod, Alleah, and Jen—in the hope that one of them might be willing to talk. I also chose a few people who'd posted the most, those who had taken the most photos, asking if they'd seen or heard anything. I had no idea if any of them would respond, but at least I felt that I was doing *something*.

Cassie. Don't forget about Cassie Wise.

It took me a moment to find her profile on Facebook. I sent her a friend request, along with a message, and hoped that she checked the site often enough that I'd hear from her soon. She seemed like a nice person, and I wouldn't mind getting to know her a little better. Goodness knows, I could always use a few more friendly faces.

That done, I closed my laptop and set it aside. The name Melanie had given me, Ivy Hammer, played over and over in my mind, but I wasn't able to find much on her, and I'd checked as soon as I'd sat down. She wasn't in the news, wasn't a prominent member of Pine Hills. Her social media profiles were private, and her profile image was of a cute kitten that looked like it was a stock photo, rather than a cat of her own.

I did find an address for her, however. I'd taken note of it but wasn't sure what I planned to do with it. I wasn't keen on showing up on someone's doorstep unannounced.

Who was I kidding? That's exactly the sort of thing I did on a regular basis.

But not right now.

I leaned my head back and closed my eyes. It was well before my normal bedtime, yet I was considering pulling on my PJs and going to bed early anyway. I didn't expect to hear from Paul, not with a murder investigation going on, though I was curious about what the call that had cut our lunch date short was about. I also wanted to tell him what little I'd learned since we'd last talked, just in case it helped speed the investigation along.

I glanced at my phone, but it was all the way across the room, sitting on the island counter. I raised a hand and tried to will it to float over to me, but alas, it remained stationary. It appeared as if my overexposure to the sun's rays hadn't given me superpowers. Oh well.

I was about to lean back and take a nap when the world exploded.

One minute, I was sitting calmly in the quiet of my own house, cat snoozing contentedly beside me, and the next, I was standing halfway across the room, and Misfit was an orange streak shooting down the hall, into the bedroom.

"What in the world?"

Crash! Boom! Clang!

And then a searing blast of noise, followed by a throat-tearing scream.

My heart climbed back down from where it was pounding inside my skull as I realized what I was hearing. No, the world wasn't ending.

Caitlin's band had begun to practice.

I'd known it was going to be loud, but I hadn't anticipated that it would be bone-rattlingly so. Turning on the TV wouldn't drown it out, nor would playing music of my own. I doubted a jet engine would override the decibel levels that were causing my windows to rattle and my insides to turn to liquid.

There was no way I was going to be able to nap through that. And I most definitely wouldn't be able to think clearly enough to work on a puzzle or come up with Glen's killer.

That was all the prodding I needed.

I snatched up my phone and keys and was out the door without another thought.

My ears only rang a little as I drove, my mind firmly on the task ahead of me. I wasn't sure what I was going to say or how I'd approach this without coming off as overly nosy. Considering my reputation as such, I wasn't sure it mattered.

Still, I was learning to at least try to make it seem that I wasn't poking my nose into other people's business, even when that was exactly what I was doing. It might not always work, but hey, at least I was making the attempt.

Of course, what I really should have been doing was letting the police handle the investigation without my intervention. Maybe someday I'd do just that.

But today was not that day.

Ivy Hammer lived in a duplex on the opposite end of town from where Melanie Johnson resided. A FOR RENT sign hung on the door next to her own, telling me that she had the place to herself for now. There were other similar houses along the street, and all of them were of a condition that was leaning toward dilapidated, Ivy's place included.

A dark blue Dodge Charger sat in front of the

duplex. It wasn't beat up, but like the houses around it, it didn't look overly cared for either. I parked behind it since there was only on-street parking here, despite what looked like an old driveway that had been left to grow over. Only a few bare patches where the gravel had been crushed into the earth remained amid the brown grass.

I climbed out of my Escape and passed by the Charger, peeking in the windows to see if I could see anything that would tell me something about the owner. The inside was immaculate. Not even a stray tissue or flake of dust ruined the pristine interior. Maybe I'd misjudged, and it was well-cared for.

A door opened, and a pretty blonde in shorts that had been cut even shorter, so that the pockets were hanging out from beneath the ragged hem, and I use that world loosely, stepped outside. Her shirt was probably two sizes too small, which meant it had to have come from the kids' section because the woman was tiny.

"Can I help you?" she asked, crossing her arms. A pair of silver bracelets jingled like wind chimes whenever she moved.

"I'm sorry," I said, stepping away from the car. "I was just looking." Before she could ask me if I was a thief—or worse, a car buff (she would learn how embarrassingly little I knew about cars)—I pressed on. "You wouldn't happen to be Ivy Hammer, would you?"

Her eyes narrowed, and she shifted her position as if she was getting ready for a physical confrontation. "Yeah?"

"Hi, I'm Krissy Hancock." I didn't want to walk

directly through her yard, so I took the ancient driveway to the front door and held out a hand.

She just stared at it. "Do I know you?"

"No." This was going great already. "But I was given your name. This has to do with Glen Moreau."

If I'd expected her to break down and cry or recoil in surprise, I would have been disappointed. If anything, her expression hardened, as did her stance, as if anticipating a physical blow.

"What about him?" Ivy asked, her voice as guarded as the rest of her.

"I'm sure you heard about what happened?" She nodded. "I was told that you two were together the night before the marathon."

Ivy snorted. "Who told you that?" She held up a hand. I noted that her nails were cut short, and her fingers had that rough look to them that spoke of someone who worked with her hands. "No, wait. Let me guess. Melanie Johnson, right?"

There was no one else outside, but it didn't feel right discussing this out in the open, just in case someone did overhear. "Would it be all right if we talked about this in private?" I asked, smiling in a way that I hoped was friendly.

The look that passed over Ivy's face made me worry that she was going to turn me down, but she relented after a glance toward the sky. The sun might be going down, but it was still hot.

"You can come in for just a minute, but no longer than that. I've got things to do."

I followed Ivy into her house. The inside mirrored her car in that it was a massive upgrade over the exterior. The walls were painted, and decorative plates hung on the walls. The floors were clean, and nothing was out of place. The room smelled of lavender.

"All right," Ivy crossed her arms again and turned to face me without inviting me to sit on the plush couch in the living room. "What did Melanie say?"

"Nothing, really. We were talking about Glen, and she mentioned that you and Glen were dating."

"Debatable."

I floundered for a moment before going on. "She said that you two were together the night before he died. I was at the marathon and was one of the first people on the scene, which is why I'm curious." It was a lame excuse, but I felt as if I needed to say something.

"Melanie says a lot of things," Ivy said. "She thinks that because her life fell apart, mine should also. I wasn't even with Glen."

"You mean before he died?"

"I mean, ever." She sighed. "Look, Glen came on to me, and I guess I was flattered. My life hasn't been easy, and it was nice to have someone look at me like he did. But this was a long time ago. And it lasted until I found out he was already married. I wasn't interested in becoming some side fling, so I left him."

"I was under the impression Glen and Melanie broke up because of you."

"They might have." She shrugged as if it didn't matter one way or the other. "I didn't tell Melanie anything about what happened, but someone must have. She texted me and threatened me for months afterward. So did"—she flushed—"her son."

"Jase texted you?"

"He did. He was upset, and he had every right to be. I told him it was nothing, and after some . . . persuading, he believed me." She looked me up and down. "Why does any of this matter to you, anyway? You said you were at the marathon, but I don't buy it. Were you screwing Glen too?"

My face flushed despite not having anything to be embarrassed about. "Oh no, I never talked to him, let alone dated him."

Ivy laughed. "I'm surprised. When you first showed up here, I glanced out the window and immediately thought that you were Ellen, though your hair . . ." I assumed that meant Ellen was blond, just like the rest of the women Glen seemed drawn to.

"Ellen?"

"I don't know her last name, and I don't know anything about her other than, as far as I was aware, she was Glen's last . . ." She frowned. "I wouldn't call anyone he dated a girlfriend. I guess *fling* does work, as much as I hate to admit it."

"Do you think she was the one he was with the night before he died?"

Ivy shrugged. "Beats me. If I were to guess, I'd say yeah. They were together last week; I do know that. I saw them talking before he headed for that place of his."

I wondered if she saw Glen and Ellen together at Death by Coffee, but something else caught my ear, something that seemed a lot more important.

"What place?"

"The one Glen always slunk off to whenever he could." Ivy's entire demeanor changed. She dropped her arms, and for the first time since I'd invaded her life, she looked scared. "You know, forget I said anything, would you?"

"Ivy." I took a step toward her, forcing her to look me in the eye. "What place? Could it have had something to do with Glen's death?"

"I don't know. Maybe." She ran her fingers through her hair, and I noted how her hand shook. "Glen was pretty secretive about it. Back when we . . . you know?"

I nodded.

"Well, we were together, and he got a call and took off. I got mad, thinking that he was running off to see some other girl. This was after I found out about Melanie, but before I knew what to do about it." She rolled her eyes, as if annoyed with herself, before she went on. "I followed him to this creepy little building. He went in and was there for like ten minutes before he left carrying a brief-case. I don't know where he went after that, and I never asked him. Something about the whole affair freaked me out."

"Did you see anyone else go in or out?"

"No. Just Glen. But I saw other people in the area, and I swear one of them was watching me. I couldn't so much as look at the guy without shaking, so I avoided it."

"What did he look like?"

"I can't remember." Before I could press her, she hurriedly went on. "Honestly. I couldn't look at him, and once Glen left, I was out of there like a shot."

That wasn't what I wanted to hear, but I suppose it was to be expected. Still, I tried not to let my excitement show when I asked, "Where is this building?"

After some hemming and hawing, she told me. I thanked her and had just stepped outside when she reached out and grabbed me by the arm. Her grip was surprisingly strong.

"Be careful, all right? A few days after I followed Glen, some strange things happened around here, and I'm pretty sure it had to do with that creepy guy who watched me."

"Strange things? Such as?"

She shook her head—unwilling, or too afraid, to say it out loud. "Just . . . be careful." And then she closed and locked the door.

9

A loud ringing filled my Escape, along with cracking and popping, telling me that something wasn't quite right. I'd had Mason help me get my phone paired to my vehicle last week and still wasn't used to it. It did allow me to make a call while driving, which was a bonus, but either I was doing it wrong or the connection wasn't what it should be.

Not that anyone ever answered when I needed them.

I tapped the touch screen on the dash, ending the call as it went to voice mail. Paul was likely busy, and I didn't need to add to the events of his day by telling him about the building Ivy had described to me. Once I'd had a look to make sure it wasn't just a local shop or a law office, then I could call him back and leave a message.

The place I was looking for was only a few streets away from Death by Coffee, on a street called Rosebud Avenue. Most of the businesses lining Rosebud offered services rather than items for sale—lawyers' offices, tax accountants, and so on. Everything was brown, boring, and so nondescript, it was the perfect place to house a criminal enterprise.

I coasted by Tellitocci and Sons, vaguely surprised it was still there. While no one who worked there had been involved in a murder, one of the lawyers there had tried to protect a client who was. You'd think that would put a damper on business, but I suppose some people are lucky.

I continued on until I reached the end of Rosebud Avenue. I glanced back over my shoulder with a frown. Somehow, I'd missed the address I was looking for.

Careful not to hit anyone—or anything—I found a place where I could turn around and, this time, took the road at a crawl. There was little traffic, foot or otherwise, meaning I didn't need to rush. One brown building melded into the next, and before long, my eyes were crossed, and I felt as if I'd gone by the same place at least a dozen times.

And then I saw it.

It was a tiny brown box of a building that looked like a warehouse that had been hit by a shrink ray so it would fit inside what was once an alley. One of those check-cashing places that always felt a bit skeevy to me sat on one side. Its QUICK logo was surrounded by dollar signs. A laundromat with dirty windows and machines that appeared to be thirty years out of date sat on the other side. There was no sign out front.

*It looks like the sort of place where more than just cloth-
ing gets laundered.*

I drove past without stopping to make sure
there were no bulky security types standing outside, but the only person I saw was a short older
woman sitting in the laundromat, reading a magazine. I couldn't tell if she worked there or if she
was waiting for her clothes to dry.

"Who's ready for a stakeout?"

Since I was the only one in the vehicle, I guess
that meant me.

I turned around and found a place to park
across the street from the small building. Thankfully, other vehicles were lined up there, so I didn't
stand out too much. I mean, the orange of my Escape wasn't subtle, so it did draw the eye, but who
would expect me to be watching a nondescript
place in a very descript vehicle? And considering it
was still light out, I hoped that whoever operated
out of that place would let their guard down and
wouldn't be too concerned about someone watching their doors.

I didn't shut off the engine since I'd roast without air-conditioning and prayed that no one would
notice the exhaust. I sat back to wait, nerves jumping.

And waited.

And waited some more.

Studying the building told me nothing. There
was a single window by the door, but heavy shades
kept me from seeing inside. Not that I could have
seen much from where I was seated anyway. Like
the laundromat, there was no sign on the door,

not even one that said whether the place was open or closed. No one went in, no one went out. Of the few people who walked by, no one so much as glanced at the place as they passed.

I picked up my phone and did an online search for the address but came up with nothing. There was no listing, nothing telling me what might be inside, let alone who owned it. It could have been a storage shed, for all I knew, one owned by Glen Moreau so he could keep trophies from his many conquests. Or perhaps a place to stash a comic book collection or some sports memorabilia.

I could always go over and knock on the door. If anyone was there, they might answer and give me a peek inside. Even if they turned me away, just having someone come to the door would tell me something.

But if I did that, I would be putting myself in danger. If this was a criminal headquarters of some kind, whoever answered might mark me for trouble, and I could end up just like Glen Moreau. Ivy had mentioned strange things happening after she'd followed Glen here. I didn't need to invite the same thing to happen to me.

Staring at the building was getting me nowhere. I tried to call Paul again, figuring that if anyone would know what the building might contain, he might. And if he didn't, he'd have the resources to find out.

Voice mail. Again.

I tapped the screen to hang up without leaving a message.

With nothing else to do, I picked up my phone.

I had a few messages waiting for me, which, if nothing else, would help break the monotony. I clicked on my Messenger app and was surprised to see Rod Maxwell's name at the top of the list. I tapped the message open.

Thank you for participating in the Pine Hills marathon. I hope to see you next year.

That was it? A stock response that told me nothing.

"A lot of that going around," I grumbled, clicking on the next message. This one was from Alleah Trotter.

What happened to Glen Moreau is a tragedy. It's unfortunate that someone decided to use our event to commit such a horrible act. I only wish I had seen something that would have allowed me to prevent it from happening. I've told the police everything I know. Thank you for your concern.

Well, that was more than I'd gotten from Rod, but it still didn't help me much. It made me wonder if both Alleah and Rod's non-answers had anything to do with what they'd discussed at the Banyon Tree. A part of me wanted to ask them, but I doubted I'd get any sort of answer, stock or otherwise.

I didn't recognize the name on the next message: Skinny Jefferson. It wasn't until I opened it that I remembered that he'd been one of the photographers at the marathon, and he'd posted a vast majority of the photos on the Facebook page.

I might have something for you, he wrote. *Here's my number. Call me.*

Excited, I did just that.

"Hey, yo."

I hesitated, uncertain what to make of that. "Uh, Skinny Jefferson?"

"That's me. What's up?"

Did he think I was someone else? I pressed on. "This is Krissy Hancock. You replied to a message I sent you about photos you'd taken at the marathon."

"Yeah, yeah."

I waited, but nothing else appeared to be forthcoming. "You said you had something for me?"

"Yeah." I almost expected him to leave it at that, but thankfully, he went on this time. "So, I was thinking you could stop by."

My senses started tingling. Something wasn't right. "For?"

"Well, I could show you the photos I took."

Again, I sensed that something was off, so I asked it, "And?"

"And I was thinking that maybe you'd be willing to do a shoot."

"A shoot?"

"Yeah. You come in and model for me. I'll be the only one here, so you wouldn't need to be embarrassed. And I wouldn't share the photos with anyone without your permission, of course. They'd be tasteful and everything. And if you wanted copies to give to a boyfriend or something, I'm cool with that, just as long as you let him know it was consensual."

Ah. I got it now. "I don't think so."

"I promise that nothing you don't want to happen will happen. I'm a professional."

Professional or not, there was no way I was going to model—nude or otherwise—for Skinny Jefferson. "How old are you?" I asked. He sounded young. His answer confirmed it.

"Twenty-two."

"I . . . no. Just no."

"I'd pay, of course."

"I'm sorry, Skinny, I'm not interested." Just the thought made my skin itch. I had nothing against people who were okay with photos of that nature, but for me, it was a no all the way, no matter how much money was involved.

"Darn." There was disappointment in his voice. I had a feeling that he was hoping more would happen than a simple photo shoot.

All from a guy I've never met. It made me wonder how often he pulled something like this. I had a feeling that any and every woman who showed the slightest hint of interest in him or his photos got the same offer.

"Look, Skinny, do you have anything for me or not? Someone was murdered."

There was a long pause. I watched the front of the building across the street, and still there was no movement. I was beginning to wonder if it was indeed Glen's storage shed or man cave or some benign, out-of-the-way locale where he could escape.

Escape from what, exactly? I wondered. Even if Glen was the only person who ever went inside, there could be evidence between those walls that pointed to his killer.

"No," came the eventual reply.

It took me a moment to remember what I'd asked. "You don't have anything?"

"I didn't look. I figured you could take a peek between sets."

I closed my eyes. As much as I wanted to find something in those photos, I didn't want to put myself at the mercy of a guy named Skinny.

"I'd better go," I said. "Thank you for getting back to me."

"Hey, if you change your mind, you've got my number."

"Understood. I won't." I clicked off.

The sun was finally dropping low enough that the sky had turned a burnt orange. It was actually kind of pretty, despite hovering over such an ugly place. My stomach grumbled, reminding me that I hadn't had much to eat yet today.

"Well, this was a bust," I muttered, suppressing a yawn. I didn't know how the police did it. Stakeouts were definitely not on my "fun" list. Even if I'd brought a crossword and snacks, I'd still have been bored out of my mind.

I was about to drive off, but I paused when I noticed a car coast to a stop in front of the laundromat. I didn't recognize it, and the windows were tinted just enough that I couldn't make out who was inside, yet a tingle of excitement worked through me anyway.

I slumped in my seat, knowing that if whoever

was in the car looked my way, they'd surely see me, regardless of whether I was sitting upright or slouched. Unconsciously, I held my breath, as if that would make me invisible, and watched to see who would emerge.

It took two long minutes before the car door opened. A short, plump man somewhere between his fifties and sixties stepped out. He didn't so much as glance behind him as he hurried toward the front of the nondescript brown building I'd spent the last hour or so watching.

My mouth went completely dry, and my heart started pounding in my chest. I knew that man.

Johan Morrison.

"Oh no, Rita," I whispered, hardly able to believe my eyes as Johan entered through the front door of the building. He didn't look furtive, like he was doing something illegal, but it sure didn't look good for him. This was a place Glen Moreau had frequented. And now Johan was here? He was supposed to be out of town.

I tried to come up with some explanation as to why Johan would be here, but nothing came to mind. How could it? I didn't even know what here was.

I clutched my phone, torn between calling Paul and just pretending that I hadn't seen anything. How could I turn Johan in? He was Rita's boyfriend, someone who made her happy. I needed to know more before I made a move I couldn't take back.

I set my phone aside and watched to see what would happen, hoping that Johan would come back out, proclaiming his mistake, before heading over to the laundromat to do his laundry. Or maybe he got lost on his way to go over his accounts with a tax consultant. Heck, maybe this place *was* a tax consultant's office.

Time crawled. The longer Johan stayed inside, the worse I felt. First, Johan was seen sneaking off with a woman near the woods where Glen Moreau would eventually die. Now this. I was having a hard time imagining any way he could come out of this looking good.

I drummed my fingers on the wheel, muttering, "Come on. Come on, Johan. *Leave*," over and over under my breath.

Finally, the door opened, and Johan emerged, carrying a briefcase he hadn't taken inside. He hurried to his car, tossed the briefcase into the passenger seat, and was on the move almost before it registered on me what was happening.

Out of reflex, I put the Escape in gear, intent on following him, but caught myself. Johan might not have seen me yet, but the moment he looked into his rearview mirror and saw my big orange vehicle following him, he'd know it was me.

And then what? I doubted he'd stop and explain himself. Even if he did, I wouldn't believe him, no matter what he said. He'd lied to Rita. He wouldn't hesitate to do the same to me.

I waited until Johan was out of sight before I pulled onto the road. No one else had left the building, and I had a feeling that no one would, not as long as I was sitting there.

My stomach growled again, but I ignored it. I really hoped this was all one big coincidence, but I doubted it.

And even if it was, there was one thing I could no longer put off, no matter how much I would like to.

It was time I talked to Rita.

10

Rita's car sat in her driveway, telling me she was home. Books covered the back seat, as if she were buying them and then forgetting to take them inside with her. Either that or she read them in her car, which, knowing Rita, wasn't as strange as it sounded.

I found myself perusing the mostly romance titles and forced myself to stop. Putting off the conversation wasn't going to make it any easier. I dreaded what I was about to do and was scrambling to come up with some way to ask her about Johan without alerting her that there was something wrong.

Or should I?

Rita deserved to know if Johan was doing something illegal, whether it was financial crimes, like Glen was rumored to be involved in, or murder. I couldn't—and shouldn't—keep that from her.

But was I really the best person to break the

news? While learning it from me might soften the blow, this felt like something the police should handle. And that's even *if* Johan was committing a crime. He might not be, which was the reason for my indecision.

But he had *snuck off with another woman.*

That was something Rita should know, regardless of whether he was a criminal or not.

Rita must have seen me lingering by her car because the door opened before I could bring myself to move toward it.

"Well, hello there, dear," she said, sounding perplexed. "Was I expecting you today?" She glanced behind her as I approached, making me wonder if she was alone, or if Johan was there with her. "I was reading and lost track of time. You know how it is. You get sucked right into the story, and the next thing you know, it's two days later."

I approached the doorway. Now that she'd seen me, there was no backing out. "Hi, Rita. I'm sorry to drop in like this, but I wanted to talk." It came out sounding mechanical.

Rita was silent for a heartbeat before she spoke. "I suppose you'd best come in then. You don't look so good, dear. I hope you're taking plenty of vitamins. The heat will sap the nutrients right out of you, and before you know it, you're as sick as a dog."

She continued talking as she led me into the living room. A Nora Roberts book lay face down on the coffee table in front of the couch. A glass of iced tea with only a sliver of ice remaining sat in a growing pool of condensation beside that.

"Can I get you something to drink?" Rita asked,

already moving toward the kitchen. "It's so hot out, I shouldn't even ask. I swear, I'm getting a suntan even though I'm sitting inside. And that's with the sun going down, mind you."

I didn't respond as she poured another glass of tea. Instead, I scanned the room, searching for . . . I didn't know what exactly. Maybe I was looking for some indication that Johan was staying at Rita's place. Why that mattered in terms of what I was there for, I didn't know. Maybe I thought the lack of his presence in her home would make this easier.

It always amazed me how tidy and sedate Rita's house was, considering how boisterous she tended to be. I tried not to look toward the bedroom, knowing a cardboard cutout of my dad would be standing just inside, looking out at me.

"Where did you go, dear?" Rita asked. She'd set the tea down in front of me and was sitting on the couch. It was obvious that she'd been there for a minute or two before she'd spoken.

"Sorry. I was just thinking," I said, forcing a smile. "How's the book?"

Rita followed my gaze to the coffee table. "It's fantastic. Nora's always are." She leaned forward and lowered her voice, as if Nora Roberts might hear her if she spoke too loudly. "She's no James Hancock, of course, but I do enjoy her novels."

"Of course."

"Do you know when the next Heart book is coming out? I've plum forgotten, and I want to know when to expect my early copy." She gave me a meaningful look.

"I'll have to check." Dad had promised to send

Rita early copies of each of the two books following the first in the series, *Victim of the Heart.* He'd also claimed he might show up and deliver them in person, which would both be a curse and a blessing, considering Rita's infatuation with my dad.

"Something is wrong," Rita said, sitting back and eyeing me critically. "I can see it written all over your face." Her eyes widened, and her hand fluttered to her chest. "It isn't James, is it? If something were to happen to him, I don't know what I would do." A pause so brief, I didn't have a chance to interject myself, before, "Or is it that woman of his? Is my James a free man again?"

"Nothing's wrong with Dad." I almost stopped there but felt the need to add, "And Laura is doing just fine. They're still together."

"That's too bad." She seemed to consider that, and added, "Not that I want her to come to harm, of course. But I wouldn't mind it if she were to find someone else to cling to. I swear, most single women her age are after something, and it's usually rectangular and green."

Laura wasn't like that, but even if I said it a thousand times, Rita wouldn't believe me. She might have Johan, but Rita always acted like she would run off with my dad if he were to ask her to. I didn't think she'd actually do it, but the thought did make me uncomfortable.

"Wouldn't Johan be upset if you were to run off with another man?" I hoped the transition wasn't too obvious or clunky. It had sounded better—and far more innocent—in my head.

If it was, Rita didn't appear to notice. "He'd get

over it. And we all know that I have no chance with a man like your father. With that mind of his . . ." She made a sound I didn't ever want to hear someone make in regard to my dad. "I could lap him right up."

Okay. Yuck. I resisted the urge to cover my ears and make gagging sounds.

"Where is Johan, by the way?" I glanced around the room as if he might pop out from behind the curtains.

"He's still out of town. I'm pretty sure I told you that." She leaned from the couch, toward where I sat in the recliner, and pressed her wrist against my forehead. "You don't feel too feverish, but your skin is drier than my mother's shortbread cookies. Are you using lotion? There are facial lotions that don't leave you looking like you've dipped your face in a vat of butter, you know."

I ran my hand across my forehead and found that, yes, the skin was cracking and peeling from too much direct sun. I had a vision of my face peeling off like one of those masks people wear at night to keep their skin pristine and suppressed a shudder.

"Is it work that's keeping Johan away for so long?" I asked.

Rita shrugged, dismissive. "I believe so."

"You don't know?"

"Why should I? Johan is his own man. And while I do miss him while he's gone, he does have a life. It's not like we're married." She shook her head sadly. "I hope you're not smothering that cop of yours. Officer Dalton deserves to have some space."

"I'm not. And I know." Was she trying to change the subject? "I was just wondering, is all."

"Wondering? Why?"

I chose my next words carefully. "I was hoping to talk to him. I thought I saw him at the marathon before it started."

Her eyes lit up. "This is about that man's death."

"It is."

"And you want to talk to Johan in case he saw something?"

"Yeah." I felt myself wince with the partial lie. I mean, if Johan had seen something, then yeah, I would love to know what it was he saw. But I worried that what he had seen were his own hands around Glen Moreau's neck.

"Well, he wasn't there," Rita sat back and crossed her arms over her ample bosom. "It must have been someone who looked like him. You know, a doppelganger? Why, I swear I saw Johan just this morning, but I know for a fact it couldn't have been him."

I considered that. Could I have been mistaken? Could there be a Johan Morrison look-alike running around Pine Hills, committing crimes?

As much as I wished it to be true, I couldn't make myself believe it. The man I'd seen walk into the building Ivy had pointed me toward had most definitely been the Johan I'd grown to know and fear.

"Where did you see this doppelganger?" I asked, figuring it best to play along for now.

"He was at a house a few miles from here. I was driving by and saw him out of the corner of my eye."

I coughed and picked up my tea to moisten my

throat. It was almost too sweet for my taste, but I gulped it down anyway.

"Was he with anyone?" I asked once I could manage it.

The look Rita gave me told me she was growing suspicious of all the questions, but there was no help for it. I sipped what was left of my tea as I waited for her to answer.

"I didn't get much of a look since it wasn't my Johan. Like I said, he's out of town. I'm not nosy, dear. What this other man does with his time is none of my business." There was a bite to her tone that made me hate pressing the issue, but press it I did.

"What does Johan do exactly?" I asked.

"For work?"

I nodded.

"Well, I can't rightly say. It involves a lot of travel, obviously. I decided it was best not to pry."

Why's that? Because you're afraid he isn't who he says he is? As much as I was curious as to her reasons, I didn't ask my questions out loud.

"What's with all these questions about Johan?" Rita asked before I could inquire about anything else. "As I've said many times now, he isn't in Pine Hills, so there's no way he could know a thing about Glen Moreau's death."

"I . . . It . . ." I trailed off, unsure how to explain without accusing Johan of, well, something.

"You think he's a bad man." When I opened my mouth to object, Rita raised a hand to cut me off. "Don't deny it. I've seen it in your eyes, have from the moment you first met him. It breaks my heart to know that you see him in such a poor light."

"I'm not accusing him of anything," I said, hating that it sounded like a lie. "I just want to talk to him."

Rita blinked her eyes rapidly, as if holding back tears. "Johan has only spoken kindly of you. I understand that he can be a bit strange at times, but aren't we all, in our own way?" She took a deep breath and let it out through her nose. "And yes, I do find it peculiar that I know so little of his life outside of Pine Hills. I'm not a complete dolt."

"I never said you were."

"I know, dear." Her smile was sad. "But I suppose I sometimes think of myself that way. It happens. But no matter what he may or may not be involved in, I do know that Johan Morrison never killed anyone. Not now. Not ever." She cleared her throat and dabbed at her eyes. "I think I'd like to go back to reading now, if that's all right with you?"

Feeling like the world's worst friend, I stood. "Thank you for talking to me, Rita. I'm sorry if I upset you."

She waved a dismissive hand. "No need to apologize. It's this book." She picked up her Nora Roberts novel. "I was immersed in a rather emotional scene when you arrived, and I think it's getting to me."

I knew it was more than that, but I wasn't going to call her on it. "Thank you for the tea. It was very good."

"Stop by anytime, dear." And despite how our conversation had ended, I could tell she meant it.

I returned to my Escape with my chest hurting. Rita already knew something was off about Johan.

I should have realized she was perceptive enough to notice his strange behavior. She knew he was odd, yet she stuck with him anyway. Shouldn't that have told me something about his character?

I started the engine but didn't back out right away. I'd upset my friend by thinking that her boyfriend was guilty of something—infidelity or murder—and I was poking around in a murder investigation I should have left for the police to handle.

It needed to stop before I ruined something I couldn't fix.

Wiping a tear away, I called Paul, fully expecting it to go to voice mail yet again. This time, however, he surprised me by answering.

"Hey, Krissy. I was just about to call you back. It's been a busy day."

"Hi, Paul, I . . ." I sniffed.

"Is something wrong?" The concern in his voice made me smile, despite how in the dumps I was feeling.

"Not really. I'm feeling kind of down, is all." I looked toward Rita's house, but I couldn't see her through the curtained windows. "It's been one of those days."

"Are you certain that's all?" Paul asked. "My shift just ended. If you're home, I could stop by."

Oh, what I wouldn't give to have Paul comfort me, but I found myself saying, "No, you don't need to do that."

"It's no trouble." He paused. "Have you eaten?"

"Not yet. I was about to go home and order a pizza." A lie, but if I told him I'd lost my appetite, he'd worry.

The pause was longer this time. I couldn't hear voices in the background, so I assumed he'd left the police station.

"How about I take you out for dinner?"

My eyes started stinging, threatening more tears. I didn't feel like I deserved a dinner with Paul, not after upsetting Rita the way I had. And yet, at the same time, I wanted nothing more than to sit across from him, to have him tell me everything would be all right.

"Yeah, sure."

"Geraldo's?"

Something in the way he said it gave me pause. It was as if he'd asked far more in that one word than simply if the fancy restaurant was okay for dinner.

Words his mother had spoken to me months ago echoed in the back of my mind.

Paul has plans. You're involved in those plans.

Until that moment, I hadn't seen any indication that Paul was planning anything more than maintaining the status quo. And now, with just the tone of his voice, I just knew there was something more going on.

"That sounds great," I squeaked. I cleared my throat and tried again. "Geraldo's would be perfect."

"I'll pick you up in twenty?"

I could easily get home and change in that time, but I also wanted a shower, just in case I was hearing his intent correctly. "Can you make it forty? I'm just leaving Rita's now."

"Sounds great. I'll see you then."

We clicked off, and I took a moment to allow my heart to slow and my head to stop spinning. With everything else in my life seemingly going wrong, it finally appeared as if I was about to take a big positive step forward in one aspect of it.

That is, unless I was reading Paul wrong. After my talk with Rita, I was truly beginning to question my ability to see what was right in front of me.

11

"What do you think?" I spun in a slow circle. "Too casual? Should I change?"

Misfit yawned, spun in a circle of his own, and settled down onto the bed for a nap.

"A lot of help you are."

Surprise, surprise, he didn't so much as twitch his tail in response.

Paul was due to arrive at any moment, and I couldn't decide on what to wear. Normally, I'm not one to worry too much about my outfit, but tonight felt like it was going to be special. Jeans and a ratty T-shirt wouldn't do. But I didn't have a fancy dress, let alone a halfway decent one.

What if he's not planning anything? I scanned my closet, panic building. Should I call him and ask him? Wing it? What if I dress up and he's still in his uniform? Or what if he's wearing jeans and a T-shirt?

Of course, Paul filled out his jeans a whole lot better than I did, so I wouldn't mind one bit.

There was a thrum of sound from next door. It was followed by the rat-a-tat of a snare drum. Misfit's ears perked up, but when nothing else followed, he settled back down. Caitlin and her band were still at it, though they appeared to be taking a break for now.

I spent the next five minutes torn between changing and just going with what I had on. Was it better to be overdressed or undressed? Would it even matter?

Before I could make up my mind—not that I ever would have—a car pulled into my driveway. I abandoned the closet and hurried to the front door. I started to open it but changed my mind and closed it again.

Why am I being so jumpy? Nothing said tonight was about anything more than dinner. Paul had more important things to worry about—namely, a murder—than his relationship with me.

But what if Glen's death made him realize that waiting entailed a risk. No one knew what tomorrow would bring.

A knock at the door caused me to jump, even though I'd been expecting it. I grabbed the doorknob and jerked the door open so quickly, I very nearly smacked myself in the face with it.

Smooth, Krissy. Real smooth.

I flashed him a toothy smile. "Paul. Hi. I'm ready." I looked him up and down. Not his uniform. Not jeans and a T-shirt. But it wasn't a suit and tie either.

"Krissy." He gave me an amused smile, as if he'd watched my half-mad preparations. "Are you all right?"

"Me? Of course. Why wouldn't I be?"

"Well . . ." He cleared his throat and covered his mouth with a fist. "Your shirt."

"What about my shirt?" I looked down, and my face immediately grew hot. "Oh. Give me one second."

I scurried back into the bedroom and closed the door behind me. I yanked my shirt off and turned it right-side out and pulled it back on before scowling at Misfit.

"You could have told me, you know?"

He opened one eye, and I swear he snickered.

I checked to make sure I hadn't somehow put my pants on backward, and then went to the bedroom door but didn't open it right away. I closed my eyes and took slow, measured breaths.

I can do this. This is just dinner. And even if it wasn't, I couldn't be a nervous wreck or else I'd botch the entire evening.

Slow and easy. Deep, calming breaths. When my heart finally settled and common sense finally started to ooze through my sun-scorched brain, I opened the door.

Paul was leaning against the island counter when I finally emerged. He smiled when he saw me.

"That's better," he said. "Though I could have helped you fix it. You didn't have to run off."

"Well, we can always save that for later." A wave of heat flashed through me, and I immediately started sweating. "If you want to, that is."

Paul chuckled in a way that told me he'd very much like to before he crooked an elbow. "Ready?"

I slipped my arm through his. "Ready."

We kept our conversation to safe subjects as we drove to Geraldo's. We talked about Death by Coffee, about how his mom, Chief Patricia Dalton, was considering retiring sometime in the next decade. Maybe. Probably not. I told him about Caitlin's band, and how we were lucky that they were taking a break when he'd arrived or else we'd have been shouting at one another over the ringing in our ears.

We didn't talk about Johan Morrison or Glen Moreau.

But deep down, I knew it was coming.

I was glad to see the parking lot was only half-full when we arrived. Even when it was busy, Geraldo's layout made every meal feel semi-private, but I knew it was only an illusion. Talk too loudly, and everyone would know what you were saying. I was hoping for a table well away from anyone else, just in case Paul had something major planned. I didn't need other people watching me pass out.

And if nothing came of our dinner?

Oddly, I wasn't quite sure how I felt about that. Disappointed? Maybe. Relieved? Perhaps that too. Was I ready for more in our relationship? I liked my life, but how much better would it be to wake up next to Paul every morning?

My toes curled, which caused me to falter on my next step. Paul caught me by the arm to keep me from falling on my face like an idiot.

"Are you sure you're all right?" he asked for what felt like the hundredth time in the last two days.

"I'm fine. I was lost in thought and tripped over my own two feet."

"Is that really it? You look kind of sick." He stopped and turned me to face him. "If you're not feeling well . . ."

"No, I'm okay. I promise." I wiped a hand across my forehead and found it coated in sweat. "It's hot out, and like I said earlier, it was a long day."

Paul didn't look like he believed me, but he let it go.

We were led to a table that wasn't quite private, but at least no one was sitting right beside us. I was cognizant of other faces, of people turning to look at us, but none of them registered. I was suddenly very thirsty and desperately needed to sit down. I jerked my chair out and practically fell into it.

Paul eased down across from me. "Maybe this wasn't a good idea."

"It is." I waved the waiter over, even though he was already on the way. "Water, please." I coughed and then cleared my throat.

The waiter's face flashed in alarm before he spun and hurried to the back. He was gone for only a few seconds before he returned with two glasses of water. He set them both down in front of me.

"Thank you," I croaked before downing the first in one go. It was cold enough to give me a cold headache. Tears leaked from my eyes as I slammed my tongue against the roof of my mouth in an effort to stop it before it caused my brain to freeze.

"I'll return in a few minutes," the waiter said before he scurried to the back again.

"Krissy . . ."

I held up a hand, forestalling whatever Paul had to say. Once the lancing pain passed, my shoulders sagged, and I was able to smile. "Drank it too fast."

"I saw."

"It was cold."

"I think you swallowed an ice cube."

Had I? It was possible, I supposed, though I didn't recall anything solid going down. "I got way too much sun over the last few days. That's all this is."

"Are you sure? Krissy, something is bothering you, something big. I can see it spelled out all over your face."

And by how I'm acting, I'm sure. I was making a complete fool of myself. I needed to get a grip. Social situations and I didn't get along at the best of times.

"I'm sorry," I said. "It's just . . ." I took a deep breath and let it out in a huff. "I'm worried about Rita."

Paul's face crinkled in confusion. "Rita? Did something happen to her?"

"No. Not yet anyway." I frowned. "I'm not worried about her health or her doing something that'll get her into trouble. It's Johan."

"Her boyfriend?"

What other Johan was there? "I saw him at the marathon, Paul. He wasn't running, and he wasn't there to watch. He was lurking near the woods." I gave him a pointed look. "With another woman."

"You don't think he had something to do with the murder, do you?" Right to the heart of it.

I started to answer, but what could I say? No, because he was Rita's boyfriend and she'd be smarter than to date a murderer? Yes, because I didn't like him and he was sneaking around all shady-like with a woman who wasn't Rita?

"Krissy, I know you don't particularly like Johan Morrison, but I haven't seen any evidence that he had anything to do with Glen Moreau." He paused with a frown. "You haven't been poking around where you shouldn't be, have you?"

"Define 'poking around.'"

"Krissy . . ."

"I didn't talk to anyone." Not really, anyway. As long as he didn't count Rita, who was my friend, so he couldn't be mad at me for talking to her.

Paul gave me a flat look.

"Really. I'm worried, is all. I mean, Rita has had it rough when it comes to men. And even if Johan isn't involved in the murder directly, he was with another woman.

"And," I added, "I saw him somewhere else."

"What kind of somewhere else?"

"I was driving down Rosebud when I happened to see him going into a building." I tried not to wince at the little white lie.

"Why were you on Rosebud?" Leave it to Paul to ask a reasonable question.

"That's not what's important," I said, ignoring his scowl. "I saw him going into a building."

Paul waited. When I didn't say anything more, he asked, "And?"

Thankfully, the waiter arrived then. We took a moment to order our drinks and food—neither of us needed to see the menu—and then he hurried away as if he thought I might have something that was catching. With the way I looked, with my sunburned face, and all the coughing, it was no wonder.

"He's a nervous type, isn't he?" I asked, hoping to lighten the mood. I felt like I was torpedoing the night, and I hadn't meant to.

"Krissy." Flat. "What building are you talking about?"

There was no way I could tell him why the building bothered me so much without telling him about talking to Ivy Hammer, who'd told me about it in the first place.

"If I tell you, will you promise not to be mad?"

"Oh boy." Paul ran a hand over his face. "Do you know what John's going to do if he finds out you're involved in his investigation?"

"He's not going to find out," I said. "And I'm not involved. Shannon and Trisha came in to Death by Coffee and told me about this place where women can go to talk about their problems. It just so happens that this place is run by Glen Moreau's ex-wife."

"Convenient," he said.

"And she just happened to tell me about another woman, Ivy Hammer, who might have been with Glen the night before his death, but she wasn't."

"And you didn't talk to this Ivy to find this out, I'm sure."

"Maybe a little." I sipped my water, hoping he wouldn't yell at me for lying earlier about not poking around.

Thankfully, Paul knew me well enough to understand that no matter what I said, I couldn't help but stick my nose where it doesn't belong. "And this ties back to Johan how?"

"Ivy told me about this place Glen used to sneak off to back when they were seeing one another. She followed him once and said it was kind of shady. And when I drove by, completely at random—"

"Uh-huh"

"I saw Johan go into this same building. It's unmarked, with no signage or indication as to what it might be. Rita swears Johan is out of town, yet he was here in Pine Hills, showing up at places connected to the murder. Rita claims that Glen might have been involved in some sort of financial scheme. I'm starting to wonder if Johan is involved in the same scheme and . . ." I trailed off as I realized I was babbling.

Paul drummed his fingers on the table. He looked thoughtful rather than angry, which was a relief. I was afraid I'd already ruined the evening, but I really needed to tell him about Johan before it ate at me. I hoped he would know what to do.

"Give me the address, and I'll look into it," Paul said after a few long minutes. He pulled his phone from his pocket, fingers hovering over it as he waited.

I told him and waited for him to type it in before continuing. "Thank you for this. I'm really worried. And if you could, don't tell Detective Buchannan. If Johan is involved in something illegal, I don't want it to come back onto Rita. And if you find something out about this woman . . ."

"I'll be careful with this," he said, putting his phone away. "Anything I learn, I'll keep to myself, unless it is important to the case." He leaned forward. "Now, I don't want you going back there, just in case you are right and something illegal is happening. If this does end up having something to do with Glen's murder, I don't want someone seeing you hanging around, asking questions."

I made a cross over my heart. "I promise to stay far away from that place. It gave me the creeps."

"Good." Paul huffed out a breath, as if pushing all the talk of murder and crimes out of his system. "Now, if you don't have any more surprises for me . . . ?" He raised an eyebrow in question.

"Nope. That's all I've got." Other than more rumors and speculation, mostly about how Glen was the cheating type. That stuff could wait until tomorrow.

"So . . ." He drew out the word and trailed off, looking anywhere but at me.

"So." I swallowed. Boy, was that second water looking good. I was sweating again, and my throat felt as if it were sunburned as well.

"Look, I . . ." He trailed off again.

My heart started thumping. "Paul." I coughed, wiped at my nose. Was the table trying to dance away from me? It sure looked like it.

A clang came from behind me. Something shattered on the floor. I was so distracted by what Paul might or might not say, it took me a moment to realize that these weren't normal sounds in a restaurant.

"You don't know what you're talking about!"

A screech as a chair was pushed back. Another shatter. This one I recognized as a glass hitting the floor.

I turned in my seat just in time to see a man staggering backward, toward me. I had just enough time to think, *Oh crap!* before he slammed into my chair, nearly knocking me from my seat. Paul was on his feet and around the table before I could fully right myself.

"I'm going to kill you!" The man who'd been shoved rushed forward, toward the man who'd shoved him.

Wait. I know those two men.

Rod Maxwell braced himself as Calvin threw himself at him. The two men grappled, arms flailing as they tried to get hold of one another. They both looked drunk and hopping mad.

"Hey! You two, stop. Police." Paul rushed forward and made a grab for Calvin, just as Calvin reared back to punch Rod.

There was a crunch as elbow met face. A collective gasp went around the room. Rod immediately raised both hands and backed away, a look of shock on his face.

Calvin spun around, saw Paul, and paled. "I didn't mean . . ." He looked wildly around the room, as if seeking an escape, before he raised both of his hands in surrender. "It was an accident."

Paul had his back to me, and his hand was covering his face, so I couldn't see how bad it was. He managed to say, "Both of you, sit," as he pointed toward the table where Rod and Calvin must have been having dinner before the fight had started. They both complied without hesitation.

The next twenty minutes moved by in a blur. There was blood on Paul's shirt, and when he moved his hand from his face, there was enough there to tell me his nose might have been broken.

He wouldn't let me fawn over him, however. He might have been off duty, but he was still a cop. He took control of the situation, keeping both Rod and Calvin in place as he called in the scuffle. I doubted he would have bothered if Calvin hadn't struck him, but his blood was up, and I think he wanted answers just as badly as I did.

"I've got to go in and deal with this," Paul said once Rod and Calvin were hauled off by a very tired-looking Officer Becca Garrison. He sounded like he had a bad cold, and I noted that bruising had started around his eyes and his nose was starting to grow in size.

"You need to see a doctor."

"There's one meeting me at the station." He handed me his keys. "I'm going to ride with Officer Garrison." He tried to sniff but winced instead. His nose wasn't bleeding anymore, which I hoped was a good sign. "Take my car. I'll stop by and get it later."

"Are you sure? I could come to the station with you."

"No, go home. Get some rest. You look like you need it."

And then he was gone, and I was in his car, driving home. Alone.

So much for a pleasant evening—and whatever Paul had to say to me. I had a feeling that after tonight, whatever plans he might have had for me would be on the back burner, at least until Glen Moreau's killer was found.

12

Paul's car was gone.

I stood at my window, my heart residing some-where around my feet. I'd tried to stay up and wait for him, but the long couple of days, as well as the heat, had me nodding off on the couch, where I'd woken early to find Misfit staring at me with the sun shining in through the window—the same window where I now stood, looking at the empty space in my driveway.

Sometime in the night, Paul had come to get his car, and he'd done so without disturbing me. My front door was locked, so he hadn't snuck in and taken the key out from under my nose. I could only assume he'd brought a spare.

It doesn't mean anything, Krissy.

Yet I felt like I'd done something wrong. Maybe I had. Instead of sticking to pleasant topics at last night's dinner, I just had to talk about Johan, which caused my snooping to come to light, which, in turn, had to annoy my police officer boyfriend. And after he'd taken that elbow to the face . . .

I turned away from the window and put it out of my mind. Paul was a busy man. If he'd been stuck at the station, dealing with the fallout from the scuffle until late, he wouldn't have wanted to wake me. It was as simple as that. My brain, which didn't much care for me sometimes, was just trying to make me feel bad.

Well, I refused to let it.

I went about my morning routine, fed Misfit and gave him some extra loving, before heading out. I was just climbing into my vehicle when I noticed a man standing outside Caitlin's house, puffing away at something that glinted in the sun. He was tall and was solid in a way that spoke of genetics more than him being fat. Long, dark hair hung into his face, obscuring everything but the glinting thing.

Teek? I wondered.

He raised a hand in greeting before taking one last drag from the metallic device, and then he turned to enter Caitlin's home.

My curiosity was piqued. I couldn't be certain this was the Teek whom Caitlin had mentioned, but something about him made me think it was. Her band had finished practicing by the time I'd come home last night, and I'd thought everyone had left since there were no unfamiliar cars in her driveway. There still weren't.

Yet someone had stayed behind. A man. Overnight.

The temptation to head over and casually introduce myself in the hopes of gleaning something from whoever answered was strong, but I was due at Death by Coffee, and there was someone working today whom I needed to talk to.

I gave Caitlin's house one last curious look, and then I was on my way.

Death by Coffee was hopping when I walked through the door. I slid behind the counter and immediately started filling orders, while Pooky Cooper took them. She was a petite blonde who stood no more than five feet with her shoes on. The last time I'd worked with her, she was peppy and had moved with a speedy grace that guaranteed customers were served quickly. Now? Not so much.

Jeff Braun was upstairs, dealing with a slew of customers eager to buy books to go with their coffees. Normally, he'd have been helping fill orders, only going upstairs when someone needed to be checked out, but today was just one of those days when both sections of the store were slammed at the same time. It created chaos, especially since Pooky and Jeff were the only two working before I'd come in.

Coffee had been spilled more than once, making footing hazardous. The counter itself was a sticky mess, and by the look of Pooky's stained apron, I knew she was responsible for much of the spillage. It might have been an accident caused by her trying to rush too much, or it might have had something to do with whatever was bothering her.

"One French vanilla latte," she said, tapping the keys on the register.

"A cappuccino," the woman said. "Not a latte."

"Right." Pooky pressed a button, causing the

drawer to fly out and hit her in the gut. She reddened, muttered, "Sorry," and fixed the order.

The rush seemed to last forever, with Pooky making a few more minor mistakes, but nothing we couldn't handle. My hair was caked to my face, and I'd spilled a coffee of my own before it was done. Any and all thoughts of Paul and Johan and the murder were wiped clean from my mind as I focused on the job. Jeff came down whenever he got a chance and cleaned up the spills. It was a good thing too, because I had a feeling that if he hadn't, I would have ended up on my butt.

Once the customers were served, we spent the next twenty minutes cleaning up, restocking, and wiping down tables. I had to correct two more orders and saw another couple toss their coffees away in disgust without bothering to come to the counter. I didn't think I'd made a mistake in filling them, but I also hoped it wasn't yet another goof made by Pooky.

Vicki had been right; something was seriously wrong with her mental state, and I was making it my job to find out what it was.

The black-and-white store cat, Trouble, meandered over to the stairs to look down upon the slowly emptying dining room. Vicki or Mason must have stopped by sometime before opening to drop him off. They were both planning to stop in later, which would signal the end of my day. Already, I was looking forward to it.

Trouble turned and sauntered toward the upstairs couch. Jeff was busy restocking books someone had brought to the counter before they'd changed their mind about the purchase. That gave me a few minutes alone to talk to my distracted employee.

"Hey, Pooky."

She quickly turned off her phone screen and stuffed it into her back pocket. "Yeah?"

"How are you doing?"

She blinked at me. "I'm okay."

Outside, a car slowed to a crawl, catching my attention. I expected someone to get out, but before anyone did, the car picked up speed and was gone.

I turned my attention back to Pooky. "Are you sure? You've seemed distracted over the last couple of days."

Another series of rapid blinks. "We haven't worked together for a few days."

"I know that." I smiled in an attempt to show her that this was just a friendly conversation, not an accusation. "But others have noticed. We're worried. Is everything okay at home?"

Pooky touched her hair, reached for the pocket with her phone, and then went back to smoothing her hair. "Yeah, sure."

That wasn't convincing in the slightest.

There was a tinkle of a bell as someone started to open the store door. Pooky spun around to the register, relief washing over her face, but the door didn't open all the way.

Rita had her hand on the handle, eyes far away, as if she were mentally somewhere else. She stood there for a long couple of seconds before she stepped back, allowing the door to fall closed again. And then, without a look my way, she turned and walked away.

It was like a punch to the gut. I knew her reluctance to enter Death by Coffee had to do with my questions—and suspicions—about Johan. I really needed to sit down and talk to her so we could clear the air.

Pooky's shoulders sagged, and she turned back to me. She was blinking rapidly again, and this time, I realized why.

"No, don't cry," I said, stepping forward and wrapping her in a hug. She leaned into it, sniffling. The tears had yet to fall, but they were coming.

"I'm sorry," she said, voice muffled into my shoulder. "I'm being stupid."

"No, no you're not."

"I am." She stomped a foot before stepping back. She wiped at her nose and took a trembling breath that looked half-angry before she continued. "I never should have told him he could move in."

Uh-oh. Boy trouble. I should have known.

"It's all right," I said, trying to sound more confident than I felt. I didn't exactly have the best track record with men, so me giving advice was, well, risky. But I couldn't stand there and do nothing.

Pooky shook her head. "It's not, though. I have no space of my own, and . . ." She trailed off, a disgusted expression crossing her face.

Well, here goes nothing. "Relationships are hard," I said. "Sometimes things work out. We manage to accept each other's differences and can often live with them, even when they feel overbearing. But there are times, in some situations, where it just doesn't work. There's nothing wrong with that.

You can't know if you can live your life with some-one until you've actually tried it."

My mind drifted to Paul and whatever he'd wanted to say last night at Geraldo's. Had our con-versation somehow made him realize he didn't want to wake up next to me every morning? Had the thought even crossed his mind?

Pooky was staring at me as if I'd grown a second head, snapping my mind back to the present. "What are you talking about?" she asked, clearly confused.

"Your boyfriend. I know you want it to work out, but if you're miserable, and if it's affecting your job and your happiness, there's nothing wrong with stepping back and reevaluating. Your happi-ness comes first. Always remember that."

"Boyfriend?" She looked toward the door just as a car slowed outside. There was a niggling of famil-iarity in the back of my mind. It took me a mo-ment to realize it was the same car that had driven by earlier. And just like before, it picked up speed and left without dropping anyone off. "Who said anything about a boyfriend?"

I could feel my face starting to grow hot. "You mentioned a guy moved in with you."

"Yeah." Incredulous. "But he's not my boy-friend. He's my *brother*."

It was my turn to blink at her. "You have a brother?"

Pooky tried not to roll her eyes at my inane question. "I do. He's fallen on some hard times, and I thought I'd do the right thing and let him move in with me until he got back onto his feet."

"But he hasn't." It wasn't a question.

"No." She clenched her fists briefly before her shoulders sagged. "I love him, I really do, but he doesn't think about me at all. He acts like he lives alone, has taken over my entire apartment. And his friends . . ." This time, she shuddered. "They stare at me like I'm a piece of meat."

"Have you talked to him about it?"

"Of course I have. He doesn't listen. In fact, he laughed at me when I complained about him leaving his underwear on the living room couch. I mean, ew! Who wants to see that? I can't have friends over. I can't date. I can't even sit in my bedroom and read a book without him or one of his friends wandering in."

The door opened, and Trisha walked in. She met my eye, nodded, and then waddled to the nearest chair, hand on her swollen belly. She eased herself down, and when I raised my eyebrows in question, she waved me off.

"I'm not sleeping, I'm barely eating." Pooky sniffed as the words tumbled out of her. "I tried to tell him to leave, that I've had enough, but he refuses to go. He thinks I'm being irrational, but I'm not. I . . . I can't live like this anymore."

I've always been a believer that family matters should be kept in the family, but sometimes outside intervention is necessary. I had a feeling that Pooky's brother wasn't a bad guy. He's, well, a brother. Siblings sometimes fight, sometimes annoy one another, without meaning any harm.

"I can talk to him," I said, thinking that it shouldn't be too much of a hassle to have a word with him. "I'll see if I can make him see reason."

Pooky looked doubtful. "You don't know Donnie."

"No, but that doesn't mean I can't talk to him. It's clear you love your brother and don't want to hurt his feelings. He probably doesn't realize how much he's disrupting your life. Maybe if it comes from someone else, someone not so close to the situation, he'll see it."

"Do you think so?"

I smiled. "I do."

"If you're sure . . ."

"I am."

After a little more hemming and hawing, Pooky gave me her address, even though I already had it on file. I promised her I would stop by after work and would talk to him.

"I'll go shopping," she said. "It'll probably be better if I'm not there for this."

Pooky went back to work, this time with a pep in her step. I caught Jeff's eye upstairs. He nodded once, having overheard snippets of our conversation and then went back to the books.

Feeling good about myself, I headed out into the dining area to check in with Trisha.

"Can I get you something?" I asked her. She was sitting in the chair, legs splayed out in front of her, hands limp atop her stomach. She looked miserable.

"An apple and mustard cake sounds good, but, no, I'm all right."

"Apple and mustard?" I made a face.

"I know. I keep finding myself wanting apple and mustard on everything. It tastes awful, but I can't help myself." She wiggled herself upright. "I sat in front of the TV last night, mustard bottle in hand and a plate full of apple slices sitting on my belly. Robert made himself scarce. He said he couldn't stand to watch me eat it."

"Sounds . . . tasty?"

"It's really not."

We shared a laugh.

"So, you don't want a coffee?" I asked. "We have apple fritters today if you're craving apple. I'm also pretty sure we've got a mustard dip somewhere back there." I jerked a thumb toward the back. "If you really want it."

"No, if I drink anything, I'll spend the next half hour peeing. I swear the little one spends all their time poking at my bladder." She shifted in her seat. "Actually, I think I'm going to need to make a stop in the ladies' room before I go."

"It's all yours. And if you change your mind, you know where to find me." I motioned toward the counter.

"Thanks." She adjusted positions again, this time with a grimace. "I did stop in to see you, however, not just to use your restroom."

"Oh?" It came out sounding worried. Robert had a tendency to overreact whenever I was involved in anything that touched on his life. Our history was one full of troubles. It made me wonder how we'd managed to end up as sorta, kinda friends. Yet here I was, talking with his wife like it was nothing.

"You know the woman I told you about, Melanie Johnson?"

"Yeah. I paid her a visit the other day. It was interesting." To say the least.

Trisha flashed me a smile that turned into a wince as she grabbed at her belly and snapped her knees together. "Woo, boy. I'm going to make this fast." She wiggled herself to a standing position. "Melanie's having a get-together at her place Friday night. It's not quite a party, but I suppose you could call it that. Shannon and I are both going, and we thought it would be nice if you came with us."

"A party?" She was asking me to go to a party with them?

"It's for the people Melanie has helped. And, well, Shannon and I, we . . ." Trisha bit her lower lip. "I guess we'd both like to get to know you better, and this seemed like the perfect way for us all to go somewhere together without any sort of commitment. You know, if you get sick of our moaning about our sizes, you could mingle without feeling like you're abandoning us. Does that even make sense?"

"It does. And, yeah, I'd love to go."

"Great!" Her eyes widened. "Okay, I've got to go. I'll text you the info, all right?"

Before I could answer, Trisha hurried to the restroom, legs barely bending as she shuffled her way through the door.

A night out with Shannon and Trisha. It was both flattering that they'd thought of me and terrifying at the same time.

I started to head back to the counter when I saw the same car I'd noticed before cruising by. I couldn't see the driver, but that familiarity was back again, this time with a force that knocked me back on my heel.

Where have I seen that car before?

And then it hit me.

I took off, scrambling for the door before the car could get away. All I needed was one good look at the driver, and it would tell me everything I needed to know.

I jerked open the door and nearly barreled into a middle-aged woman with a squirming corgi tucked under one arm. The dog barked once as the woman leaped aside. We didn't collide, but they'd made me hesitate.

The car engine revved, and before I could get a peek at the driver, it shot down the road, tore around a corner, and was gone. Too late, I thought, to check the license plate so I could give it to Paul. I managed to spot an "L" before the car was out of sight.

I sighed in frustration, but all was not lost. I'd seen that car before. I was sure of it.

And the last time I'd seen it, it was parked in front of the laundromat on Rosebud Avenue, and Johan Morrison had been driving.

13

The car didn't drive by again for the rest of the day. I watched for it, my attention more on what was going on outside the store window than on what was happening within. At some point, Jeff clocked out and was replaced by Eugene, who tried to talk to me, but I was so distracted, I barely managed much more than a few grunts before he wandered upstairs to help some customers.

The tiny part of me that was aware of what I was doing felt bad. The rest of me was more concerned with the idea that Johan might be stalking me. It sounded ludicrous, and the more I thought about it, the more I felt I had to have been mistaken, that the car had indeed belonged to someone else and I was blowing everything out of proportion.

But what if I wasn't? What if Johan had seen me outside that building he'd gone into? My Escape wasn't hard to spot, so there was a good chance he'd seen it parked at the side of the road long before he'd gotten out of his car.

And then what? He decided to pretend not to see me and then keep an eye on me afterward? If he'd wanted to do that, he could have coaxed Rita into stopping by Death by Coffee, as she often did anyway. And yeah, she was upset with me, but if Johan asked her to do something, I had a feeling she wouldn't hesitate to accommodate him.

Vicki and Mason arrived just as Pooky left and was replaced by Beth Milner. Pooky gave me a meaningful look as she slipped out the door, one Vicki didn't miss.

"I take it you talked to her?" she asked. Mason wandered upstairs, cooing to Trouble, who was rubbing up against the bookshelves and prancing from foot to foot at the sight of his owners.

"I did. I'm going to try to help her."

"Good." Vicki didn't pry any more deeply, for which I was grateful. I doubted Pooky would want her business gabbed about, even by Vicki and me.

"I'm about to head out and do that now," I said. "Unless you need me to stick around for a little while longer?"

"No, you go ahead." Vicki waited until I'd gathered my things, and then she walked me to the door. "Are you doing anything tomorrow night?" she asked before I left.

I almost said no before I remembered my promise to Trisha. "Surprisingly, I am."

"Paul?" Her smile was playful, if not mischievous.

"Actually, no. Trisha asked if I'd go with her and Shannon to a party."

"Really? I didn't realize you three were friends."

"It's sorta happened recently." I was still shocked by it. "And this event is being hosted by the ex-wife of Glen Moreau, so I suppose I have ulterior motives for going." I thought about that for a few moments and realized that wasn't entirely true. "I guess I'm just glad they invited me. It'll be nice to put any hard feelings we've had about one another behind us once and for all."

"That's nice to hear. You need to make more friends. Maybe one of us can keep you out of trouble."

"Hey!"

She nudged me with her shoulder.

"If Paul can't manage it, I don't think any of you will."

"No, I'm sure you're right." Vicki stepped back. "You go and have fun. We can get together another night."

"I'm free Saturday?" I made it a question. "We could watch a movie at my place. Bring Trouble. I'm sure Misfit would love to see his brother." Though the last time we'd gotten the cats together, they'd sat across the room from one another, glaring.

"Sounds like a date. I'll call you later, and we can hammer out the details."

I left Death by Coffee, but before I stopped by Pooky's, I decided I needed a little sugar pick-me-up. Besides, Phantastic Candies was on the way, and it would be rude not to at least pop in and thank Jules for the lemonade.

Phantastic Candies was as bright and colorful as its owner. Chutes of candies lined the walls as though the place was a funhouse. Bin upon bin of chocolates and sugars and caramels took up the remainder of the space. It was, in a word, bliss.

Behind the counter, Jules was working at the books with a faint scowl. He typed into a calculator, one finger running down the page as he did. When he got to the bottom, he paused, and then started all over again.

"Is everything okay?" I asked, plucking a bag of dark-chocolate-covered cherries from a bin and setting them on the counter.

Jules closed the book and then cracked his back. He was wearing a lime green overcoat, and when he moved, his shoes made a clacking sound that told me he was wearing tap shoes. The store's air-conditioning was working overtime to keep the chocolate from melting, but Jules still looked hot in his coat.

"It's nothing," he said, waving a dismissive hand toward the book. "We've had some of our more expensive chocolates grow legs and sneak out the door on their own. I was trying to figure out exactly how much we've lost, but it's impossible to know for sure without sitting at the computer."

"Do you have security cameras?" I glanced around but didn't notice any.

"There's one over there." He pointed toward the corner, but I still couldn't see it. "But the quality is bad, and it's aimed at the counter and doorway more than the rest of the store. Candy always vanishes. Kids." He shrugged, as if that said everything. "But the numbers have grown recently, and it's starting to affect the bottom line."

As he spoke, the door opened, and a handful of

teens walked in. Jules rang up my chocolate while the kids perused the shelves. I watched them, as if I thought they might be the candy thieves. The kids settled on handfuls of sugar straws and bubble gum, and dropped them onto the counter for Jules to sort out.

Once they were gone, I resumed my place. "Do you have any suspects for the thefts?"

"A few." He grinned as he leaned on the counter. "I'm not the detective you are, but I'd like to think I have a few tricks up my sleeves."

"I hope you catch them." And I meant it. While stealing candy was a long way from murder, it was still a crime.

And besides, if it got bad enough that Jules had to close up shop, *I* might have to murder someone.

As if he gleaned something from my expression, Jules shifted subjects. "Has any progress been made on Glen's killer?"

"Not really," I said. "There's all sorts of rumors flying around about Glen, and a couple of the suspects got into a fight at Geraldo's. One of them hit Paul in the face."

"Oh no! Is he all right?"

"I know he's bruised, and he might have broken his nose, but I can't be sure. I haven't seen him since it happened."

"That's awful. I wish there was something I could say that could help. I didn't know the victim or any of his friends well enough to know if anyone has been acting strangely recently."

"Paul and Detective Buchannan are doing their best. Hopefully, they'll have it figured out soon." I started to change the subject to ask about Donnie Cooper but caught myself. If I didn't want to talk to Vicki about Pooky's problem, then I shouldn't talk to Jules either.

"I'm sure they will." He winked before going back to his books. He knew, just as much as I did, that I wouldn't be able to let the police handle the investigation on their own. It wasn't in my DNA to stand aside when I thought I could help.

Speaking of helping . . . "I'd best get going." I opened my bag of cherries and popped one into my mouth.

Oh, yeah. Bliss.

"And thanks again for the lemonade," I said once I swallowed. "It's really helped me get through this heat."

"Don't mention it. Lance might stop by again this week and drop off some more. I swear, I think he's looking to single-handedly keep the lemon market booming. He's made so much lemonade, I don't think I'll ever stop smelling lemons."

I laughed, waved, and then was on my way.

Pooky's apartment wasn't far from downtown, so the drive was short. Too short, actually. I was sitting outside the brick, two-story complex within a few minutes of leaving Phantastic Candies with no idea how I was going to approach this. I didn't know anything about Donnie Cooper outside of what little Pooky had told me. I didn't even know if he was her older brother or if he was fresh out of high school.

A kid I thought I could handle. But if he was some sort of middle-aged slob who was so set in his ways he was immobile, I wasn't sure how I was going to help. It wasn't like I could evict him. Or pick him up and toss him out myself, even if he weighed nothing. Now that I was here, I was beginning to realize how difficult this might be.

Only a handful of vehicles were parked in the lot. The spaces were numbered, though there was a section for visitors that was entirely empty. I pulled into one of the spaces there, climbed out of my Escape, and then headed for apartment 24B, which was on the second floor.

I could hear thumps coming from the apartment, even before I reached the door. It sounded like someone was throwing a ball against the wall. Muffled voices that could be people talking or could be coming from the TV were just barely audible over the steady *thump, thump, thump.*

I knocked on the door, already knowing this was going to end badly. There was an aura to the place, a vibe that made me feel icky just standing there. The complex was nice enough, so it wasn't that. The feeling didn't start until I was standing outside the door. A pungent, spicy smell was in the air. I couldn't identify whether it was someone's cooking or if it was something else.

When no one answered, I hammered harder. The thumping stopped, and before it could resume, I knocked again, just in case they hadn't heard me the first couple of times. The voices cut off abruptly, telling me they'd likely come from the television, but the smell remained.

A minute later, the door opened, and Pooky's brother, Donnie, stood before me, wearing nothing but a pair of dark blue boxer shorts.

"Yeah?" he asked, scratching at his hairy belly.

I wanted to avert my eyes, to run in the opposite direction as fast as I could, but it was like his torso was a black hole, drawing my attention deep into his overlarge bellybutton. He was slightly over-weight, like someone who spent a lot of time sit-ting around, but not so much that they grew fat. But the hair . . . it was everywhere.

"You looking for something, lady?" Donnie asked when I didn't say anything.

"I, uh . . ." I cleared my throat and forced myself to look up into his face. "Donnie Cooper?" I was al-most positive it was him. He and Pooky had the same blue eyes, the same facial structure. If he'd been a couple years younger and maybe a foot shorter, I might have thought they were twins.

"Yeah?" His eyes narrowed. "Who's asking?"

I noted the pungent smell was growing stronger. I still couldn't pinpoint exactly what it was, but I did know that it was coming from the apartment. Between the smell and her brother's state of un-dress, it was no wonder Pooky wanted him gone.

"I'm a friend of Pooky's."

He snorted a laughed. "Right." He started to close the door.

"Really," I said, wedging my foot in the frame before he could close it all the way. "We work to-gether." I couldn't bring myself to tell him I was her boss, worried he'd use it against her somehow. The guy gave me weird vibes—the same kind I felt when I'd approached.

"Okay." He eased off the door. "So?"

"So, I've noticed she's been off recently."

"Off, huh?" He rolled his eyes. "She's fine."

"She hasn't been sleeping or eating properly," I

said. "It's been affecting her work, and I guess we're getting a little worried about her at the store. I stopped by in the hopes I could help out somehow." And then, for appearances, "Is she here?"

"Help." Flat. "No, she's not here, and no, I don't know when she'll be back." He tried to close the door again, but I hadn't moved my foot.

"Donnie," I said, opting for my most diplomatic tone of voice. "She needs her space. Don't you think it's time that you let her have it?"

Another laugh. It sounded as rude as he'd intended it to be. "Look, lady, Claire's fine. We're good here and don't need anyone's help. This is my place now, and she just needs to accept that. If you're so concerned about making sure Claire eats and sleeps right, maybe you should invite her to come live with you."

Not only did he use Pooky's given name—something she'd made clear when we'd hired her that she didn't like—he was claiming the apartment as his own. The weird vibe I'd been getting had turned hostile.

"Donnie, please see reason—"

"Move your foot." He reached behind the door and came back holding a bat. "Or I'll smash it so flat, I'll be able to close the door whether it's there or not."

I jerked back, opened my mouth to say something, to plead or beg, but before I could utter more than a grunt, he'd slammed the door in my face. Locks tumbled, and the voices resumed at twice their previous volume.

And then the *thump, thump, thump* began once again.

Well, that didn't go as planned.

I wandered back to my car, stunned. How in the world had Pooky managed to live with a guy like that for as long as she had? I understood that he was her brother, but if he treated her even half as awfully as he'd just treated me, I would have sent him packing long ago.

I didn't have a brother of my own. Or a sister. I supposed that would make a difference in how much crap I would take, so I couldn't entirely blame Pooky for letting Donnie stay, even though it was obvious he'd worn out his welcome.

But this . . . this was something else.

As I climbed into my Escape, my phone pinged. I checked the message and was happy to see it was from Cassie Wise. I'd also missed a message from Jen Vousden as well. Maybe something good would come out of this day after all.

I checked Jen's message first.

I wish I'd been at the marathon, but unfortunately, I've been sick and hospitalized, so I was unable to attend. Thank you for your concern.

The cynical part of me instantly wondered if it was a lie. It would be easy enough to find out if Jen was in the hospital, and I planned on checking that out at some point.

Not sure what else I could do yet, I sent her a quick *Thanks for getting back to me. Feel better,* and then moved on to Cassie's message.

Hey, Krissy! I'm so glad to hear from you! I'd love to meet up and chat sometime soon. I don't think I saw any- thing that day, but who knows? If we put our heads to- gether, then perhaps something will come out of it. It's terrible what happened to that man. And to have it hap-

pen during an event that was supposed to be for a good cause. Awful.

Anyway, get back with me soon. Let's set up a lunch, have a chat, all right?

Cass

I considered asking her if we could meet right then and there, but decided I wanted a shower more. I sent her a reply, asking if tomorrow morning would work, and telling her she could choose the place. I hit SEND and then set my phone aside.

I needed time to think. About Pooky's problem, about Glen's murder. And about Johan's odd behavior. That's not to mention Paul and our abbreviated dinner date.

But before I did any thinking, a shower, because whatever that smell that had come from apartment 24B was, it was now on me.

14

"How do I . . . ?" I clicked on a tab that I thought would expand the window, but I must have hit something else entirely because all of my windows abruptly minimized. I made a sound low in my throat that had Misfit's head jerking up from where he napped on the couch.

"Sorry," I muttered, bringing the window back up. Misfit watched me for a long couple of seconds before lowering his head once again.

I was due to talk to my dad on video chat in five minutes, and I had no idea what I was doing. It was the first time we'd ever attempted such a feat, and I was regretting agreeing to it. I knew how to use a computer, but I wasn't as proficient with it as I should be. I could handle the word processor and the internet just fine, which meant this should have been a piece of cake.

I took a deep breath and settled my mind. I wasn't focusing on the right thing, and it was causing me to make mistakes. This time, when I clicked, everything worked as it was supposed to.

I created the chat room, sent the access code or link or whatever it would send to Dad, and then sat back to wait. That lasted all of two seconds before I realized the camera placement on my laptop was less than ideal. It was placed close to the keyboard, rather than at the top of the screen, so when I leaned back, the image was angled to go right up my nose.

"Just great," I muttered, adjusting positions. Sitting forward didn't help all that much, but at least I couldn't see into the depths of my skull. I lowered my chin so far, it was practically resting on my chest, scowled, and then gave up. I was sure Dad had seen worse in his time, especially from me.

I sipped lemonade—the last of the batch—careful not to drip any onto the keyboard. Condensation had created a small puddle on the table. I grabbed a napkin to use as a coaster, and within seconds, it was stuck to the glass, a sopping, dripping mess.

"I'll be glad when this heat is over," I said, glancing at the snoozing cat. He'd been lethargic ever since I'd gotten home, which worried me some. Misfit wasn't a kitten anymore, and I hated seeing him so miserable.

But he seemed okay now. I just hoped he would stay that way.

Light reflected off the screen of my laptop, nearly blinding me, as a car drifted by. Thinking back to the car I'd seen outside Death by Coffee, my nerves started jumping. I rose from my seat and checked the window to make sure the car wasn't the same one as before, but it was only Caitlin coming home, a bag of groceries in her arms.

"Buttercup?" Dad's tinny voice came from my pathetic laptop speakers. "Krissy, are you there?"

"I'm here!" I called, hurrying back to my chair. "Sorry. I thought someone might be here and got up to check."

Dad looked great for a man his age. It must have been the Californian sun or perhaps his girlfriend, Laura Dresden, keeping him active. There were still moments when I couldn't fathom him being with anyone else other than Mom, but she'd passed years ago, and Laura was clearly good for him. Without her, I'm not sure where he'd be.

"You can hear me, right?" Dad asked, squinting into the camera like he thought he could see me in it.

"I can. You can hear me?"

"Yep." He breathed a sigh of relief. "I was worried that this wasn't going to work. Laura assured me she had it set up right, but you know me. I like to do things myself so I know how to do it." He paused. "You're looking rather crisp, Buttercup. Get too much sun?"

"You could say that. I ran in that marathon I told you about."

"Oh! Right. How did that go?" He must have seen something flash across my face because he laughed. "That good, huh?"

"It was really hot that day," I said, mentally debating whether to tell him the rest. "And someone was murdered."

His eyes widened briefly before he settled back into his chair. I noted he was in his office, which shouldn't have come as a surprise, considering he was using his laptop. A bookshelf behind him gave me a good look at most of the books he'd written. He called it his "ego shelf," but at this point, the shelf was plural.

"Did you know this someone well?" he asked.

"No." I gave him the details as best as I could figure them. Glen Moreau was the victim. He'd threatened one of the organizers, Rod, going so far as to post a Facebook message in the middle of the marathon. He was there with two of his friends. And then there were the women he'd used and tossed away, and the possible financial scheme. The only thing I left out was Johan Morrison.

"That sounds complex," Dad said, whistling through his teeth.

"It is. I'm not sure where to start with him. Glen appears to have cheated on every woman he's ever been with, was into some shady stuff, and didn't get along with most of the people I talked to about him. I feel like everyone who knew him had a reason to want him dead."

"Other than his friends."

"As far as I'm aware, they're the only people who actually liked him." But I hadn't talked to either of them yet either. Would I come away feeling the same way after a conversation with Trevor or Calvin? I wondered.

"Sounds like you've got your work cut out for you."

"The police do," I said. "I'm not going to get involved."

Dad laughed. "If you say so." When I started to protest, he patted the air. "All right, all right. I get it. Just remember to be careful, whether you're involved or not. This guy sounds like he was a piece of work, and if he upset a lot of people, chances are good that he upset some dangerous people right along with your normal, everyday sorts."

No kidding. "I'll be careful," I promised.

"Good. You need to take care of yourself, Buttercup. I can see the stress on your face. I'm not sure if it's the murder, or if it's something else, but I don't like it. You have a tendency to obsess."

"I know. I think I might take a vacation sometime soon. Get away from Pine Hills for a bit." With Paul, hopefully. Somewhere with cool waves, a beach. And if that place just so happened to be clothing optional . . .

Dad cleared his throat, jerking me back to the here and now.

"I, uh . . ." I could feel my face redden.

Thankfully, Dad didn't pry, though he did smile in a way that made me worry that he'd gleaned my thoughts from my expression. "If you talk to your police friends, consider telling them to focus on the victim's personal life. He might have been involved in a financial crime, but this isn't a television show. A murder in a small town like Pine Hills likely has more to do with the guy being a no-good cheat and a jerk than it does with him ripping people off."

I wasn't so sure, but I nodded anyway. Ivy had said something about weird stuff happening after she'd followed Glen to that building I'd watched Johan go into. And now, after watching the same building, someone had driven by Death by Coffee multiple times, looking suspicious. That couldn't be a coincidence.

"I—" My head jerked up as the sound of an engine caught my attention. A moment later, a car door slammed. "Someone's here. I should go."

"All right, Buttercup. Let's do this again sometime soon."

"Of course." There was a knock on the door. "I'll text you later."

We said quick goodbyes, and I closed my laptop lid before I rose to answer the knock. My mind raced through the possibilities of who might be paying me an unannounced visit, each worse than the last. I was half convinced that when I opened the door, Johan would be standing there, a silenced pistol in his hand.

I slowed, unsure I wanted to answer. If I checked the window and it wasn't someone I knew, what would I do? And what if I did see a gun? I could call Paul, and then what? Wait until he got there to save me?

"Krissy?" Paul's voice came from the other side of the door.

I let out a pent-up breath as relief washed through me. I was working myself up for nothing. I answered the door. "Sorry," I said, feeling like a dope. Paul had his head down, one hand on the doorframe as if it was the only thing holding him upright. "I was talking to my dad. Come in." I stepped aside.

Paul was in uniform. He removed his hat as he stepped into my house, and he visibly sagged when the cool air hit him. His shirt was stuck to his back, and a trail of sweat rolled down his neck before he turned to face me.

I winced. Both of Paul's eyes were blackened. A butterfly bandage was strapped across the bridge of his swollen nose. There was more bruising than I felt there should be, but then again, I'd hoped for none at all, so even a little was too much.

"It looks worse than it feels," he said.

"It looks like you got hit by a baseball bat." I grinned, unable to contain myself. "I thought *I* was the one who was supposed to stop catching criminals with my face."

"Funny." He flashed me a smile before sagging down onto the stool by my island counter. His eyes drifted to my lemonade. "You wouldn't happen to have more of that, would you?"

"No, sorry. But you can have the rest. It's still cold." I peeled the damp napkin from the glass before handing it over.

He took a small sip, and then a longer gulp. "This is good." He smacked his lips and then polished off the remains.

"Lance made it. Jules promised they'd bring more over soon."

"If he does, let me know. I'll have to stop by for that."

"What? I'm not a good enough reason to visit?" I said it playfully, but Paul flinched anyway, as if I'd insulted him. "I'm just kidding," I said, sitting across from him.

"I know. It's just . . ." he sighed. "I wish dinner had gone better." He glanced at me, then away.

"Me too. Did you figure out what the fight was about?"

"Not really. The two men claim they were having dinner to honor Glen's memory. They had too much to drink, and one thing led to another, and before long, tempers were flaring."

"Do you believe them?"

Paul shrugged. "Hard to say. John took over at the station, and since I was the one who took the elbow to the face, I wasn't permitted to sit in on the interviews."

I could see why. There had to be a conflict of interest in there somewhere, though you'd think Calvin might be a little more forthcoming being confronted by the cop whose face he'd bopped.

"John let Rod Maxwell go after an hour or so, but he's still holding Calvin Davis. Apparently, this isn't the first time he's gotten into trouble, though I think it's stuff like unpaid fines and public intoxication. John's probably holding him more because he assaulted me, even if it was an accident, than his past infractions."

"Do you think any of it has to do with Glen's murder?" I asked.

"Unlikely," Paul said. He sniffed and winced. "If John had something solid on him, he'd have told me."

I wondered, but that likely had more to do with Buchannan's history with me, rather than Paul.

"But that's not why I'm here." Paul picked up his glass, saw it was empty, and set it aside. "I checked on that building you told me about."

"The one I saw Johan go into?"

He nodded, brow furrowed. When he spoke, he did so while looking down at the top of the counter.

"I couldn't find anything on it. No owner, no business filing. Nothing."

"Like it doesn't exist?" Kind of like Johan Morrison. A creeping dread worked its way through me.

"It exists, but as far as anyone in Pine Hills knows, it's just an empty building."

"Did you go to it? Check it out in person?"

"I stopped by." He shifted on his stool. "Krissy, are you sure you gave me the right address?"

"It was between a laundromat and one of those places you cash checks?" At his nod, I went on. "Then, yes, I gave you the right address. That's the place Johan went into, and the same place Glen Moreau had frequented."

Paul met my eye, stared hard at me. "You're sure?"

"Paul, I'm positive." The dread worked its way up my throat. "Why? What did you find?" Images of dead bodies atop piles of money flashed through my mind. How in the world could I explain that to Rita?

"Nothing."

I blinked at him. "Nothing?"

"Absolutely nothing," Paul said. "The building was empty."

"Empty?" My brain couldn't seem to grasp the concept. "But Johan went in. He came out with a briefcase."

"Are you positive he didn't enter with it? Could you have overlooked it and only noticed it once he left?"

"No. I . . . I don't know." I was pretty sure Johan hadn't gone in carrying a briefcase, but what if I was wrong? I hadn't been feeling my best lately, so it was possible I wasn't as attentive as I should have been.

Paul reached out and put a hand on my own. "Maybe there's nothing to this. Maybe you thought he went into that building, but he'd really gone into the one next door."

"To cash a check." It came out sounding flat, dead.

"The doorways aren't that far from one another. And it's been brutally hot out there these last few days. You've gotten more sun than what is healthy and . . ."

"And what?" Anger flared through me, and I pulled my hand from his own. "I imagined it?"

"I didn't say that—"

"No, but you implied it." I crossed my arms, and then, realizing it made me look like a petulant child, I dropped them and stood. "I know what I saw. Johan went into that building and came out carrying a briefcase he hadn't gone in with."

Paul's worried expression only made me angrier.

"I'm not hallucinating. I'm not sun-sick or whatever you're implying. That place is tied to Glen Moreau and Johan Morrison, I'm sure of it." And that meant it had to be tied to Glen's death, didn't it? "A car was following me," I blurted.

Paul's face grew serious, and he stood. "Someone followed you? When? From that building?"

"No. And I guess it didn't follow me as much as it lurked outside of Death by Coffee. I noticed it slow a few times and then speed off."

"Did you see the driver? Get a plate?"

I shook my head. "Well, I did see one letter. An

'L.' " I thought that's what I'd seen, but now, I was second-guessing everything. "I . . ." I bit my lower lip, uncertain I wanted to say what I was thinking, and then deciding that I needed to. Not just for my sake, but for Rita's. "I think it was Johan's car."

Paul stilled. He knew what I thought of Johan, and I was pretty sure he felt the same way. "Are you positive?"

"Positive? No. But I'm pretty sure it was the same car Johan climbed out of outside that building." I described the car as best I could. Paul took notes silently, letting me speak without interruption. "It's possible they could just be of a similar make and model, but I don't think so."

Paul was silent a long moment before he said, "I don't like this."

"Neither do I," I said. "Ivy Hammer claimed some strange things happened around her place after she'd followed Glen to this same building, and now a car is driving slowly by Death by Coffee. It can't be a coincidence." Even if it wasn't Johan, I felt it had to be connected.

Paul picked up his hat and carried it to the door with him. There was a dangerous look in his eye.

"What are you going to do?" I asked as he pulled open the door.

"I'm going to look into Johan Morrison again, check out this car you saw."

"And then?"

He looked at me, and then surprised me by kissing me hard on the lips.

"Don't you worry about that," he said. "Call me if you see this car again. I don't want something to happen to you because you thought you could handle it on your own."

I was too stunned to argue. My lips were tingling, and my toes were curling. A large part of me wanted to grab him and drag him inside and keep him locked up inside my house for the foreseeable future.

But if I did that, I might never know who had driven by Death by Coffee, or if Johan was indeed a criminal mastermind.

Paul put his hat onto his head and then headed for his car. If it had been a horse, he would have looked like a cowboy about to ride off to do battle with the villain who'd threatened his damsel in distress.

Of course, I wasn't exactly a damsel who sat around waiting for a man to save her, no matter how romantic the idea might be.

15

I've got something for you! Hit me up!!
I frowned at the message, not sure I wanted to bother. Skinny Jefferson had sent it, exclamation points and all, less than an hour ago. It was entirely possible he'd spotted something in one of his photographs, something that might break the case wide open, but I had a feeling it was far more likely he was still looking for a nude model.

I drummed my fingers lightly on the keyboard before typing a reply.

Send me what you've got. I read the short message five times before hitting SEND to make sure there was no way Skinny could misinterpret my meaning.

While I waited to see what he might have, I went back to perusing the internet, searching for anything that might explain the now-empty building I'd seen Johan enter. When I wasn't doing that, I would flip over to Facebook and check the marathon page, looking for a post, a photo, anything that would tell me what might have happened to Glen Moreau.

I found nothing on either count.

Scrolling down to where Glen had made his own post before his death, I reread it, hoping to spot something in the way it was worded that would help solve his murder.

I'm going to make sure Rod Maxwell gets what's coming to him.

If Rod Maxwell had been the victim, the post would have painted Glen as the most likely killer. Could it work in reverse? The two men argued during the marathon—or more accurately, Glen threatened Rod, who didn't do much to defend himself before Trevor stepped in. Then Glen posted his threat. Both the verbal sparring and the post hinted that Glen knew something about Rod, something the other man wouldn't want to get out.

That sounded like motive to me.

Add in the chat Rod had had with Alleah Trotter at the Banyon Tree, and then later, the fight with Calvin at Geraldo's. It sure seemed like Rod was involved in more than just organizing a marathon. And Alleah sounded as if she were a part of whatever it was Rod was trying to keep secret. Could that have been what the fight between Rod and Calvin was about, despite what the men claimed?

My phone pinged twice, telling me I had a pair of waiting messages. I used my laptop to check them.

The first was from Cassie.

Scream for Ice Cream? Tomorrow at about tenish? I know it's early, but I've got some errands to run and finish before noon. Let me know!

I considered it, and then agreed. Ice cream sounded great, and I was pretty sure I'd have enough time to get everything else I planned on doing in the morning done before then, despite ten being a smidge early for ice cream.

Who was I kidding? It was never too early for ice cream.

Before checking the second message, this one from Skinny, I picked up my phone and texted Vicki. We'd already made tentative plans, but I wanted to hammer down the details now. I was making time for Cassie and Trisha and Shannon. I could definitely make time for my best friend.

Confirming Saturday night, my place, with Trouble. Anytime after six would work. It was Thursday now, and with Melanie's party Friday night, I'd probably need the downtime.

That done, I clicked the message from Skinny, expecting disappointment.

I don't want to send it, but you do need to see it. Come to my place. Here's the address.

Sure enough, Skinny's address followed.

I started to answer but caught myself. This felt like an obvious ploy to get me into his house, where he could attempt to coax me into posing for those photos. Telling him off would be easy, but if he did actually have something, doing so might cause him to shut me out completely, and I'd never know what it was he had.

Instead of replying, I closed my laptop. I'd sleep on it. If I felt there was some value in showing up at Skinny's place, then I'd do it—with Paul in tow. Otherwise, I didn't want to encourage him to keep in contact.

Vicki texted back a thumbs-up emoji. So far, so good. Now I just had to remember all my appointments. Considering the state of my mind as of late, it wasn't going to be easy.

Misfit wandered into the living room and rubbed against my leg as I stood. It was getting late, and while I could stay up for a few hours more, I decided against it. With a good night's sleep, I could face tomorrow refreshed. I had a huge list of things I wanted to get done, and sleepwalking through them wouldn't cut it.

As I prepped for bed, I kept thinking about what Paul had told me about the mysterious building on Rosebud. The place was supposedly empty. Glen had gone into there and come out with a briefcase. The owner was a mystery. Johan had gone in and left with a briefcase, just like Glen.

Something had to be in there.

I stood in the middle of my bedroom with my PJs in my hand. Misfit had followed me in and was already curled up at the foot of the bed, watching me with sleepy eyes.

The building was empty.

Checking out an empty building wasn't nearly as dangerous as walking into Skinny Jefferson's place alone.

Right?

Before I knew what I was doing, my PJs were discarded on the bed, and I was putting on black slacks, a dark shirt, and a pair of near-black tennis shoes. I tied my hair back to keep it out of my face and then was out the door.

If the building was indeed empty, no one should care if I had a look around. I could check it out from all sides, try to peer in through the windows. It wasn't like I planned on breaking into the place. A quick look, just to satisfy my curiosity, and then I'd go home and go to bed. That's it.

I drove to Rosebud a jumble of nerves. It wasn't that I didn't believe Paul and thought that I'd find a constant stream of shady characters going in and out when I arrived, but I was pretty darn sure that building hadn't been empty when Johan had entered. He'd left with a briefcase. If nothing else, there might be some evidence lying around that would hint at what was in it or who had left it there.

Could it be a drop spot? An empty building owned by no one. It seemed like as good a place as any.

I parked in the same spot I'd parked the last time I was there. Most of the businesses, lawyers and all, were closed up tight. Only the laundromat appeared to be open. The same older woman sat in the same chair, reading what could very well be the same magazine. She didn't glance up as I killed the lights and shut off the engine. If she hadn't reached up to scratch her nose, I would have begun to think she was a mannequin.

I sat in my darkened Escape, eyes scouring the

street, which was lit up by streetlamps. No cars cruised the area, and no pedestrians strode down the street, making it eerily quiet. A light cloud cover obscured the sliver of moon peering over the tops of the buildings. If I was planning on breaking in, all I'd need to do was knock out a few streetlights and avoid walking in front of the laundromat, and I'd be able to approach unseen.

But I wasn't breaking in. I wasn't approaching the building. I was . . . what? Sitting in the dark, staring at a lifeless building?

The back of my neck started to itch. I thought back to all those books I'd read where that was a sign you were being watched, but if someone was there, they were well concealed, because I couldn't see anyone other than the oblivious older woman.

"There could be cameras." I jumped at the sound of my own voice. My heart was racing, and I wasn't entirely sure why. I could start up my Escape and drive away like nothing had happened because nothing *had* happened.

And nothing will. I winced as I opened the car door, and the overhead light popped on. As soon as I was on the sidewalk, I closed the door and then just stood there, listening for a sign that someone had seen me and was on the way to investigate.

I heard nothing but the faint bleat of a dying car alarm a few streets over. It cut off, leaving me standing in silence.

All right, Krissy, one look, and then you're out of here. I strode down the street until I was across from

the Quick Cash—or whatever the name meant
with all those dollar signs—before crossing. If the
older woman were to look up from her magazine
and crane her neck, she'd be able to see me, but
otherwise, I felt invisible. I didn't spot any cameras
anywhere, though I was pretty sure that was the
point.

*And I'm not doing anything illegal. I'm just walking
by, a pedestrian out for a stroll in the middle of the night,
on a street no one had any reason to be walking on.*

Peeking into the window of Quick Cash as I
passed, I saw nothing alarming. Some tables, a
counter, and closed doors. My heart was thunder-
ing in my ears, and my legs felt rubbery. If someone were to walk down the sidewalk now, I wasn't
sure what I would do. Run, most likely.

"It's just a building," I muttered, leaving Quick
Cash behind. I approached the target of my night-
time escapades, not sure what to expect. Up close,
it was just as small and boxy and bland as I'd already noted. The window by the door was still obscured by heavy shades, which meant peeking in
that way was pointless. There were no side windows because the sides butted up against the laundromat and Quick Cash. An alley ran along the
backside, but the only way to reach it would be to
walk down the street until I found an access point.

Which would look far more suspicious than me
standing out front, looking lost.

This was a waste of time. It was almost a relief,
really. I didn't know what I would have done if the
shades were gone from the window and I could see

in. What if I saw something? A clue that needed investigating? Signs of a scuffle?

Or worse, a body?

I glanced up and down the street. Still no one. There was definitely no camera here because there was no place for a camera.

The old lady might know something. I could go into the laundromat, ask her about her neighbors, and then go home. If she worked there, chances were good that she'd taken note of some of the people who'd gone in and out of the building next door. If she was simply someone who spent a lot of time doing laundry, well, then there was no harm in talking to her either. She might be more willing to talk if that was the case.

My brain was ready to do just that, but my body had other plans. Without conscious thought, my hand reached out and tried the doorknob, fully expecting to find it locked.

It wasn't.

The ominous creak that followed had all the hairs on the back of my neck standing up.

"Hello?" My voice was pitched at a whisper. If someone was inside, they might not have heard me, but they surely would have heard the door. "Anyone there?"

Crickets. Not the literal kind, but my mind supplied the soundtrack anyway.

Another check up and down the street. Still no one. The laundromat lady wasn't visible through the window at this angle. I was alone.

I stepped over the threshold.

Darkness enveloped me. If there was a back window, it was covered, just like the front. I could see a few feet of tiled floor thanks to the light coming in through the open doorway, but that was it. I fished out my phone, found the flashlight app, and turned it on before closing the door behind me.

I'm not sure what I expected to find, but whatever it was, my heart sank when I saw the stretch of empty tile and the single table pressed against the wall. There were three doors across the room. The first was hanging slightly open and a sign on the door proclaimed it to be a universal bathroom. The other two were unmarked and closed.

My footfalls echoed in the empty space as I crossed the room. A quick peek in the bathroom showed me a toilet and sink. A toilet paper roll sat atop the back of the toilet, but there was no hand soap, no paper towels.

I moved to the second door and noted both the lock and deadbolt. *An alley door?* Opening it, I saw that, indeed, it led to an alley void of anything of interest. I stepped back inside and closed the door.

I moved to the last remaining door. I was almost positive I'd find it locked when I tried the knob, but like the others, it opened without resistance. I shone my phone into the room and . . .

And nothing. More of the same tile. A few dust bunnies. I took a deep, disappointed breath, and then froze.

Something wasn't right.

It took me a moment to realize what that something was. My eyes scoured the floor, ears perked for any sound, but it wasn't until I saw the pattern on the floor that I realized what was bothering me.

Yes, the building was empty now.

But it hadn't been until recently.

The small room had square imprints on the floor made of dust and by something heavy that had lined the back wall. It didn't take a genius to figure out that filing cabinets had stood there. There were no files to be found now, let alone the cabinets that had once stored them, but it was a clue.

I turned and hurried out to the table resting against the wall. It was long and had immobile legs. It wasn't the kind that you could break down easily. It would have taken some work to get it out through the door, unlike the filing cabinets, which could have been wheeled out through either door using a handcart. You wouldn't even need to empty them to do it.

I ran a finger over the table and looked at it in the light supplied by my phone.

No dust.

When I'd taken that deep breath, I'd noticed that, despite being empty, the building didn't smell stale. My footfalls didn't cause dust to fly either. There were no footprints. I'd seen Johan go in, so if this was just a drop spot, then you'd think it would be dusty. I mean, who sweeps the floor of a room no one ever spends time in?

I walked slowly around the room, checking every corner, looking for something—anything—

that might have been missed when they'd cleaned the place out. I didn't smell disinfectant or anything that would indicate that whoever had worked out of here had wiped it down. The cleanliness was of the usual sort, with swept floors and basic dusting, but nothing excessive.

It was as if someone had worked here.

I'd made a full circuit around the place and was about to investigate the bathroom in the hopes that whoever had emptied the building had dropped something into the toilet and forgotten to flush, when I heard a sound that most definitely didn't belong.

Sirens.

My body and brain froze at the same instant. I was standing a foot from an alley door, yet when the police car screeched to a halt just outside the building I was currently snooping around in, I didn't make for the alley and freedom.

I rushed into the bathroom and closed the door.

Almost immediately, the front door opened, and I heard footfalls as someone entered the premises. There was absolutely no way I was going to shut off my phone and stand there in the pitch-black dark of an unfamiliar bathroom. There could be anything in there, including hand-sized spiders lurking in the corners.

Seconds passed, and then Buchannan's voice drifted through the door. "I know you're in there, Ms. Hancock. Come on out."

My first thought was, *How did he know it was me?* It was quickly followed by three words:

My orange Escape.

I considered remaining hidden, but what would that accomplish other than to annoy the detective even more than he already was? He knew I was here, and even if I locked the door, he could wait me out. Besides, that itch on the back of my neck had grown eight legs as my imagination started taking over.

I pushed open the bathroom door and stepped out. I was immediately blinded by a flashlight. I held tight to my phone as I raised my hands, showing Detective Buchannan they were mostly empty.

"Hi," I said. "I, uh, was just looking."

"Right." Buchannan lowered the flashlight. I had to blink to clear my vision, but I could hear the scowl in his voice. "I honestly don't know what to do about you." A beat, then, "Let's go."

I didn't object as I followed him out of the building. Two young cops stood out front, their car parked at the curb. I didn't know either officer, which didn't bode well for me.

"The door was unlocked," I said. "So, I technically didn't break in. I'll go home and leave you alone now."

"No you won't." Buchannan waved a hand, and both of the young cops approached. One of them was holding a pair of handcuffs.

"Come on!" I pleaded. "There's nothing in there. You don't have to arrest me for walking into an unlocked and empty building!"

But no one was listening to me. The cops handcuffed me, albeit gently. I was deposited into the back seat of the cruiser with one of the cops murmuring apologies. He probably knew my connection to both Paul and the police chief.

As soon as I was settled, they closed the door and conferred with Buchannan for a few long minutes before they got into the car. Buchannan remained standing, arms crossed, as I was driven off. Just before we turned the corner, he slammed a fist down onto the hood of his car, telling me I'd made a huge mistake.

16

A constant *click, click, click* came from a fan facing the couch in the Pine Hills police station interrogation room. I was currently alone, but the balled-up blanket and flat pillow on the couch—as well as the fan aimed at said couch—told me that someone had been here before me.

The two officers had deposited me in the room without much more than a "Wait here." The station was quiet to the point of being practically abandoned. Pine Hills wasn't normally a place of high crime—outside of the occasional murder, of course—so it wasn't much of a surprise that the police force worked with a skeleton crew this late.

But it did mean there was no one to deal with me in a timely manner.

I'm not sure how long I waited. I sat in the plastic chair at the table in the middle of the room for a little while and then paced from one wall to the next to break the monotony. I checked out the coffeepot, which held sludge I doubted anyone actually drank, and even went so far as to throw a couple of darts at the dartboard above the couch before returning to my seat.

Yawning, I considered the blanket and pillow and wondered if Buchannan would mind if I took a nap. The adrenaline from my late-night jaunt had worn off, and exhaustion was seeping in. The heat didn't help. The fan circulated hot air, which did little to cool me down.

The door opened, and I popped to my feet out of reflex. My heart gave a lurch, which sent a zing through me that quickly dissipated as Detective John Buchannan entered. He looked as pooped as I felt.

"Sit down," he said, dispensing with "Ms. Hancock" and other pleasantries.

Without a word, I did as he said.

Buchannan dropped into his chair before rubbing at his face. I wondered if he'd been on duty when he'd learned of my infiltration of the empty building or if someone had woken him up. I couldn't resist glancing back at the couch. Could he be the one sleeping here? The blanket and pillow had been there for a while, and as far as I was aware, he and his wife weren't fighting, but what did I really know about John Buchannan's life outside of his job?

"What in the world were you thinking?" Buchannan asked, drawing my attention back to him.

"I guess I wasn't." I gave him a sheepish smile. "Sorry."

"Sorry?" He laughed. There was no amusement in it. "I . . ." He shook his head. "What are we going to do with you?"

I lowered my head, face burning. I felt like a kid who'd just been caught sneaking into the wrong locker room. "I hear that a lot."

He rubbed at his face again and continued to shake his head. "You're going to give me a stroke, I know it."

Another smart remark was on the tip of my tongue, but I thought better of it. "I didn't intend to go in," I said instead.

Buchannan dropped his hands and gave me a flat look.

"Seriously. I heard that the building was empty, and since I saw someone go in the other day, I figured I'd take a peek. I didn't expect it to be unlocked, and when I found it was . . ."

"You heard it was empty?" Disbelieving. "I think you'd best start at the beginning. Pretend I haven't heard anything about what you may or may not have done over the last few days."

I took a deep breath to organize my thoughts, and then I told him, starting with Glen Moreau's murder. I hedged around naming my sources, and I was careful not to mention Johan, but I told him pretty much everything else, right up until the moment he'd shown up at the empty building's front door.

"How did you know I was there?" I asked when I was done.

"You aren't as sneaky as you think," he said. "We got a call about someone lurking around, acting suspicious. I was hopeful we'd caught a break, but when I got there, I saw your vehicle." He scowled.

It took me a moment to catch what he was implying. "Wait. A break? You knew about the building?" Of course he did. I'd asked Paul to look into it for me, and while he wouldn't have blabbed about my involvement, he would likely have used police resources to investigate it.

Buchannan sighed, went to rub his face again, but paused halfway there. He dropped his hands heavily onto the table. "We've known about that location for a little while now."

The words "And I'm just finding out about it now?" nearly burst from my lips, but I caught myself. "Because of Glen Moreau's murder?"

Buchannan stared at me as if weighing the benefits of telling me anything at all. I mean, I wasn't a cop. I wasn't a private investigator or a lawyer or anyone who should have anything to do with the murder, let alone any sort of police investigation.

But he also knew I wasn't going to simply let it drop. If he didn't tell me, I'd ask Paul. And if Paul wouldn't tell me, I'd just find some other source. Rita and her gossip buddies, Georgina and Andi, were always a possibility.

"No," he finally said.

"You've known about it longer?"

"Let's just say that the activities that have gone on around that place have been noticed. It's been a project of mine, a personal one I've worked on my own for quite a while now."

A flare of anger shot through me, but quickly dissipated. I'd asked Paul to check the place out, and he'd come back and told me it was empty and that there was no record of who the owner might be. Had he known when I'd asked that Buchannan was investigating it? Had Buchannan instructed him on how to answer?

Had he lied to me?

The possibility caused my heart to ache. There was a chance Paul hadn't known—Buchannan did say he'd worked it on his own time—but if he had . . .

"Here's the deal," Buchannan said after letting me stew for a few moments. "There's no one to press charges against you, so you don't have to worry about that. I could come up with a few reasons to toss you into a cell, but that would become a headache I don't want to deal with."

I supposed my relationships with Paul and his mother were protecting me here. Buchannan had tried to lock me up more than once in the past, and Chief Dalton almost always let my infractions slide.

I was beginning to wonder how long that would last.

"However"—Buchannan held up a finger as though I were about to speak—"this is going to be your only warning. Stay out of these investigations. If you insist on showing up where you don't belong, I'll have no choice but to arrest you. If I didn't know you as well as I do, I would have already."

I nodded, keeping my eyes on the table in front of me. I wasn't just pretending to be ashamed; I actually was. I should have known better than to go strolling into a building that might be tied to a crime. No, scratch that. Was tied to a crime.

"Can you tell me one thing at least?" I asked, glancing up through my lashes.

Buchannan narrowed his eyes but didn't tell me not to ask.

"Is Johan Morrison in trouble?" When his lips thinned, I hurriedly added, "I don't want Rita to be hurt. If he's involved in this in any way, she should know to be careful with him." I'd avoided his name until now, but I had to know.

Buchannan tapped a finger on the table that was in time with the *click, click, click* of the fan. Seconds passed that felt like minutes before he answered.

"He's being watched. That's all I can say about it right now. And *you*"—he leveled a finger at me—"are not to say anything to Rita Jablonski or anyone else about this. Do I make myself clear?"

"Very."

"Good." Buchannan sighed and rose to his feet. "I'm going to have someone drive you back to your car. I hope your time sitting in here has gotten through to you." He started for the door, stopped. "Wait here. And, please, just . . ." He shook his head and left the room.

I sat there, numb, and stared at the open door. Johan could be . . . what? Involved in crimes that got Glen killed? Murder? I'd wondered about him myself in the past, and then again more recently when I'd seen him with that woman, but a part of me had thought that I was overthinking it, that there was no way Rita's boyfriend could be involved in anything other than being a bit weird.

A shape appeared in the doorway. Frazzled hair, a too-long Metallica T-shirt with a tear under the left arm hanging loosely on a body sagging as if exhaustion were going bury her. Becca Garrison looked like a woman who'd just been torn out of sleep, and I knew exactly who was responsible.

An "I'm sorry" was on my lips, but a harsh look stopped me.

"Don't say it," she said. "Let's go."

I stood and followed her out of the room, but not before taking one last look at the makeshift bed on the couch.

Garrison's the one who's been sleeping here?

We took her personal vehicle, rather than a police cruiser, for which I was thankful. I was about to climb into the back seat out of habit, but a terse "Don't be silly" brought me to the front. Garrison waited until I was buckled in before we were on our way.

"I'm sorry about this," I said, despite her objections. "I figured Buchannan would have had one of the on-duty officers drive me back."

"I need to make a stop anyway." She patted at her hair but didn't bother trying to tame it.

"At home?" Casual.

She glanced at me out of the corner of her eye. "No."

I was dying to know why she was sleeping at the police station, but asking her would feel too much like a violation of her privacy. We weren't exactly friends, though I hoped we were closer than mere acquaintances. I'd seen the blanket and pillow months ago, so whatever had happened wasn't a recent development.

Garrison must have felt my curiosity because she heaved a sigh and explained without me having to ask.

"I've had some . . . monetary issues lately," she said. "A bad deal on my place. Loans." She snorted. "Whatever. It was a scam. and I fell for it."

"Can you arrest the person who scammed you?"

"I wish. They technically did it all legally, hitting just the right loopholes so I can't do a thing about it. I'll be all right. Sucks right now, but . . ." She shrugged one shoulder. "I feel stupid. I'm a cop. I should have—" She sucked in a breath, and though I couldn't tell by her face, it sounded like she was close to tears. "The department's doing what they can to help."

Hence the couch.

I didn't know Becca Garrison all that well, and our relationship was rocky at best, but that didn't mean I wanted to see her struggling. And sleeping on a police department couch couldn't be good for her back. I know mine hates it whenever I sleep anywhere but my own bed.

I cleared my throat, self-conscious, but concerned. "I have a spare room if—"

She cut me off with a slash of her hand. "I don't need anyone's charity." Her voice, which had been as harsh as the hand gesture, softened. "I appreciate the offer, but I'm okay. I just need some time, though maybe I deserve this. I should have seen it coming, but I guess I'm not cut out for . . ." She glanced at me, changed what she was going to say. "At least I don't have to get up early for work this way. I'm already there."

We finished the relatively short drive to Rosebud Avenue without saying anything more. My Escape was right where I'd left it. All the cop cars were gone, and the door to the empty building was closed and, I assumed, locked up tight.

"Thanks for the lift," I said, but I didn't get out right away. There was something I needed to ask, something I couldn't have asked John Buchannan but felt I could ask Officer Garrison. "Did Paul know?"

She turned in her seat to face me. "About?" I could tell by the tone of her voice that she already knew.

"This." I waved a hand toward the building. "About the investigation into this place?"

Garrison scratched at her cheek, looked past me, toward the laundromat, which was now closed. The lights were off, and the older woman was gone.

"I'm not going to get into that," Garrison said after a moment. "This place is part of Detective Buchannan's investigation. Only those who needed to know knew anything about it."

"And Paul didn't need to know?"

Garrison spread her hands. "It wasn't up to me to tell him."

It wasn't an answer, not really, but I got the point.

"I understand," I said, unease creeping in. What if I was the reason Paul didn't make detective? What if my meddling ended up costing him his job? I might have helped catch multiple murderers in my time in Pine Hills, but that didn't mean my actions didn't have consequences.

I slid out of the car and was about to close the door when Garrison leaned across the seat.

"Don't take any of this personally," she said. "John does what he thinks is best. Sometimes, he's right. Sometimes . . ." She left the rest hang before driving off and leaving me to consider whether Buchannan was right in this instance, or if I was causing more trouble than I was worth.

17

I shot straight up in bed, heart hammering in my chest, with no idea what had woken me.

Seconds ticked by while I just sat there, barely breathing. Hearing nothing, I turned on the bedside lamp. Misfit was standing in the bedroom doorway, back arched, so whatever had woken me, he'd heard—or sensed—it too.

My mouth felt like it was filled with cotton as I slid from the bed and padded barefoot across the room to the door. Misfit looked at me once and then hid under the bed, a sure sign that he was as spooked as I was.

"Hello?" I nearly smacked myself, but the word slipped out anyway. *Good work, Krissy. Let the ax-wielding maniac know where you are.*

But if there was an ax murderer in my living room, he didn't come running, nor did he reply. If I wanted to know if he were actually there, I'd have to go investigate myself.

Oh, goody.

I stood in my bedroom doorway for a good long minute, listening for the slightest creak of a board, of a knife sliding from the block, or the click of my front door opening, but there was nothing to be heard. The minute stretched into two, and then I eased out into the hallway. A few more steps and I was peering into my darkened living room and kitchen.

"Hello?" This time with more confidence. "Is anyone there?" After a tick, I muttered, "Not that you'd tell me if you were."

Memories flooded the back of my mind, kept my heart racing. Of killers breaking in, of being assaulted in my own home. Every second that passed in which nothing happened only made my tension rise, waiting for that moment in which someone would leap out from behind the counter, machete in hand.

But standing there would get me nowhere, nor would it dispel the notion that someone was hiding somewhere in my house. I crept into the kitchen, peeking carefully around the counter as I went, and checked the knife block. All the knives were accounted for. I slid the butcher knife free and then moved to the wall so I could flip on the light.

That was a mistake.

If a killer was waiting for me somewhere in the house, the moment the light turned on was the perfect time to attack since I'd just blinded myself. I blinked away tears and waved the knife in front of me, just in case someone did come at me. Chances of me hitting anyone were slim, but it was better than nothing.

The world came back into stark, bright focus, and I found myself standing there, swinging a knife at nothing.

Unsatisfied, I took the next few minutes to scour the living room and the little dining area, including checking under the table, and then went back down the hall to check the laundry room, the spare room, and my bedroom and bathroom, just to make sure they were empty.

I was alone. Whatever had woken me hadn't come from inside the house.

"All right." I breathed a huge sigh of relief, though I was still worried I'd missed something. "Let me think." Talking out loud helped ease my mind, though it did make me seem a little looney.

My mind was still heavy with sleep, but I began to mentally sort through my evening.

I'd come home from my little escapade and had gone to bed almost immediately, making sure to fill Misfit's water dish before I did. I'd been exhausted, so I was out within minutes of my head hitting the pillow, and then . . . ?

I had a vague recollection of a dream, but it was nothing I could describe. I could have been dreaming of Paul and a beach, or I could have been having a nightmare, which might explain why I was so jumpy when I woke.

But a nightmare didn't explain Misfit's nervousness, not unless I'd screamed myself awake with no recollection of doing so.

No, that wasn't it. I'd have remembered a nightmare, and if I'd startled Misfit awake, he would have been afraid of me, not the rest of the house.

I wandered back into the living room and looked around. Could something have fallen? I wasn't much of a decorator, so I didn't have photographs or paintings hanging on the walls. I didn't even have one of those LIVE, LAUGH, LOVE signs or any sort of inspirational quotes nailed above the door or hanging in the kitchen. The fridge was free of magnets, so nothing fell from there either.

My eyes landed on the front door. Could it be? Gripping the knife tightly in my fist, I went to the door and opened it, ready to jump back if someone was waiting out there.

My driveway was empty of all but my Escape. It was also late enough that all the lights in the neighborhood were off, including Caitlin's, so it wasn't her playing her guitar that had woken me—though I imagine I would have still been hearing it, if it had been.

"You're going crazy, Krissy." I guess that sort of thing happens when you spend all your time chasing after killers. It made me wonder if Paul struggled to sleep at night, and if he did, would having someone sleeping next to him help? I thought it might because I surely could use someone to cuddle up to right about then.

I was about to step back into the house when I noticed a single sheet of paper fluttering against my front door.

A wooden-handled knife was holding it in place.

I blinked at it uncomprehendingly at first, not quite sure what I was looking at. My brain supplied an inane "How did that get here?" and then my heart started racing. Someone *had* been to my house. Someone with a knife. I suddenly felt like I had a target painted on my back and hunched my shoulders, fearing that a gun would go off at any moment.

Without thinking, I snatched the paper off the door, leaving a chunk stuck to the knife, which was still jammed into the wood. I scuttled back into the house and slammed the door closed, locking it in one swift motion.

I didn't need to read the words on the page to know it was a threat, but read it I did.

If you know what's good for you, you'll stop interfering. This is your first and only warning.

It was, of course, typed, and it wasn't signed.

Reading the note could have sent my paranoia and fear through the roof, but instead it grounded me. Anger took the place of my panic, and I had to fight the urge to ball the page up in my fist.

Someone had threatened me. This wasn't the first time it had happened, and I was positive it wouldn't be the last.

Yet, this time, it felt almost cowardly. Most people were willing to threaten me to my face. I wasn't physically intimidating. Whoever had left this had pinned it to my door and then had run away before I could see them. Was I supposed to be scared of someone like that?

I set the page down on my table and weighed it down with my butcher knife before I headed into the bedroom for my phone. I unplugged it from the charger and then dialed as I wandered back into the living room. A sleepy Paul Dalton answered.

"Krissy? What time is it?"

I didn't know, and I was kind of afraid to look. If I'd woken him up at three a.m., I'd feel bad, but this was important. "Paul, someone was here."

"What?" He sounded much more alert now. "Are you at home?"

"I am. They left a note pinned to my door. I think you should come get it." I was being vague, but I was so angry, it was a struggle not to scream. "I'm fine, and whoever was here is gone, but they left evidence behind."

"I'm on my way."

He clicked off before I could say another word.

Misfit crept out from beneath the bed and wandered into the living room. I gave him a treat before I started pacing, trying to deduce who could have left the threatening note.

The killer was the obvious first choice, but that didn't really tell me anything. It could also have come from someone involved with that now-empty building. Even John Buchannan's name crossed my mind, though I dismissed it almost immediately. I mean, he wanted me to quit interfering with his investigation, sure, but he'd just tell me that to my face—and did. Often. No need for knives and creepy notes.

What about Johan?

I hated to admit it, but I found him just as likely as the killer, which made me sad, not just for me, but for Rita.

I'd calmed considerably by the time Paul pulled up. As soon as his headlights lit up my windows, I opened the door to wait for him. I was in my summer PJs, which were on the ratty and too thin side, but he didn't seem to notice. His eyes immediately latched onto the knife stuck to my door.

"I didn't touch it," I told him before he could ask.

He wasn't dressed in his uniform, but he produced an evidence kit from his pocket anyway. He took a photo of the knife with his phone, pulled on a pair of gloves, and wiggled the blade out of the wood, leaving behind a rather deep cut.

"It looks like it was hammered into place," he said, peering at the knife through the bag. "See the marks here?"

I could. There were circular dents at the base of the knife where the hammer had struck. That was likely the sound that had woken me.

Why not use a nail? I wondered. I guess a knife was a bit more intimidating, but still . . .

"You said there was a note?"

I crossed my arms over my chest as I nodded and led Paul inside, to the table. He produced another baggie and slid the note inside it before reading it.

"I wasn't thinking, and I did touch that," I told him.

"It's fine. I doubt we'll get much since we aren't exactly a high-tech department. I'm guessing whoever left it was careful enough to use gloves, but if not, I'll let you know." Paul set the meager evidence aside and then turned to me. "Are you all right?"

"I'm fine." Or I thought I was. When I tried to drop my arms to show him how fine I was, I couldn't bring myself to do it. "A little spooked, I guess."

"Did you see anyone? A car maybe?" Paul glanced toward the door, as if he could see through it, into the driveway beyond.

"No. I was asleep when it happened, and when I came to, I wasn't sure what had woken me. It took me a while to think to check outside, and by the time I did, no one was there. I—" My eyes widened. "Caitlin!"

Paul looked confused, and then worried. "Do you think someone is after her?"

"No, it's not that." Excited now, I all but dragged Paul to the door. "She has a camera!"

Caitlin had once been stalked by a friend of hers who used to peer in through her windows and scare the bejesus out of her. It was part of the reason she'd moved to Pine Hills in the first place, to get away from that friend. She kept security cameras aimed out her windows, just in case the woman ever found her.

One of those cameras was pointed toward my house.

Paul didn't resist as I led the way to Caitlin's house and started hammering on her door. He did try to talk some sense into me, considering the time—whatever it was—but I wasn't hearing him. I didn't know the range on Caitlin's camera, but if it caught the note-leaving culprit, it could very well lead to the apprehension of a killer.

A light snapped on inside, and a curtain swished, revealing the briefest glimpse of a face. Then the door opened, and Caitlin Blevins stood in her doorway, hair a mess atop her head, in a black tank top and black shorts, which revealed a few lines of a tattoo on her upper thigh.

"Do you know what time it is?" she groused before she noticed Paul standing beside me. "What's going on?"

Paul opened his mouth to speak, but I butted in, too excited to stay quiet. "Your security camera, the one facing my house. We need to see if it caught something."

Caitlin's face reddened. "It's not facing your house to spy on you."

"I know." I wanted to shove her out of the way, grab the camera, and . . . what? I didn't know how it operated. "Someone left me a threatening note, and your camera might have recorded them hammering it in place."

A skeptical look passed over her face, but she stepped aside. "I'm not sure it reaches that far, but we can look."

"Did you get an alert?" Paul asked, following me into Caitlin's house. A guitar was sitting on a stand beside the television. A cord ran from it to the gaming console next to the TV.

"I'm not sure." Caitlin stifled a yawn. "I was listening to music when I fell asleep. The alert would have been drowned out." She turned toward the hall. "Let me get my phone." She headed for her bedroom.

"This might not amount to anything," Paul said at a whisper when she was gone.

"I know. But if it does . . ."

He nodded. We both knew what was at stake, and it was more than just my peace of mind.

Caitlin returned a few minutes later, hair pulled back in a messy ponytail. She handed her phone over to Paul. "I brought up the app but didn't look. I wasn't sure if I was supposed to."

"Thank you." Paul started to check the footage, but I bumped into him trying to look over his shoulder, causing him to nearly drop the phone. He took a few steps toward the kitchen, leaving me alone with Caitlin while he checked whatever footage might be there.

"So," I said, drawing out the word. I needed to talk, and I needed to do it about something other than killers. "I saw someone standing outside your house this morning. Was it one of your bandmates?"

Caitlin didn't look embarrassed when she said, "That was Teek. He needed a place to crash, and I let him stay."

I glanced at the couch. There was no sign that anyone had slept there, though she could have removed the evidence earlier in the day.

"Are you two . . . ?"

Caitlin snorted. "Not hardly."

"I think I found something."

Both Caitlin and I moved to where Paul was looking closely at Caitlin's phone. The footage was black-and-white and grainy, but it *was* there.

As soon as we were in position, Paul pressed PLAY.

A furtive shape was climbing into a car, which was parked, not in my driveway but at the side of the road, close to Caitlin's house.

"It starts here, so I'm guessing it didn't pick him up until he'd already run across the yard to get back into his vehicle," Paul said. "And there's no footage of him going to the house, so he must have taken the long way around."

I barely heard him. The shape was too indistinct to make out body type, let alone if it was female or male, but the latter seemed more likely. It was in the way the person moved, the set of their shoulders.

But while the footage was grainy and the person too indistinct, I could make out enough of the car that I thought I recognized it.

"That's the one," I said, jabbing a finger at the phone. "That's the car I saw, the one that drove past Death by Coffee yesterday."

"You're sure?" Paul asked.

"Positive." Mostly. I mean, I suppose it could have been a similar car. I couldn't make out the make or model, let alone the color, so it was entirely possible I was wrong, but I didn't think so. "That's it."

"Can you send this to me?" Paul asked, turning to Caitlin. "I can't make out the plate, but we have someone who might be able to clean it up for us."

"I think so." Caitlin took her phone back. After a few tense seconds during which she grumbled and tapped at her screen, she asked, "What's your email address?"

Paul gave it to her, and a moment later, there was a ping. He checked his phone, and sure enough, the footage was waiting in his inbox.

"Great," he said, pocketing his phone. "Thank you." He took me by the arm and led me to the door. "We'll get out of your hair now, but someone might be back in the morning. I'm not sure if they'll need to use your phone, but if we can't clean up the footage at the station, perhaps they'll be able to do something here."

"Sure. I'll be here."

After apologizing for waking her, I allowed Paul to lead me all the way back home.

"Do you want to come to my place tonight?" he asked as soon as we were back inside. "You could bring Misfit if you want. I can lock up Kefka and Ziggy." His two huskies. "They wouldn't hurt him on purpose, but they sometimes forget how big they are. I'll likely be at the station for a while but should be home before daylight."

The thought of spending the night at Paul's was appealing, but not without him there.

Besides, abandoning my house would admit that the threat had gotten to me, and I wasn't ready to do that quite yet.

"I'll be fine," I said.

"Are you sure? I could always come back here if—"

"No," I rested a hand on his wrist. "I'm okay. We're okay." I motioned toward Misfit, who was watching us as if he could follow the conversation. "Promise."

Paul frowned before he nodded. "All right. I'll check in with you in the morning." He collected his evidence and started for the door.

"Hey, Paul," I said. "I do have a question for you."

He turned to face me.

"Did you know Buchannan was watching that building I told you about?"

He stood there for a long moment, giving nothing away. I could almost see him come up with, and discard, multiple answers. He finally settled on, "Not when I first looked into it."

Which wasn't the same as saying he hadn't known when he'd told me about it, but I let it go.

"Thank you for coming," I told him. And then to prove there were no hard feelings, whether he'd left things out or not, I stepped forward and kissed him on the cheek.

A faint smile flashed across his face. "Anytime." And that was a promise that I hoped he would keep, no matter how many times—and ways—I screwed up.

18

Zombies looked more alive than I felt as I dragged my way into Death by Coffee. I wasn't scheduled to work, but Pooky was. A conversation about her brother, Donnie, was on the docket, and I wasn't going to avoid it just because I felt like death warmed over.

A short line led to the counter. Instead of skipping it, which would have been my right as co-owner, I slid in behind a young couple hanging onto one another in a way that told me they'd just started dating. The man—boy, really—kept sneaking sly glances at his companion. There was a hint of shock on his face, a "How did I get so lucky?" that made me smile.

Mason was working behind the counter, with Jeff helping him fill orders. The morning rush was winding down, and both men looked ready for a break. That meant Pooky was upstairs with the books, which would make the conversation easier.

Dragging her to the back would draw attention. Sitting with her on the couch reserved for readers—a couch that was currently empty of anyone but a cat—would look natural.

"Good morning to you, Krissy. How are you on this fine sunny day?"

I stuck my tongue out at Mason as I sidled up to the counter, causing him to laugh.

"That good, I see. A coffee and a cookie?"

"Yes, please." Call me strange, but nothing beat the gooey remains of a cookie at the bottom of a coffee cup. It added just the right amount of sweetness to the drink, while providing a delicious reward at the end.

Jeff was readying my order, cookie included. "Hello, Ms. Hancock," he said over his shoulder.

"Call me Krissy." Not that he ever would. I'd tried since he'd started working here to get him to call me by my first name, but to no avail.

"Long night?" Mason asked.

"You could say that." I took the coffee when Jeff offered it and sipped. I could feel a knot in my neck ease as it went down. I also broke out into a sweat. It was going to be another scorcher.

Mason leaned on the counter, propping his chin on his hands. "Tell me more."

Upstairs, Pooky was dealing with a woman I recognized as a regular but didn't know her name. I had time.

"Well, first, I snuck into an empty building and got caught by the famous detective John Buchannan. I spent the next few hours in the charming Pine Hills police station interrogation room sorting that out."

Mason's mouth twitched, but he held back the smile.

"Then, after I went to bed, someone pinned a threatening note to my door." I paused for dramatic effect. "With a knife."

The smile vanished as his eyes widened. "A knife? Someone threatened you?"

"I'm fine. And Paul's on the case. He took the note and the knife as evidence, and thanks to my neighbor's security camera, we have the car—and culprit—on video. It's grainy, and you can't really make anything out, but Paul hopes the footage can be cleaned up. It's only a matter of time before he has the guy in custody." I hoped.

"It sounds like you did have an interesting night. And here, all I did was sit at home and watch *The Expanse*."

"You need to get out more." I winked at him before asking, "Can I get a water with this?"

"Sure." Mason filled a cup and handed it over. "Is there anything I can do to help?"

I knew he meant about what happened last night but chose to pretend I didn't. "I can drink this just fine myself, but thanks."

"Ha-ha," he deadpanned as I carried my coffee and water up the stairs, to the bookstore portion of the store.

The woman was gone, leaving Pooky alone, shelving a few wayward books, while Trouble lounged on the couch. I waited for her to finish before speaking.

"Hey, Pooky? Can I talk to you for a minute?" I motioned toward the couch. The black-and-white cat looked as if he'd had as long a night as I'd had. "It's about Donnie."

"Whew boy. All right." Pooky ran her fingers through her hair before crossing the room and taking a seat. "Hit me with it."

I handed her the water. "Just in case," I told her as I sat down with Trouble between us.

She sipped and clutched at the cup as if it were a lifeline. "Did you talk to him?"

I was surprised she didn't know. "I did. He didn't say anything about my visit?"

Pooky rolled her eyes. "Right. When I got in, he told me to order a couple of pizzas because his friends were headed over and they'd be hungry. That was the extent of our conversation."

"Well, I talked to him." I took too large of a gulp of coffee and choked on it. I tried hard not to spray it all over the couch—and Trouble—and mostly succeeded.

"Are you all right?" Pooky was halfway to her feet.

"Fine," I managed between coughs. "Wrong tube."

Breathing in water was painful. Hot coffee was like snorting one of those alcoholic drinks they set on fire—with it still aflame. My eyes were watering like fountains, and I was pretty sure half the store was staring at me. I ignored them and took the water Pooky offered me. I sipped and soon was breathing regularly.

"Sorry about that." One more cough, and I thought I was ready. "I think Donnie needs to find a new place to live."

"You're telling me. I know he needs to go, but he won't listen to me."

"You're going to have to put your foot down and make him go. He's using you, using your hospitality and relationship to take advantage of you. Ask him nicely if you can. Then more forcefully if you can't. And if that doesn't work . . ." I considered it. "Change the locks when he leaves to go to the store or a friend's place. Call the police if you must."

"The police?" Her nose scrunched up in a way that was awfully cute. It made her look half her age, and she was already young. Without her brother holding her back, I had a feeling Pooky would have dates lined up for months. "I don't know if I could do that."

"You might have to." I thought back to how Donnie had treated me, how he'd claimed Pooky's apartment was now his. "If you don't make him go, he'll push you out, and likely make you pay for the apartment, regardless of whether you're living there or not."

"He wouldn't." But I could tell by her tone that she thought he very well might.

"I know it's not a great situation," I said. "And I know you care about your brother. But it's time for him to go."

"It is, is it?"

I jumped at the sound of Donnie's voice coming from the stairs behind me. My coffee had a lid, so I only spilled a little of it on my hand.

The water, on the other hand, didn't.

When I jerked, the entire contents of the cup flew straight up into the air. As if in slow motion, the water descended, but not back into the cup or onto my hand, where it would have caused little to no damage.

Instead, it landed on Trouble.

He'd barely twitched when Pooky and I sat down. And when we'd started talking, he'd only settled in deeper, placing one paw over his eyes, as if our presence caused the light to grow.

But when the water hit him, he shot off the couch like he'd been coiled to spring. There was a tearing sound as his claws dug in and he leaped onto the coffee table. He slid off that, hit the floor running, and skidded sideways, slamming into a bookshelf before he righted himself and was gone.

Donnie laughed, a big guffaw that caused my blood to rise. "Stupid cat," he said. "That's why dogs are better. Someone should just—"

I didn't want to hear whatever he was about to suggest. I surged to my feet, careful not to spill what was left of my water, and spun on him.

"What are you doing here?" I demanded.

He snorted and stepped past me as if I didn't exist. "We're out of milk," he told Pooky. "Since you no longer work here, you need to pick some up."

"Excuse me?" I asked, at the same instant that Pooky said, "I don't think so."

"This lady is trying to control your life." Donnie jerked a thumb at me. "I'm telling you to get out of here before she takes over completely."

"*You're* telling *me?*" Steam practically shot from Pooky's ears. "Oh, I don't think so, Donnie." She gave me a look, one I interpreted as "Leave us be so I can murder my brother."

I nodded once and then headed down the stairs, leaving them to it.

"What was that about?" Mason asked when I returned to the counter. He was watching the animated conversation going on by the couch. Since there was no wall blocking them from view, everyone could watch, and they were. Voices weren't raised—yet—so we couldn't hear what was being said, but I figured it was only a matter of time.

"Pooky is taking care of a problem." She jammed a finger into Donnie's chest, sending him back a step. "I don't think it will be a problem for much longer."

Less than five minutes later, Donnie slunk out, head down, a proverbial tail between his legs. I didn't need to ask Pooky if Donnie was moving out. His body language, and her defiant grin, told me all I needed to know.

Trouble slunk toward the stairs and then plopped down to lick the water from his fur, all while shooting me death glares. I decided not to risk my skin and apologize to him. I hoped he wouldn't hold my actions against Misfit tomorrow or else my house would be a wreck by the time the two cats were done with one another.

I finished off my coffee, tossed the cup into the trash, and after waving to Mason and Jeff and shooting Pooky a thumbs-up, I left Death by Coffee and climbed into my Escape. I checked the time and decided I had a few minutes before my early lunch date with Cassie. I checked a number online and then dialed.

"Hi, I need the number to Jen Vousden's room," I said when it was answered. I spoke as if I had every right to inquire in the hopes that I did.

"One second." There was a click as the bored-sounding woman put me on hold. She returned a few moments later, rattled off the number, and then fell silent.

"Uh, thanks?" It came out as a question, though I didn't mean it to.

"Right. You need anything else?"

"That's it."

A grunt, and then the line was disconnected.

It sounded like someone had had as long a night as I had. I wondered if I could have asked to be connected to Jen's hospital room but decided it didn't matter. I typed in the number the nurse had given me and waited for it to be connected.

"Hello?" The gravelly voice on the other end of the line caught me by surprise.

"Hi, um, Jen Vousden?"

"Speaking. Who is this?"

"Krissy Hancock. I sent you the message about the marathon?"

"Oh."

She didn't sound impressed, yet I continued. "I thought I'd call and see how you were doing." It sounded better than "I called to see if you were actually in the hospital."

"I'm getting by." An audible swallow. "Throat's sore. Talking hurts." I could almost hear the "hint, hint."

"I won't keep you." And then, because I couldn't resist, "I'm sorry about Glen Moreau."

There was a long stretch of silence. When she spoke, it was carefully. "It's a shame. I'm sure Rod and Alleah were devastated."

"Rod and Alleah?" I didn't expect their names. "Why's that?"

Another pause, this one longer. "It happened at the marathon."

I could tell there was more to it, something she wasn't saying. "How well did they know one another?" I asked. "Glen and the other organizers?"

I could hear Jen licking her lips, almost incessantly. Nerves? Or a by-product of whatever was wrong with her? "I've got to go. The meds are kicking in."

"I didn't mean to keep you. Thank you for talking to me, Jen. I hope you get better soon."

"Thanks." I thought she was hanging up, but a moment later, she spoke again, "Glen showed up during one of our organization meetings for the marathon. Rod and Alleah weren't happy and just about shoved him out the door. That's all I know."

I wanted to press, to demand to know more, but I'd already taken up enough of Jen's time. "Thank you."

A grunt, and the line went dead.

I drove the short distance to Scream for Ice Cream, my mind a million miles away. What had Glen wanted to talk to Rod and Alleah about? Obviously, it was something they didn't want to get out. Between them not wanting Jen to hear them at the meeting, to the conversation at the Banyon Tree, I was pretty sure Rod and Alleah were into something shady, and it had carried over to the marathon.

I found a parking spot, setting aside my thoughts on Glen's murder, and went inside the ice cream parlor. As soon as I was through the door, Cassie Wise stood and waved me over.

"I hope I'm not late," I said, joining her.

"Nah, I was here early." She motioned for me to sit before taking her own seat. A gigantic metal mixer cup sat in the middle of the table. There were two glasses. One was half filled with a chocolate milkshake. The other was empty. "I ordered this monstrosity without realizing how big it was. If you want some, feel free. If not . . ." She stuck out her tongue and patted her flat stomach.

"I wouldn't want you to get sick." I filled the empty glass with the milkshake and took a drink. It was rich and creamy and made my head throb in a good way.

"So, this thing with that guy, Glen Moreau." She shook her head. "I can't believe it happened right in front of me."

I nearly choked on my milkshake. So much for not thinking about Glen and his murder. "You saw something? I thought—" I cut off at the wave of her hand.

"Not in front of me, in front of me. But, you know, just before I got there."

Right. "You ran past him, didn't you? I don't remember you in the crowd."

She nodded, looked at her milkshake like it suddenly had made her sick, and pushed it away. "I wonder if I could have done something. Like, if I'd been paying more attention, I might have heard it happening and could have stopped it."

"I don't think you would have wanted that."

She thought about it, and then paled. "I guess not. It's just . . ." She frowned at her hands. "I didn't know Glen, but I hate that something like this had to happen to him." She leaned forward. "Do you think Rodney Maxwell could have done it?"

"I'm not sure." I matched her posture. From the outside, it probably looked like we were conspiring together. "Did you see anything that might hint that he did?"

Cassie thought about it briefly. "There was the fight, of course." We'd both seen that. "And I don't know if you saw it, but as soon as the marathon started, Rod hurried away like his pants were on fire."

Getting into position? I wondered. "Which direction did he go?"

She leaned back and tapped her lower lip with a finger. "There were these sheds back by the trees. He went that way."

My stomach dropped, and like Cassie, I pushed my milkshake away. *Johan was back there with that woman.* "Was he alone?"

"As far as I know, he was. But he was definitely anxious about something. He wasn't the only one who was acting strange."

I waited her out, my mind racing. Johan snuck off with a mystery woman and was later joined by Rod. Had Rod seen them sneak off and was checking to make sure they weren't . . . what? Trying to sabotage the marathon? Getting hinky? Murdering someone?

Or was he there to help them?

"I overheard someone talking on the phone," Cassie went on. "He sounded worried, and when Glen started scuffling with Rod, he watched them with, I don't know, a sort of hopefulness that seemed out of place. It was weird."

I thought back. The only person I'd seen on the phone that I knew had any connection to Rod and

Glen was Glen's friend Calvin Davis. "Do you know what he was talking about? Or with whom?"

She shook her head. "Not really. Whatever was said surprised him. It was none of my business, so I didn't eavesdrop, and with the fight going on . . ."

"I understand." Though I was curious. Did Calvin learn something in that call? If there was a plan to kill Glen Moreau, and Rod Maxwell was involved, it would make sense that Calvin would be worried for his friend. He would have warned him, might even have led him off the posted route to tell him about it.

Could Calvin have seen the killer?

He'd later fought with Rod at Geraldo's. Both men acted like there was nothing to it, but what if Calvin knew Rod had killed Glen? You'd think he'd go to the police if that was the case, but if he thought he could get something out of it, could he have tried to blackmail Rod but it backfired, causing the fight? Calvin had shouted that he was going to kill Rod, as if Rod was the one with the dirt and planned on using it against him. If that was the case, then Calvin couldn't reveal Rod's secret without his own coming to light.

Mutually assured destruction.

Cassie was still talking. I snapped back to the here and now.

"I'm sorry," I said. "I zoned out there for a minute. What were you saying?"

"I asked if you've thought about joining a gym. A new one is opening up downtown, and I thought I might join, but I really don't want to do it alone."

If I'd been in my right mind, I would have balked at the idea. Me? A gym? The mere thought was enough to make my muscles wilt and my knees go weak.

But I found myself smiling as I said, "That sounds great."

"Fantastic!" Cassie beamed. "I'm glad we ran into one another at the marathon. I don't have a lot of friends around town, so it's nice to have met someone I connected to right away."

"I feel the same way," I said.

"This is going to be great."

What did I just get myself into? I pulled my milkshake back in front of me and drank it like it might be my last.

19

My phone rang as I was climbing back into my Escape.

"Paul? I was just about to call you. What's up?"

"I'm sorry," he said. He sounded out of breath. "I was going to check in with you earlier, but something came up, and I haven't had a chance until now."

Something that has to do with the murder? I wisely kept the question to myself. "That's all right. I had a few errands to run and was meeting with a friend, so if you called earlier, I might not have answered."

Silence filled the air.

"Really," I said. "I helped one of the new hires at Death by Coffee with a personal problem and had stopped in to let her know how it went, and then I met with Cassie Wise for ice cream. We met at the marathon and are going to join a gym together."

Paul did good not to laugh at the mention of

me exercising. He didn't comment on it at all, actually, which was probably smart. "Did you have any other problems last night?"

Problems. He meant threats or stealthy visitors. "No. I didn't sleep, but nothing else happened."

"Good."

"Any luck with the plate or make of the car?" Or its owner.

He hesitated before saying, "We're working on it."

I wondered if by working on it, he meant he'd just run down the culprit and was in the process of dragging him to the police station.

No, Paul wouldn't hold that back. I was the victim here, and if he'd caught the culprit, there was no reason not to tell me.

Unless it was someone I knew.

Someone like Johan Morrison.

"You don't have to protect my feelings if you know something," I said. "I can take it."

"I know you can. I'm not holding anything back. One sec." There was a muffled sound as he covered his phone. I could just barely hear the mumble of voices but couldn't make out what they were saying. "Sorry," he said when he returned. "I need to go."

"Hey, before you go, I have one quick question."

"If it's about the investigation—"

"It's not," I cut in. "Not really." I winced. I was bad at this lying thing. "I was wondering what happened to Calvin Davis. Cassie and I were talking about him over milkshakes."

This time, I didn't fill the silence when it began to stretch out.

"He's still here," Paul finally said.

"Here? As in, he's still at the police station?"

"He is. There were . . . circumstances."

Beyond elbowing Paul in the nose and whatever reason Buchannan had to hold him in the first place? I wondered what those circumstances might be, and if they extended to murder.

Once again, it was better not to ask.

"I see." If Calvin had indeed seen something, such as Glen's murder, and was blackmailing the murderer, or was being threatened himself, then jail would be a good place for him. There, he was safe from said murderer. And there was always a chance he might break down and end up talking.

But would the police ask him the right questions?

"Krissy." I could hear the warning in Paul's voice.

"I'd better let you go," I said. "You've got work to do, and I still have a few errands to run. I've got a thing tonight. A party, actually. It's with Trisha and Shannon. I'll call you later and tell you all about it, okay?"

Before he could respond, I clicked off.

I sagged back into my seat and considered my options. Paul's words hinted that he was at the station now, so going there would be a risk, but I wanted to talk to Calvin. It wasn't illegal to visit inmates, was it? It wasn't like he was locked up in a maximum-security prison or anything.

I decided to take a chance but didn't do it right away. I *did* have a few errands I wanted to run, and there was no sense in putting them off. Misfit needed food, and I'd seen an ad for a fountain water dish—the water came out of a fish's mouth—

that I thought he would like. I drove to the local pet store, took my time to pick up the supplies, including a basketball-size rope ball that he could use for both play and to sharpen his claws. Maybe then he'd stop using the couch as a scratching post.

Once that was done, I made for the Pine Hills police station, hoping that when I got there, Paul Dalton would be long gone.

Paul's car was sitting in the corner of the lot when I arrived, but that told me nothing. All that meant was that he was on duty. He drove a patrol car while on, well, patrol. I didn't know which one was his, or even if the department assigned cars to its officers, or if it was a first come, first served sort of thing. All I knew for sure was that there were a few patrol cars on the lot, and there was a fifty-fifty chance I'd run into Paul inside.

Of course, I supposed I'd much rather have to talk my way around Paul than Detective Buchannan. Paul might hear me out, would warn me against interfering, all while leading me toward the cells where Calvin was being kept. Buchannan, on the other hand, was apt to take me to those same cells and toss me inside.

But hey, even there, I'd get a chance to talk to Calvin, so I supposed I'd call it a win either way.

When I entered through the station front doors, I immediately scanned the area. No Paul. No John Buchannan. So far, so good.

I knew where the cells were located—both the old overflow cells downstairs and the newer ones on this level—so it was possible that I could sneak in and have a chat with Calvin and sneak out again without anyone knowing. My eyes found the security cameras, and I scratched that idea before it could fully form. I didn't know if the cameras were continuously watched or if the footage would be checked only if something were to happen. I was guessing it was somewhere in between.

"Do I want to know?"

I jumped and then turned to find a firecracker of a woman heading my way. Chief Patricia Dalton was short and fit and moved with a determination that made me think that while she might be considering retirement in the next decade or two, it wasn't because she was tired of the job.

"Hi, Chief." I very nearly saluted in my nervousness. "Fancy meeting you here."

She raised a single eyebrow.

"I don't mean that I didn't think you'd be here or that you shouldn't be working. I . . . you . . ." My shoulders sagged, and I ceased babbling.

"Something tells me you aren't here for Paul." A smile tugged at the corners of her mouth. It warred with the warning in her eyes.

"No, I'm not."

"Care to fill me in as to why you are here, then?"

There was no sense in lying to her. For one, she'd sniff it out right away. And for two, she was Paul's mom. I didn't want to screw up our relationship by lying to her. She was kind of the reason we'd gotten together in the first place.

"I want to talk to Calvin Davis. Paul told me he was still locked up."

Chief Dalton's brow furrowed. "Why are you wanting to talk to him?"

"There's a chance he saw something."

"The murder?"

"That, and something about my friend Rita." I took a breath to steady my nerves. "Her boyfriend snuck off with another woman at the marathon. Calvin might have seen who it was."

Chief Dalton's expression didn't change. "Why do you think that?"

"I'm not sure. I was talking with another friend, Cassie Wise, and, I don't know"—I shrugged—"it's worth a shot. If he didn't see anything, I'll thank him and leave."

"And if he did?"

"I'll find out who Johan was with, and hopefully why. Then, when I take the information to Rita, I won't be sabotaging their relationship without reason."

"And the murder?"

My smile was bashful. "If he wants to confess, then, hey, I helped out, and we all win."

"Why do I feel like there's more to this than you're letting on?" Patricia sighed, scratching at her neck. "But it's not like Mr. Davis is off-limits. He hasn't talked much since he's been here. Has been rather vague, if you ask me. Maybe you can shake something loose."

"Really?" I cleared my throat and toned down my excitement. "Thank you. I just want to know if he saw anything. I'm not going to trample all over Detective Buchannan's investigation." Again.

"No, you're not." She waved a hand, and Becca Garrison strode over in full uniform. She looked a lot better than when she'd dropped me off at my car, though the exhaustion was still weighing her down. "Officer Garrison will keep an eye on you."

"Calvin might not talk with a cop around," I said.

"He might not," Chief Dalton agreed. "But Officer Garrison knows how to keep out of sight when she needs to. She'll be listening in, just in case something important to the investigation crops up. That way, you won't have to remember to tell someone."

I caught the accusatory tone and didn't take offense. I had a tendency to keep things to myself if I thought it would keep me or one of my friends out of trouble. I mean, who wouldn't? And considering I'd been doing just that when it came to Johan and his possible involvement with a murdered man . . .

I agreed to the babysitter without complaint.

"Remember, you're here to inquire about your friend's boyfriend," Chief Dalton said. "I'd like you to keep to that as much as possible."

Was that a wink? Maybe her eyelid just twitched.

"I'll try."

She grunted, and then, with a nod to Garrison, she returned to her office.

"This is going to be fun," Garrison muttered when she was gone. "Come on, let's go."

Officer Garrison led me down the hall to the standard cells, which were much nicer than the ones that Buchannan kept throwing me in downstairs. She stopped at the corner, just out of sight; apparently, that was where she was going to eavesdrop. She nodded me forward.

I took a calming breath and said, "Wish me luck," before I turned the corner.

Only one cell was occupied. Calvin was sitting

on his bunk, studying his hands. He was wearing the same clothing he'd worn when he'd elbowed Paul, which I suppose shouldn't have been a surprise, considering he'd been here since then. He looked ragged and angry and in no mood to have a pleasant conversation with anyone, let alone a nosy stranger.

As soon as he heard footsteps, he jerked upright. "When can I go? You've kept me here long enough." He scowled when he realized I wasn't a cop. "Who are you?"

I scrambled for an alias and came up empty. "I'm Krissy," I said. "I just want to talk."

"Talk?" He snorted and sat back down. "I don't feel like talking to no one."

"I was at the marathon."

He didn't so much as shrug. "So?"

"So, I was wondering if you might have seen something strange happen while you were there?"

Calvin laughed without a hint of amusement. "This some sort of new interrogation technique? Can't get me to cop to something I didn't do, so they send some random chick to try to trick it out of me? It's not going to work. I didn't do nothing, and I didn't see nothing. You've got nothing on me, and I want to go home and shower and get to work before I get fired."

"The police didn't send me," I said. And then I threw out a name to see what he'd do. Besides, it was supposed to be why I was back there. "I know Johan Morrison."

"Should I know who that is?"

"I don't know. Do you?"

"No."

"He's got this creepy smile, and he—"

"I said I don't know who that is," Calvin snapped.

"But you do know Rod Maxwell."

Calvin's fists clenched. "You know I do."

"You fought with him at Geraldo's. I was there."

Calvin's jaw worked as he chewed over what to tell me. There was something there; I could feel it. The only question was, would he tell me? I was no one, especially to him.

"Rod killed Glen."

I started. "You saw him do it?"

"No, of course not." He glared at me before shaking his head, as if to clear it. "But I know. Glen had a beef with Rod, which was obvious if you ever saw the two of them together. I don't know what it was about." He glanced at me quickly and then looked away. "But I knew they didn't get along. It's why I asked Rod to meet me. I wanted to hear it from him, to ask him directly if he killed Glen."

That wasn't what Paul had told me, but I didn't want to say that out loud. "Did he admit to it?"

"If he had, we wouldn't be having this conversation now. I'd be locked up somewhere far more secure, and the morgue would have one more body to contend with. If I hadn't been so distracted by Trevor—" He clamped his jaw closed so fast, I heard his teeth clack.

"Trevor?" Glen's other friend, the one who'd found the body. "He distracted you? When?"

"It's nothing." Calvin shifted on his cot. "Trevor was going to confront Glen about something personal between them. And, no, I don't know what. I never got the chance to talk to him about it, and after what happened . . . I haven't talked to Trevor, and I'm not so sure he wants to talk to me."

"Did you two have a falling out?" I tried to recall if there was any obvious animosity between them at the marathon but came up blank.

"I don't know what happened. I don't know why Glen was murdered. And I don't know why I'm still here." He crossed his arms over his potbelly. "I'm done talking about anything other than how and when I'm getting out of here."

I didn't press him on it. Calvin had said more than I'd expected, and asking for anything else might push it too far. I didn't want him to clam up entirely for the police, because I was pretty sure Detective Buchannan would have a slew of new questions for him now.

I thanked him, earning myself a grunt, and then headed back to where Officer Garrison waited. She had a notebook in hand and was scribbling into it. I waited for her to finish, and when she did, she shook her head in amazement.

"I don't know how you do it," she said.

"Neither do I," I said, catching her meaning. "People just like talking to me." Though I had a feeling it wasn't because of my winning personality. They just figured that if they told me what I wanted to know, then perhaps I'd go away that much sooner.

At least, that's how I explained it, anyway.

Garrison continued to shake her head as she took me back to the front of the station. Chief Dalton was still in her office, but I didn't want to bother her. Officer Garrison could fill her in once I was gone. It was probably better that way.

"Thank you for doing this," I said, though Garrison hadn't been the one to allow it. "And if you change your mind about staying at my place for a few days . . ."

"Thanks, but no." She looked eager to get going. "I'll be fine."

I was worried, but Garrison was strong. She'd get through her troubles and would somehow come out the other side looking even stronger.

20

"I promise it won't hurt you."
Misfit gave me side-eyes before rearing back and swatting at the stream of water coming from the fish's mouth. He jumped back, shook off his paw, and then crept slowly forward again. The fountain was quiet, making only a slight hum, along with the constant tinkle of water that made me want to pee as soon as I'd hooked it up.

"You drink out of it," I said, urging Misfit forward. "It'll keep your water from growing stagnant."

Another sideways glance followed by another swat and leap.

I threw my hands up into the air, turned away, and left him to it.

Melanie Johnson's party was tonight, and I wasn't looking forward to it. A part of me wanted to cancel, and if it was just me going, I might have. But I wasn't going to bail on Trisha and Shannon, not when we were just starting to become friends. Besides, going would give me a chance to talk to Melanie about Glen some more—and ask her about Johan. The last time we'd spoken, I didn't get a chance to ask her about Trevor or Calvin either. I planned on doing that this evening.

I'd already spent much of the day puttering around, looking for something to keep me occupied that wouldn't end up with me sitting in the cell opposite Calvin. I was just as lost as the police seemed to be on the case. Rod had ties to most everyone involved in the marathon and murder, so he was clearly top of the most-likely-to-be-a-murderer list. Trevor was the one who'd found Glen's body and, according to Calvin, had wanted to confront Glen about some unspecified personal issue. Was that enough to consider him?

No, not really.

And honestly? I just wanted to know whether or not I should be worried about Johan.

A message was waiting for me when I plopped down onto the couch and opened my laptop. Skinny Jefferson. Again.

I debated whether or not to open it, and then gave in, just in case it wasn't another attempt to coerce me into a photoshoot. I clicked on it, skepticism high.

You really need to stop by. I promise I won't try anything hinky, though if you happen to change your mind about the photos, I'm not going to say no.

I drummed my fingers on my laptop, thinking. This could still be a ploy to get me to undress for him, but what if it wasn't? I could be ignoring an important piece of information because I was (rightfully) weirded out by the creepy guy with a camera.

How about I stop by tomorrow morning? I didn't expect to be needed at Death by Coffee, so I could see Skinny and then pop into the store afterward. *No photos, but I would like to see what you have.* I considered that and added, *The stuff from the marathon.* I didn't want to give him the wrong idea.

I hit SEND, and after perusing a few websites, including the marathon's Facebook page, which was a bust, I closed my laptop lid. I wasn't going to find anything online tonight.

Misfit was still stalking the water as I headed down the hall to get changed. I opted for casual wear, keeping in mind that because of the small size of Melanie's house, this get-together was likely to be held outside. A tank top and shorts later, I decided not to wait around any longer and left for Melanie's. It was still a little early, but if I wanted to talk to her alone, now would be the time.

On the way, I found myself not heading for A Woman's Place, but rather toward Rita's house. I didn't like how we'd last parted, and that image of her changing her mind about entering Death by Coffee haunted me.

When I arrived, however, her driveway was empty. I sat there, engine idling, and considered calling her. If nothing else, I could apologize, tell her that I didn't want anything to come between our friendship. But this was a conversation I wanted to have face-to-face, not over the phone.

I backed out of her driveway and turned toward Melanie's.

My stop at Rita's hadn't taken long but had delayed me enough that when I pulled up to A Woman's Place, four other cars were already there. Smoke coiled into the air from behind the house, telling me I'd been right about the outdoor event. I parked behind a new Impala and then made my way up the drive, past Melanie's PT Cruiser, and to the door.

Women's voices came from around the house, and I decided that knocking would be pointless. I went around back and found Melanie standing around a fire pit with three other women. I recognized none of them.

"Krissy!" Melanie said, breaking off from the conversation to come over and greet me. "It's so nice to see you here."

"Trisha and Shannon invited me. I hope that's okay."

"Of course, of course." Melanie led me toward the fire. "They aren't here yet but should be shortly. Let me introduce you."

"You don't need to—"

She spoke over me. "Everyone, this is Krissy Hancock. Krissy, meet Yolanda Barton, Avery Mills, and Hanna Newman."

Yolanda was a large, redheaded woman with a wide, gracious smile. She took my hand and pumped it twice. "It's so good to meet you."

Avery, a wiry teen who looked as if she'd just graduated from high school, nodded once, and then looked away as if afraid I might scold her. A faint yellowing around her eye socket told me why she'd sought Melanie's services.

Hanna was Avery's opposite, an elderly Black woman, who eyed me with suspicion before flashing me a half smile when I turned to her.

"I need to get a few more things ready before everyone else arrives," Melanie said. "You all get to know one another while I'm gone." She patted me on the shoulder and then hurried through the back door, into the house.

"This is nice," Yolanda said, holding her hands toward the fire, which was strange considering it was already hot enough to cook a hot dog without the flames. "I never have cookouts at home."

"We used to all the time," Hanna said. "Back when Benjamin was still with us."

"Was he your husband?" I asked.

She gave me a look like I was a complete idiot. "He was my dog."

"Most men are," Avery smirked before ducking her head to avoid eye contact.

An engine that sounded as if it was moments from exploding warned of more incoming guests. If I planned to get Melanie alone, I was quickly running out of time.

"Excuse me a moment," I said. "Need to visit the ladies' room."

Yolanda nodded and winked, as if she'd caught on to some big secret, while the other two simply ignored me and went back to chatting with each other.

I didn't bother knocking as I slipped in through the back door. Melanie was in the tiny kitchen, chopping veggies. She glanced up when I entered and then went right back to cutting.

"You get a chance to talk to Ivy?" she asked. She tried to make it nonchalant, but I caught the tension in her voice.

"I did."

"And?" *Chop, chop, chop.*

"And I was curious about Glen's other friends." Melanie paused mid-carrot. "Why?"

"I've heard rumors. What do you know about Trevor Conway?"

"He's harmless."

"I heard he was planning to confront Glen about something during the marathon."

The chopping resumed. "If he was, it was probably about Ivy."

"She claims she never actually dated Glen."

The next chop was so violent, the end of the carrot shot clear across the room. "I don't care what she says. Ivy is a liar, a cheat, and she would say and do anything if she thought she could get something out of it." She tipped the cutting board over a bowl so the carrots could slide into it.

Melanie set the knife aside and picked up the bowl, which was filled with chopped veggies. "I've got to run this outside. We can talk later."

She pushed past me and left me standing in her living room, most of my questions unasked. More voices had joined the others—all women. I recognized Trisha's voice among them and decided it was time I went out to socialize.

Both Shannon and Trisha were talking with Yolanda when I stepped back outside. The crowd had grown to three times its previous size, and more women were trickling in with every passing minute. As soon as Trisha saw me, she waved me over.

"I'm glad you made it," she said, giving me a side-hug since her belly made a normal one impossible. "I wasn't sure you'd come."

"I wasn't going to miss it." I turned and hugged Shannon in a similar hip-bump fashion. "There's a lot more people here than I expected."

"Melanie helps out a lot of people," Shannon said. "It's one of Pine Hills's best-kept secrets."

There were at least twenty people here now, and still more were trudging through the yard. I wondered how many of these women had told husbands and boyfriends that they were going to visit their parents or were going to hit up the grocery store but had come here instead.

This might be a good place for Pooky. She might not have a romantic relationship problem, but I still thought she'd benefit from talking to some of these women about her brother. I made a mental note to say something to her the next time I saw her.

I noted the woman who'd stopped by the last time I was here, Cora Lynn, making her way toward the group, head constantly on a swivel, as if she was afraid someone might leap out of nowhere and attack her. It made me wonder what had happened to her that had brought her to Melanie.

"I was thinking of starting a board game group," Yolanda said, drawing my attention back to the conversation. "Just women. We just need to find somewhere to hold it. I've checked with the library and the church, but scheduling a good time for it has been a bear."

"Board games?" Trisha asked. "Like Scrabble?"

Yolanda made a face. "I've got better games. Catan, Pandemic, and three versions of Ticket to Ride, for starters. We could move on to more complex games once everyone is comfortable with those."

"What about Death by Coffee?" Shannon asked.

"I've never heard of that game," Yolanda said. "Is it new?"

"No, the place. Downtown. Krissy owns it." She turned to me. "I don't mean to put you on the spot, but you've got that space upstairs, or if it is after hours, all the tables. Even if it's just temporary until she can find a better location, do you think you might be willing to let them use the space?"

Yolanda's eyes widened. "Wait! I've seen that coffee shop. You own it?"

"Yeah. Well, co-own it. I'd have to talk with Vicki about it, but—"

"We wouldn't get in your way," Yolanda said, cutting me off in her excitement. "And you're welcome to join in whenever. And we'd buy stuff, you know, always buy our drinks and food there, never bring any in."

"There's no nee—"

"And we'd clean up afterward, so you wouldn't have to worry about the mess." She bit her lower lip, and I swear a tear started to form in her eye. "If it wouldn't be too much trouble, that is. I get that this is a big commitment since you'd want someone there until we left. I wouldn't presume to ask for a key or anything."

"I'm sure it'll be fine," I hurriedly said when she took a breath. "Let me talk to the other owners, and I'll get back to you."

Yolanda clapped and started babbling about board games to Trisha and Shannon; the latter mouthed, "Thank you," to me as if I'd done the world a great service by offering to at least consider the idea of hosting a board game night for Yolanda's fledgling group.

With my good deed done, and since I wasn't required for the current conversation, I wandered over to the snack table for a few veggies. I filled a napkin and then looked for Melanie, hoping to resume our earlier conversation.

She didn't appear to be outside with the group, though with so many women there, it would be easy to overlook her. I made a circuit around the small yard, munching on carrots and celery as I went.

It wasn't until I reached the side of the house that I heard her voice. It was raised in a harsh whisper that was meant to be quieter than it was. A man's voice followed.

I crept around the corner, pocketing what was left of my snack. Melanie was standing in her driveway, hand on the forearm of a man with long hair and a tattoo of a snake on his neck. He appeared to be in his twenties, though it was a hard twenty. He was not a happy camper.

"All right, *Mom*." He sneered the word. "I'll let you get back to your precious women." He ripped his arm from her grip and turned to walk away.

"Jase, come on. You know it's not right. After what she—"

But he wasn't listening. He raised a hand, made an obscene gesture with it, all without looking back.

Melanie watched him go, heaved a sigh, and then turned. I ducked back around the side of the house before she could see me. The front door opened and closed, telling me she'd gone inside. Now was my chance.

With a purposeful stride, I hurried toward Melanie and Glen's son.

He'd just reached a black Firebird that looked as shiny and new as if it had been teleported straight from the factory in the '90s to now. He was about to open the door when I called out to him.

"Jase? Can I talk to you for a moment?"

He glanced back, eyes hardening. "If Mom sent you, I don't want to hear it."

"She didn't." I panted to a stop. The short jog had reawakened the fire in my legs. I had to put a hand atop his Firebird to keep from falling over.

He glared at my hand before crossing his arms. "What do you want?"

"I'm sorry about your father."

He snorted. "He deserved what he got."

That caught be by surprise. I knew he was angry

about his father's cheating ways, but outright hostility after the man was murdered? It seemed a tad, I don't know, insensitive.

"Your mom thinks it had something to do with Ivy Hammer," I said, deciding not to press too much on Jase's feelings about his parents. At least, not yet. "That she was with Glen before he died."

The grin that spread across Jase's face was pure hostile amusement. "She said that, did she?" A short laugh. "I guess I shouldn't be surprised. She's always trying to blame Ivy for everything, as if her own inadequacies are somehow Ivy's fault."

"You don't think Ivy is responsible?" I wasn't sure if I was asking about the murder, or the failure of his parents' relationship.

"Let's just say Ivy has treated me far better than either Mom or Dad ever did. Mom resents it, so she tries to get Ivy into trouble every chance she gets. She used to call her workplace, make up stuff about drugs and alcohol and sleeping around. She's probably told the police that Ivy killed Dad, even though I know for a fact she didn't."

"How can you be so sure?"

Jase's posture shifted to be less aggressive and more defensive. "I just know, all right? Ivy didn't do it. And she most definitely wasn't involved with Dad beyond those first few weeks when he came on to her."

I was getting some really strange vibes from Jase. I'd have figured Ivy Hammer would have been on his crap list, right along with his parents, but he sounded like he respected her. More than that, even.

"Tell Mom to lay off, all right? I'm done with her, and I don't want to hear from her ever again. About Dad, about Ivy. I came here to say my piece, and that's it. I'm not looking for a reconnection." He turned, opened his car door, and slipped inside. "No more." He slammed the door, gunned the engine, and sped off in a flurry of thrown gravel that just missed hitting me.

I stood there, watching him go, before I returned to the party, mind whirling. Something wasn't right about Jase. I got that he was mad at his mom, and that he still blamed his dad for what happened between him and Ivy. I mean, who wouldn't?

But there appeared to be more to it. A lot more.

"Hey," Cora waved as I rounded the corner. "I remember you."

"Hi." I gave her a smile that was as distracted as my mind. "I hope you're doing better. You seemed pretty upset the last time you were here."

Cora bobbed her head in what I took to be an affirmative. "Melanie works wonders." She turned, and we both spotted Melanie at the same time. She was leading another woman into her house, whispering to her, eyes shooting all over the place, as if she was nervous about being seen with her.

"What's that all about?" I wondered out loud. It seemed like Melanie was having a lot of private conversations considering this was a party.

"That's Ellen," Cora said. "After the last time she was here, I didn't think she'd come back."

The name took a moment to register, and when it did, it was like a sledgehammer to the back of my head. "Ellen?" I asked. That was the name of the woman Ivy had said was Glen's last girlfriend, the one he might have been with before his death.

"Yeah. She showed up crying last week while I was in a session with Melanie. I didn't hear much, but from what little I did hear, I got the impression that she was romantically involved with someone, and that she was afraid it was going to end badly."

21

"Hey, Krissy, something on your mind?"

"Hmm?" I turned away from the door to find Shannon giving me a concerned look.

"You've seemed distracted all night." Behind her, the party was dying down. The fire wasn't quite embers, but it was well on its way there. Yolanda had left an hour ago, as had Hanna. Trisha was having a conversation with a few other women who were taking turns touching her pregnant belly.

"Sorry," I said, as guilt welled up. "There's been a lot going on lately. I didn't mean to abandon you two." Or four, I supposed.

"Is it something I could help you with?" Shannon asked. She groaned as she shifted her weight.

"No, it's nothing, really. You should get off your feet." There were plastic chairs set up around the yard, and nearly all of them were empty.

"I'll be fine. In fact, Trisha and I were about to

head out. I wanted to come over and check on you before we did."

"Well, I'm glad you did." I lightly touched her arm. "But I'm okay. Once I get a good night's sleep, I'll be even better."

Shannon didn't look like she believed me, but she nodded. I had a feeling it had more to do with her sore feet and swollen belly than anything.

I walked her over to Trisha, who'd just extracted herself from the other women. She looked exhausted.

"I think I've had more people touch me uninvited today than I've had in the last decade," she said.

"At least it's women who are interested in your baby who are touching you. Try working evenings at a diner where half the men have spent most of the day drinking and are well on their way to sloshed." Shannon shuddered.

Trisha made a face. "No thank you." She turned to me. "I'm sorry we didn't get to hang out all that much. Pregnant women tend to be popular. Every time I thought I'd have a moment to myself, someone else would show up, and I'd have to go through the cooing and touching all over again."

"No, it's my fault," I said, and I meant it. I'd spent most of the party watching the back door in the hope that Ellen or Melanie would return, but to no avail. I had questions. A lot of them, and they were the only two who could answer them. "We should do this some other time."

"But maybe on a smaller scale," Shannon said,

making a face. "I'm not big into huge groups of people I don't know."

I nodded in agreement.

Across the way, a pair of women were talking and looking directly at us. I got the distinct impression they were considering coming over. Shannon noticed them too.

"We're going to head out," she said, stifling a yawn that was more for show than real. "I desperately need to lie down."

"Tell me about it." Trisha grimaced as she flexed her legs as best as she could without tipping over. "Those chairs were made for someone who weighs a whole lot less than me. I thought I was going to pop through one of them."

An image of Trisha, legs and arms skyward, as she struggled to extract herself from the middle of a broken plastic chair flashed through my mind. If I hadn't been so mentally distracted, I might have laughed.

"I think I'm going to go too," I said, glancing around. There was hardly anyone else there except for us and the curious women, and while Melanie had poked her head outside a couple of times, it was clear she had no intention of rejoining the festivities. And Ellen? A quiet exit out the front door was my best guess.

I walked Trisha and Shannon to Shannon's car and helped them get in. There was a lot of grunting and cursing in very unladylike ways, but they managed to squeeze into the too-small vehicle and drive off without too much difficulty.

I paused at my Escape, wondering if it would be prudent to walk in on Melanie and force her to talk to me. But the vibe I'd gotten from her wasn't an honest one, at least when it came to her son or her failed marriage. I doubted she'd have anything useful to say to me now, about Ellen, Johan, or otherwise.

I'd intended to stop by Rita's on the way home, but I found myself sitting in my driveway, having driven home without recalling doing so. Talk about being distracted. It was too late to turn around now, and besides, tomorrow would be better anyway. It was getting late, and I wanted to be able to stay with her as long as she needed me.

If she wanted me to, that is. After what I had to say about Johan, I wasn't sure she would want me to stick around.

Misfit was sitting in the living room, glaring, when I entered the house. He immediately marched over to his food dish, which was empty. I'd given him some dry food before leaving earlier, but he'd scarfed that down, likely the moment I was out the door.

"I'm sorry I'm late," I told him. "You won't starve, you know."

His whiskers twitched in warning.

I scooped some more dry food into his bowl and turned to grab a can of his favorite pâté, when I hit a slick spot on the floor. My foot went out from under me, and if I hadn't been in the kitchen, I would have gone down hard on my back.

Instead, I managed to whack my elbow on the counter just before I grabbed onto it, holding on for dear life. The scoop went flying across the room, hitting the far wall and then bouncing onto the floor with a clatter. Thankfully, it was empty, or food would have been everywhere.

Misfit, who normally lets nothing deter him from food, shot from the room as if someone had lit his tail on fire. I was left alone in the kitchen, legs splayed awkwardly, chin mere inches from the top of the counter, and with an elbow barking like mad.

Once my heart settled, and I was able to work my way back to my feet, I investigated what had caused the near disaster.

The floor around the new water fountain was soaked. At least half the water I'd put into it earlier was gone, splashed in a semi-circle around the dish. I must have stepped over it on my first pass through, but that second time . . .

Grumbling to myself, I cleaned up the mess before grabbing a spare towel. I spread it out on the floor and then put the water fountain atop it.

"There," I said. It was ugly, but it would have to do until I could get to the pet store and find a suitable pad.

Misfit returned, eyeing me with distrust before he went to his still-empty wet food dish. He turned an incredulous kitty eye on me and plopped down to await his dinner.

"It's coming." I opened a can, filled the dish, and then left him to it. I rubbed at my elbow as I grabbed my phone and sat down on the couch. I was going to look like a walking bruise by the time the week was out.

I tapped my phone against my palm as I debated what to do. I'd promised to call Paul, and I intended to do just that, but what was I going to tell him? That Jase and Melanie didn't get along? He already knew that. That a woman Glen was supposedly seeing, a woman whose last name I didn't know, was seen talking to Melanie both before and after his death?

The latter seemed the most important. Why would Melanie be seeing one of Glen's flings? Because she thought it would hurt Ivy somehow? And speaking of Ivy, why was Jase so determined to defend her? Hadn't she been the reason his parents had broken up?

And did any of this matter when it came to what Johan was into or Glen's murder?

With no answers in sight, I went ahead and called Paul.

"Krissy, hi."

"Hi, Paul. I'm home."

There was a pause during which I knew he was considering all of the horrible things I could have been getting myself into while I wasn't safely ensconced inside my house. I hadn't exactly been forthcoming in our last phone conversation, so his mind had to be all over the place.

"I was with Trisha and Shannon," I reminded him. "We went to a party."

"A party?" I could visualize the raised eyebrows.

"It was women only, or I'd have invited you. Remember me telling you about A Woman's Place?" At least, I thought I'd told him. Like my arm, my brain felt bruised. I blamed the heat. "Trisha invited me to go with her and Shannon, and I thought it would be a good idea. It was kind of like a cookout. We just stood around and talked."

"Sounds fun?" He made it a question.

"It was okay. I met some interesting people." *Careful now, Krissy.* "Melanie Johnson runs the group. Glen's ex."

"I know who she is."

"Her son, Jase, showed up. I overheard him fighting with his mom about Ivy Hammer. Melanie told me that she hadn't seen Jase since he'd moved out, yet there he was." I paused, considered. "There's something hinky going on between Jase and Ivy, but I don't know what."

"Because you didn't pry?" Flat, almost amused.

"No, I didn't." Not really, anyway. "And a woman who was supposedly seeing Glen showed up. All I know is her name is Ellen. She snuck off with Melanie, which I found kind of strange."

And then something else hit me.

"They're all blond."

"The women?"

I nodded, and realizing Paul couldn't see me, I said, "Yeah. Melanie is blond, as are Ellen and Ivy." And Alleah, though she wasn't at the party. Did that matter? "Glen was seen at Death by Coffee with a blonde. And the woman Johan snuck off into the woods with was as well."

"There are a lot of blond women, Krissy. It's a popular hair color."

"I know." Between the natural blondes and the bottled ones, it was impossible to go anywhere without seeing a blond head or two. "But one of those women is far more involved in this than the others. She has to be, right?"

"Or Glen had a type," Paul said. "Don't over-think it. I'm not saying we don't want to talk to the women, especially if they were seen with him be-fore his death, but you can't start thinking that every blond woman might be a suspect."

No, I couldn't. "It was just a thought," I said, a little too defensively for my liking. "Anyway, the big thing I wanted to mention was getting to know Trisha and Shannon. I think we might be becom-ing friends."

"Really?" I could hear the disbelief in his voice. "Shannon is a good person, so I'm not entirely sur-prised, but both her and Trisha? With your histo-ries?"

"I know! It caught me by surprise too, but here we are. And there's that other woman I've been talking to, Cassie Wise. It's taken me a while, but I think I'm finally making more friends." Of course, thinking of friends, I immediately thought of Rita. I really needed to talk to her.

Misfit sauntered into the room, licking his lips. He considered me on the couch for a moment, but instead of jumping up, he turned and headed for the bedroom. Apparently, I wasn't yet forgiven for getting him his dinner late. Or for scaring him.

"I'm glad," Paul said. "Maybe with more friends, you won't feel the need to chase after every crimi-nal Pine Hills produces."

"Maybe." Though I doubted it. Sticking my nose where it doesn't belong was a part of my DNA. I could thank my mystery-writing dad for that.

"I do have some news for you," Paul said. "We were able to clean up the footage we obtained from Caitlin Blevins enough to get a good look at the car from last night."

Excitement thrummed through me. "And the guy who knifed my door?"

"No, but we could read the plate, which gives us a possible ID. The car is registered to Rodney Maxwell."

I sucked in a breath. "Rod?" There he was again, stuck smack dab in the middle of some shady dealings.

"We're looking for him now. He hasn't been home, and no one seems to know where he is now, but we'll find him."

I eased up from the couch and peered out my window, half convinced I'd find Rod's car idling in my driveway.

No one was there, of course.

"Rod threatened me?" I'd thought the note had to do with that strange, empty building on Rosebud. But what if it didn't? What if Rod had killed Glen and knew I was poking around, looking for the murderer? I said as much to Paul.

"If he did, we'll find out," he said, meaning the police, not me and him. "I want you to make sure all your doors are locked, and keep an eye out for any prowlers. I don't think Rod would risk coming after you now, but you never know."

That was not reassuring in the slightest.

"Another thing," Paul went on. "The license plate had an 'L' in it."

It took my brain a moment to make the connection. "Like the car that drove by Death by Coffee."

"Exactly."

So, not Johan then. I wasn't sure if I felt relief or if I was more worried now.

"Be cautious, Krissy, but don't stress yourself out over this. I'm pretty sure Rod is laying low. And nothing I've seen on the guy hints that he's a violent man."

"Other than jamming a knife into my door."

"Better your door than the alternative."

He had me there.

"Just . . ." I could feel him struggle for the right words. He settled on the tried and true, "Be careful."

I didn't bother with the usual "I will." I could say it all I wanted, and we both knew it wouldn't be true. I always found a way to end up exactly where I didn't belong.

But now, knowing Rod was the one who'd threatened me, knowing that he was whispering to Alleah at the Banyon Tree and had gotten into a fight with Calvin at Geraldo's, I was leaning toward him as the killer. And I couldn't forget that Facebook post in which Glen had said Rod was going to get what was coming to him. Could Rod have seen it and decided to return the favor in advance?

But what about Melanie and Jase and this mysterious Ellen woman? Or Johan. Could I dismiss them so easily?

No, I couldn't.

"I didn't know, by the way," Paul said, cutting into my ruminations, "about Buchannan's investigation. Not until after I'd already looked into it. He didn't tell me about it because I wasn't going to be working on the case. It was only a theory of his, something he was exploring on his own time. It's not an official investigation yet, but more . . . speculative. He didn't keep it from me because of you."

It didn't take a genius to figure out that Paul must have spoken to Officer Garrison. "I understand," I said, not quite sure what else I could say. No matter the reason, I wasn't thrilled that Buchannan was keeping anything from Paul, official or not. I mean, they worked for the same side.

"I don't want you to think you're a detriment to my career."

Okay, he'd definitely talked to Garrison. "I don't think that." Not really.

"Good."

I wanted to ask him why exactly Buchannan had been looking into the building in the first place, and if Rod Maxwell had anything to do with it, considering he was seemingly involved in everything else, but I didn't.

"Krissy, I . . ." I could tell by his tone that Paul was changing the subject to something far more personal.

My heart gave a little leap, and I realized that right then, after everything, I wasn't ready for whatever he had to say.

"We should meet up and talk," I cut in before he could continue. "Maybe dinner and a movie or something. After the murder investigation is done."

A pause. "All right," he said. And was that relief in his voice? That was more worrisome than if he had pressed the issue. "A date, then."

A stretch of silence. I broke it. "Good night, Paul. I'll talk to you soon."

"Good night, Krissy."

We clicked off, and with my heart feeling oddly heavy, I headed for bed.

22

A light rain pattered my windshield as I stared at the house in front of me. The property was surrounded by trees, giving it privacy that would be the envy of any recluse out there. The house itself had once been a log cabin but had been updated with modern technology that made it look more . . . I don't want to say futuristic, but yeah.

The road leading to Skinny Jefferson's house was quiet, allowing me to pull off to the side without worrying about getting in someone's way. The driveway was short, paved, and hidden from view until you were practically upon it.

In a word, it was the perfect place for a serial killer to live. Okay, a few words.

I'd promised myself I'd take Paul with me when I stopped by Skinny's to check out whatever he had for me, but Paul was busy. If I'd told him my plan, he would have tried to talk me out of it, and then, when he realized I was too stubborn for that, he would have insisted on joining me, which is exactly what I should have wanted.

But I didn't. Dragging him away from his job to protect me was not going to happen, not after our last conversation. I'd already done enough to hurt his standing with the department, whether he believed it or not.

My windshield wiper sluiced away the rain, which was cooling for now, but I knew that once it burned off, the humidity would rise to unbearable levels.

Here goes nothing. Putting the Escape into gear, I pulled into Skinny Jefferson's driveway.

A tall, strangely proportioned man carrying an umbrella hurried out of the house before I'd coasted to a stop. His legs were stick-like, as were his arms, but his mid-section was barrel-shaped. If I'd squinted, I could see why people called him "Skinny," but I imagine the name had been given to him back in high school, when he was actually, well, skinny.

"Sorry about the rain," he said, holding the umbrella over my car door.

"It's not your fault." I weighed him with my eyes, and then decided he looked mostly harmless. That didn't mean he was, but hey. He looked younger than his claimed twenty-two years. But his smile appeared genuine as he stepped back to allow me to exit my car and join him in the driveway.

"Yeah, but it feels like it is. I wish you had gotten with me before now." He looked me up and down. I could almost hear the calculations going on in his head. Weight, height, skin tone, all combined with what lens to use, lighting, and so on. "Let's get inside."

"I'm just here to see your photos," I reminded him.

"Yeah, yeah, I get it." He jerked his head sideways, toward his house. Then he started walking.

And since I didn't want to get drenched, I hurried along beside him, safely hidden beneath his umbrella.

"Place used to belong to my uncle," he explained as we walked the short distance to his front door. "He never used it. It was his getaway cabin, but I guess he never managed to get away." He glanced back at me and grinned. "So he let me have it, and I've done what I can to make it livable."

"It's nice," I said, though from the outside, I couldn't really tell if that was true or not.

"Thanks." He opened the door and stepped aside, keeping his umbrella over me the entire time. "After you."

I hesitated only a moment before entering the house. If Skinny was a serial killer, I was in trouble no matter where I stood. I hadn't seen much in the way of neighbors on my way in. I could probably scream my throat raw, and no one would hear me.

And yet I am here, walking into what could be a killer's den, anyway.

My sense of self-preservation wasn't all that well developed. And besides, if you started thinking of every person you met as a prospective killer, you'd never make friends.

The inside of Skinny's house was much like the outside. You could see vestiges of the old log cabin hidden behind the technology. The living room—the only big room, from what I could tell—was set up to be Skinny's studio. Lighting, a backdrop, and a couple of tripods took up most of the space. A small love seat was crammed into the corner, facing a wall-size television across the room.

"Cozy," I said. The walls already felt like they were closing in.

Skinny grinned as he shook off his umbrella and shoved it into a small wooden barrel by the door that looked as if it had been made for that precise purpose. "It suffices. I sometimes wish I had more space, but you work with what you've got." He motioned toward the couch. "Go ahead and have a seat. I'll get the photos."

The couch looked clean enough, but I made sure not to touch it with my hands as I eased down. Knowing Skinny's desire for nude models, I didn't want to touch anything, just in case he'd had a few over recently.

There was a chest sitting beside a shelf filled with cameras of all shapes and sizes. The chest looked kind of like it might have belonged to a pirate, and it was open, revealing wisps of fabric that were supposed to be clothing, but were so see-through, I didn't know why anyone would bother. There were also other props tossed inside. Some were of the sort that made my face redden and reinforced the idea that I didn't want to touch anything, while others were more generic. The top half of a bowling pin showed through the jumble, which seemed both out of place and horrifyingly appropriate at the same time.

"Here we are," Skinny said, returning with a thick book in his hand. "I went ahead and put them in an album." He dropped down onto the couch beside me. His shoulder and thigh were pressed against mine as he flipped open the book and set it atop both our laps, essentially trapping me.

I tried to scoot away, but there wasn't any room. It was either get up or suffer his closeness and see what he had to show me.

"What am I looking for?" I asked, looking down at the photos. The page he'd opened to showed images taken at various angles during the pre-run gathering. The crowd. The runners getting prepped under the tent. A few shots of the trees and route. Honestly, they weren't half bad, though I wasn't an expert.

He flipped a page, paused, and then turned another. "Here." He pointed a finger at the middle photo. I noted he had a single drop of black polish in the middle of that fingernail and wondered if it meant something or if it was a style thing.

I started with the faces in the photo, but nothing jumped out at me. It was just a shot of a small portion of the crowd. "Okay?" Even as I said it, I finally saw it.

"There," Skinny said, moving his finger to point at what should have leaped out at me the moment he'd pointed the photo out. "In the background."

It was Johan and the blonde, heading for the

sheds. The photo had been taken from somewhere in the crowd, meaning it was a long-distance shot that showed me absolutely nothing I didn't already know.

"Oh." I couldn't keep the disappointment out of my voice. "I knew about that."

"That's just the first image," Skinny said, a triumphant tone to his voice. "I saw those two sneaking off in a few of the photos in this series. Here." He pointed at another photo that showed the same indistinct blonde with Johan from the back and far away. "And here." Another. "I started thinking about what they might have been up to, and when I realized that the guy got killed in those woods, that whatever it was, it might be connected to the murder. That's why you're here, right?"

I nodded. My heart had started thumping hard. "I'm not sure they had anything to do with it, but they might have seen it."

"That's what I was thinking." Skinny turned the page a couple more times, pausing to look at the photos before he did. "I don't have a good shot of the guy. He wasn't mingling with the crowd at any time before or after the marathon. It's like he just showed up out of nowhere and then vanished." He scoured a page. "Here we are."

I looked. The photos were of dozens upon dozens of people. Runners, spectators. "I don't see it."

"Wait." He flipped back to the first photo, keeping his finger in place to mark the other. "Notice the outfit?"

I did. It hit me like a slap. "The dark, tight clothes."

"Yeah, which looks a lot like the other runners. But note the colors."

Black and hot pink. I'd seen it before.

Skinny turned back to the marked page. "And here."

There it was, front and center. Tight black shorts and shirt, hot pink accents. Blond hair.

Alleah Trotter.

Johan had been meeting with Alleah. And Rod Maxwell had joined them not long afterward.

It was all starting to make sense. Somehow, Johan had gotten involved with Alleah and Rod. Glen was already working with them somehow. Or against them. I wasn't sure on that point quite yet, but I was getting there.

They'd all met up before the marathon started. Maybe even before that, considering what Jen had told me about Glen showing up at a meeting. And then I saw Alleah and Rod together at the Banyon Tree. I should have noticed then that her outfit was the same one as the woman who'd snuck off with Johan. If my brain had been functioning properly, I might have.

Alleah had said something about making sure Glen didn't tell his friends about whatever it was that Rod was worried about. Did that mean that she killed him to silence him?

And Johan is tied to it as well.

"Can I have this?" I asked, already fumbling for the photo. "For the police. And one of the others for comparison?"

"Yeah, sure, I can print more." He took the book from me and removed the photos. "Here you go."

"Thank you." I took the photos and stood. "I should go."

Skinny followed me to the door and opened it for me. He looked disappointed when he noted the rain had already stopped and he wouldn't need to escort me back to my vehicle. "Hey, if you change your mind about the photos . . ."

"I'll let you know," I said, hurrying out the door. "I'll call you."

"All right, cool."

I had my phone out and was dialing before I was fully into the driver's seat. The call went to voice mail. "Hi, Paul, I might have something for you. Photos. I know who Johan snuck off with. Call me, and I'll get the pictures to you. Thanks." I clicked off.

Backing out of Skinny's driveway, I considered my options. I could take the photos to the police station and leave them with someone there. But if they were to get lost, it could be days before I found out that no one else had seen them, and then I'd have to come back to Skinny's for new copies. No, I wanted to make sure to put them into Paul's hands directly. I'd wait until his call.

Until then, there was someone else who needed to know about Johan's meeting with Alleah Trotter and Rod Maxwell. Someone who wasn't going to like it one bit.

This time, when I pulled into Rita's driveway, her car was there. I took a moment to steel myself, and then I grabbed the photos and headed for her front door.

"Why, hello, dear," Rita said as soon as she answered. There was an odd lilt to her voice, as if the jovial greeting was forced. "I wasn't expecting a visitor so early in the day. Shouldn't you be at Death by Coffee, making sure it's running properly?"

"Hi, Rita. Sorry to drop in unannounced." Again. "Can I come in for a minute?"

"Of course." She stepped aside to allow me to enter, before leading me to the living room. I sat in the same chair I'd sat in the last time I was there, while she chose to stand by the couch, arms crossed. It made me feel like an intruder. "What is it that brought you here?"

The house fell eerily silent. The bedroom door behind Rita was closed, saving me from having to look at the cardboard cutout of Dad. Thank goodness for small blessings, because I wasn't sure I could do this with him staring at me, real or not.

"It's about Johan."

She paled, even as she said, "I see."

"He was in Pine Hills the day of the marathon. I saw him. And I have proof." I handed over the photo. "He's in the background with the woman. I know it's hard to make out clearly, but I'm positive it's him."

Rita showed no expression as she looked at the photo. She handed it back without a word.

"That woman is Alleah Trotter." I handed her the next photo. Like the first, she looked at it and then gave it back to me with no comment, which was unlike her. Normally, you couldn't keep her from babbling.

"I don't want to upset you—"

"I'm not upset, dear. Not at you. Never at you." She smiled, though it wasn't her usual bubbly one. "I know."

It took me a moment to understand what she was referring to. "You know about Johan?"

"I didn't until recently, but I do now." Rita sighed in such a way that her entire body jiggled with it. "When I told you I saw a man who looked like Johan at that woman's house on Elmore, I meant it."

"But now?"

"Now I know I was wrong. I fooled myself into believing what I wanted to believe, but it was my Johan."

I took a stab in the dark since, at this point, it was pretty obvious. "Alleah Trotter lives there, doesn't she?"

Her nod was stiff. "It was nothing romantic, mind you. Johan and Alleah were in cahoots—the non-romantic kind—along with another man."

"Rod Maxwell." The man who'd threatened me, and who had been seen arguing with far too many people not to be involved.

"The murdered man, Glen, was involved too, but in a more indirect way. I don't know the details, and I don't want to know." Which was extremely out of character for Rita. "But apparently he found out about what the others were into, and things snowballed on him."

Dread worked through my gut. How did she know all of this? "One of them killed him for it?"

"What?" Rita's eyes grew wide in shock, and her hand fluttered to her chest. "Of course not, dear. None of them would have done that."

I wasn't so sure about that, but I didn't want to press her too hard, considering Johan's involvement. She was holding up pretty well, but how long would that last? "What happened then?"

"Nothing happened, not really. They talked about what to do, and before they could come up with a solution, he was dead." She paused, and I caught a subtle glance behind her, toward her closed bedroom door.

Johan is in there. The thought struck me hard.

"Are you doing all right?" I asked with an obvious look toward the bedroom door. "Do you want to go for a ride or something? Get out for a bit?"

Rita waved me off. "I'm fine, dear. But I do have a few things I need to take care of." And then with a pointed look. "Personal things."

I rose from my chair and pulled my phone from my pocket. I mouthed, "Call Paul?" and held up the phone to show her that he was but a button-press away.

Rita shook her head, her expression clearly annoyed. "I'll talk to you later. It was nice of you to stop by. I do appreciate it." She walked me to the door, using her body to urge me along. "Tell that hunky boyfriend of yours that I'm okay and that no one needs to worry one bit about me."

She all but shoved me out the door. "I'll check

in on you later," I said, not liking leaving her there with Johan, but what could I do about it? I wasn't about to drag her out of her own home.

"You do that, dear." This time, her smile was kind, sincere. "Thank you for thinking of my well-being." And then she closed the door, leaving me to wonder if I was doing the right thing or if, by walking away, I was doing more harm than good.

23

I coasted down Elmore Street, feeling a bit like Rod must have felt when he cruised by Death by Coffee. My blood was up, and anxiety over leaving Rita alone with a man involved in some seriously shady dealings had me wanting to scream at someone.

And what better outlet than the woman Johan had snuck off with?

I didn't have a lot to go on when it came to finding her house, other than the name of the street. Thankfully, I didn't need much else because as I crept down the road, I saw Alleah standing by her car, phone pressed to her ear. She was talking frantically, and the back door of her car was open, as if she'd just shoved something into it or was planning to do so. She smacked the door once, shook her hand like it hurt, and then started for her house.

Not wanting to miss the opportunity, I pressed

on the gas and pulled into her driveway before she reached the front door. She turned, said something hasty into the phone, and clicked off. The glare she turned on me rivaled the one she'd given me at the Banyon Tree when I'd eavesdropped on her conversation.

I parked behind her car, shut off the engine, and climbed out of my vehicle.

"Alleah Trotter?" I asked, even though I already knew. She wasn't wearing her black-and-pink outfit, but it was her.

"Yes?" She looked me up and down. A flare of recognition flashed in her eyes, and her face hardened all the more.

"I'm Krissy Hancock." I couldn't bring myself to extend a hand to shake. I didn't care what reason she had for sneaking off with Johan, but her presence had caused Rita distress, which put her squarely on my crap list. "I was hoping I could talk to you for a moment."

Alleah glanced at her watch. "I'm in a hurry. We can do this some other time."

"I don't think we can."

She paused mid-turn. "Excuse me?"

"I saw you," I said. "I have photos."

She blinked at me. "You're taking pictures of me? Are you stalking me?"

"No, but you aren't as sneaky as you think you are."

Alleah checked her watch again and then turned to face me fully. "And what do these photos show that would make you think I'm trying to be 'sneaky?' " She made air quotes.

The photos in question were still in my car, and I wasn't about to grab them. "Let's just say I know you met with Johan Morrison and Rod Maxwell at the marathon. I also know it had something to do with a building on Rosebud, which was hastily emptied recently. It was a place where Glen Moreau used to go. You know, before he was murdered."

Alleah's expression never changed an iota, yet something about her stance told me I knew far more than she'd expected.

"Care to comment?" I pressed. "Because if not, I'll just take everything I have to the police, and they can sort it out and determine whether or not you had anything to do with Glen's death."

"I didn't."

"But you did sneak off with Johan and Rod."

She thought about it a moment before answering. "I didn't sneak, but I did meet with them."

"About?"

"That's none of your business."

"Johan came here."

Another pause as she considered that. "He did."

"He's dating another woman."

The laugh that burst out of her was so abrupt and loud, it startled me. "You think I'm sleeping with him? Please."

"Then why would he come to your house after telling Rita that he was going to be out of town?"

Alleah's amusement evaporated as if it had never been there in the first place. "He was planning on leaving town, but he didn't get the chance. He didn't lie on purpose."

I just stared at her, willing her to keep talking.

After a few long seconds, she did, "Something came up."

"Something? Like Glen's death?"

"Before that." She frowned, eyes going distant. I could see cracks starting to form, could see the worry growing by the way she kept biting at her lower lip, which was already chewed raw. She was worried about something and had been for a while.

"Alleah, a man is dead," I said. "You are connected to this man. I saw you at the Banyon Tree with Rod afterward, heard a little of what you said to him. I know about Johan. The meeting with you, him, and Rod. The building on Rosebud." I wasn't positive that she was connected to that, but considering that the others were, it was a pretty safe bet she was too. "It's only a matter of time before the police show up here to ask you about all of it."

Another glance at her watch, and then her shoulders sagged. "Okay." She didn't extrapolate.

"Okay what?"

"I worked with Rod Maxwell. We . . ." Her eyes dropped to her phone, and I instantly made the connection.

"You were just talking to him?" Which meant he still wasn't in police custody.

"Everything has gone sideways," she said, not answering the question directly. "Glen was starting to ask questions, which sent the rest of us into a frenzy."

"Is that why you had iced coffees with Glen at Death by Coffee?" A stab in the dark, but I thought it was a pretty good one.

Alleah's face screwed up in confusion. "I never met with him there. I avoided Glen as much as possible. He was . . . unpleasant."

Which, based on what I'd seen from him, and heard from others, was an understatement.

"We used Glen," she went on. "We told him as little as possible because we didn't fully trust him, but he got the job done, so it felt like it was worth it. All he knew was that what we were doing wasn't completely on the up and up, and he was fine with that, just as long as he was getting paid."

"And what were you doing?"

Alleah shook her head. She wasn't going to answer that. "I never had any romantic interest in Glen or Johan or Rod. It was pure business. I made a decent living." She gestured toward her house, which was nice, but not extravagant. "Things were going great, and then Rod came up with these new ideas, ones that hit a lot closer to home than any of us liked, which caused Glen to get curious. Next thing we know, he wanted more money."

"So you had him killed?"

She laughed. "You don't get it, do you? We didn't kill him. Not me, not Johan, and definitely not Rod Maxwell. He doesn't have it in him."

I thought back to the knife in my door. "He threatened me."

"And? I bet that's all he's done. Rod is a coward when it comes down to it. Sure, he'll throw out a threat or two, but as soon as you step up to him, he'll back down."

I still wasn't convinced. Rod had brought a knife to my house. Sure, he'd only stabbed my door, but that didn't mean he wouldn't have stabbed me if I'd caught him in the act.

And then there was the fight with Calvin at Geraldo's. That was a physical altercation. What would have happened if it hadn't taken place in public, but somewhere private?

"What does Calvin Davis know about all of this?"

Alleah looked at her watch yet again and started tapping a foot. "Nothing."

"Nothing? He got into a fight with Rod."

"If you want to know what that was about, ask the two of them. I've had no interactions with Calvin. I've got to go."

"I already talked to Calvin." I watched her carefully, but Alleah didn't flinch. "He shrugged it off like it wasn't anything to be concerned about."

"Then talk to Rod if you don't believe him. At this point, it doesn't matter what either of them says anymore. I've already taken care of everything." She turned and opened her front door.

"Alleah?"

She paused, glanced back at me.

"I'm going to find out. About the murder. About whatever it was Glen and Johan were doing in that building. All of it."

She shrugged. "Good luck with that." She entered her house and closed the door, but not before I saw the suitcases waiting inside.

She's going to run.

And there wasn't a thing I could do about it, not unless I was willing to sit in her driveway and block her from backing out.

Actually, that wasn't entirely true. There *was* something I could do.

I hurried back to my Escape and called Paul the moment I was behind the wheel. Like before, it went to voice mail. Unlike the last time, however, I didn't leave him a message, nor did I simply give up. Instead, I did something I never thought I would do.

I called Detective John Buchannan.

I don't even remember why his number was in my phone in the first place. Had he given it to me? Did I pick it up somewhere else?

The phone rang twice before he answered with a gruff, "Yeah?"

"It's Krissy Hancock."

"I know."

Maybe he had my number saved, too. "You're going to be mad at me, but hear me out, okay?"

A grunt was his only response.

"I have it on good authority that both Alleah Trotter and Rod Maxwell are going to flee Pine Hills." Alleah, I saw for myself. Rod . . . well, considering he'd already avoided the police to this point, it seemed likely.

"You know this how?"

"I spoke to Alleah."

"Ms. Hancock—"

"She was seen sneaking off with Rita's boyfriend, and I wanted to make sure he wasn't cheating." It wasn't entirely a lie but still felt like one. "I think she was talking to Rodney on the phone when I pulled up. I also saw the suitcases in her house when she went back inside. She's going to run." Her front door hadn't opened since I'd climbed into my car, but that could be because I was still sitting there.

"Where are you now?" Buchannan asked with a huff in his voice. By the sound of it, he was on the move.

"At Alleah's. I'm sitting behind her car. She's inside right now, but I don't think that will last much longer."

"All right, listen to me." A pause. "Are you listening?"

I straightened in my seat. Was he about to give me commands as though I was an officer working with him on the investigation? I was ready to create a full-on blockade if that was what he wanted. "I am."

"I want you to go home."

"What?"

"Go home, Ms. Hancock. I have officers on the way there now to pick her up."

"But if I move, she might leave—"

"We'll get her."

"But—"

The sharp breath he sucked in cut me off.

"My officers are close. We know what car she drives. She won't get away."

"Just like Rod Maxwell?"

"We're looking for him."

"You know what car *he* drives, and you still haven't caught him," I pointed out. Maybe it was small of me, but I couldn't help myself.

"Go. Home. If officers get there before you are gone, I will make sure they take you into custody as well."

And he'd do it, too. I slammed a finger into my car's START button so hard, I nearly bent the nail back. "Fine," I said. "But if she gets away, I'm holding you responsible."

"You do that." He sounded relieved and completely unconcerned about my feelings toward him. "Is there anything else you need to tell me before I hang up? I don't want any surprises."

I almost told him no, but when I turned to start backing out of Alleah's driveway, I saw the photographs on the passenger seat.

"I have pictures," I said. "They show Alleah sneaking off with Johan at the marathon." Looking at them now, I realized how insignificant they were. Glen wasn't with them. They weren't standing over his body or arguing with him or miming killing him. They just showed two people walking off together.

"Bring them to the station," Buchannan said. "I've got a mess to deal with here that's forcing me to release an inmate, so I'll be here."

The only person I knew they were holding was Calvin.

"You're letting Calvin Davis go?"

"Not today, but tomorrow morning." He didn't sound like he was happy about it either. "Bring the photos here."

The line went dead.

I hung up, feeling as if I'd failed somehow. In a few short hours, I'd made connections between Alleah, Rod, and Johan. Connections with Glen Moreau. I'd seen that Alleah was scared enough to want to flee town, knew that Rod was doing the same. Johan was hiding at Rita's.

But none of it told me who'd actually killed

Glen. A conspiracy of some sort? Sure. But not murder. Not even a good solid reason, outside of the fact that Glen was starting to ask questions. Depending on what those questions were—and how dangerous the answers—did that really add up to murder?

In many cases it did. In this one? I wasn't so sure.

24

Misfit's eyes were huge black pits as he pressed himself against the floor as flat as he could manage. He was stationed beside the coffee table, tail swishing back and forth. He was trying to remain motionless otherwise, but he couldn't help but quiver all over in uncontrolled excitement as he waited for movement.

Around the corner and down the hall, a black-and-white face appeared, eyes just as large and black and Misfit's own.

And then, chaos.

Misfit shot across the room, claws tearing into the carpet for traction. Trouble didn't wait for his littermate to reach him. He spun, flipping midair, and then he tore down the hall, toward my bedroom. The thumps and bangs that followed told me I was likely going to spend half the night setting my house back to rights.

"Should we do something?" Vicki asked. She held a bowl of popcorn in her lap. We'd sat down twenty minutes ago to watch a movie but had yet to turn on the TV. The cats were entertainment enough.

"No, they'll be fine."

The thump that followed sounded like someone had shot a pillow-wrapped cannonball at my wall. I winced, but let the cats have their fun.

"I haven't seen Trouble this active since . . ." Vicki chewed on some popcorn as she considered it. "Since he was a kitten maybe?"

"Misfit's always been high-strung but has mellowed out over the years." Until now. It made me wonder if he would be better off in a two-cat home. Or was his unfettered excitement because it was Trouble, and a new kitten would only make him jealous?

"I really should be recording this." Two streaks shot down the hall, toward the laundry room. More crashing and banging ensued. "I could see it getting a lot of views on YouTube."

"People do love their cat videos," I said, half-tempted to get up and separate the kitties for their own sake. Neither of them was as young as they used to be, and while the exercise was good for them, I didn't want one of them breaking a leg. Or my furniture.

But I remained seated, reaching for my own bowl of popcorn. Sometimes, you just had to let the kids wear themselves out.

Besides, despite the noise and inevitable breakage of valuables, watching the cats play was relaxing. I'd dropped the photos off at the police station to a tired-looking Officer Garrison—not Buchannan, who'd been nowhere in sight—before coming home and stewing. I didn't know what to do. About Rita. About Johan. Or Alleah or Rod or anyone else, actually. People were getting hurt, and I didn't mean physically, like Glen Moreau. Emotional pain was often just as bad as physical hurt, and I had a feeling Rita was suffering pretty badly right about now.

"You've got that look on your face," Vicki said.

"Huh?" I reddened. "Sorry. I was thinking."

"Is it bad?"

"I'm not sure." I recounted my visit with Rita, along with what little I knew about Johan and his less than legal activities. "I feel like I should be helping her somehow, but what can I do?"

"Not much, I don't think." Two more streaks, back to the bedroom. They did appear to be slowing down, which was a good thing. "She's got to deal with her relationship with Johan in her own way."

"But if he's involved in a crime . . ."

"Let her deal with it. You've done what you could. If he's mixed up in something and the police find out, that's one thing. Rita still needs to come to terms with Johan and whatever he's done. And then she'll need a friend." She gave me a look that said, "That's you," just as loudly as if she'd spoken it.

"Yeah, but . . ." I trailed off. Vicki was right. Rita

would be hurt—anyone would be—but she'd get over it. I mean, she'd dealt with tragedy before. What was a little money laundering, or whatever it was that Rod and Alleah were up to?

Whatever it is, it has to be a lot better than murder.

The thumping stopped. A moment later, two exhausted kitties sauntered into the living room and plopped over onto their sides like felled trees, chests heaving. Misfit reached out once and batted Trouble on the nose, earning him a casual bonk on the top of his head. Neither cat had enough energy to continue sparring after that.

"Looks like the show is over," Vicki said with a mock pout. "I guess we'll have to find that movie after all."

"Yeah. It might take them a little while to rev up for act two." Though I was hoping that if they started up again, they'd do so in a room without anything breakable in it.

The next ten minutes were spent flipping through Netflix, rejecting movie after movie. I wasn't in the mood for something dark, and a comedy seemed wrong somehow, like watching one would be minimalizing the impact of what was going on in Pine Hills, Glen's murder included.

Vicki passed by the movie *Clue*, which reminded me about something.

"What do you think about hosting a board game group at Death by Coffee?" I asked.

Vicki paused in her scrolling. "A board game group? Like Scrabble?"

"Sort of." I explained about Yolanda and her group. "It would be temporary. If they got in the way or were too loud, we could always ask them to find somewhere else. I don't think it'd come to that, but you never know." And considering I knew nothing about the board games Yolanda had mentioned, I had no idea what it would be like.

Vicki thought about it briefly. "It actually sounds like a good idea. Maybe it could be something of a draw. You know, games might bring people in. We could expand on it a little, make it something to help drive business. Like, have different games on different nights."

That sounded nice, but I wasn't sure what Yolanda would think of that, considering she planned on making it women only. But, hey, nothing said we couldn't host our own game night if it were to bring in more customers.

"We could sell board games," I said. "Along with the books." I wasn't sure where we'd keep them, but I'd find a spot, even if we had to shelve them behind the upstairs counter.

Vicki was nodding, her eyes distant as she mentally mapped it out, when there was a knock at the door. As one, Misfit and Trouble popped up, swished their tails, and vanished down the hall, toward my bedroom, where they'd likely collapse once again.

"One sec," I said, rising, half expecting it was Paul come to talk to me about Rod or the photos I'd obtained. When I opened the door, however, it wasn't Paul's pleasant face that met me.

It was Johan's dead-eyed stare.

I choked back a scream as I backed quickly away. My eyes darted to Johan's hands, but they were simply hanging at his sides, empty.

"May we speak?" he asked, his face passive, as if I'd just stood there instead of recoiling from him.

Vicki, recognizing his voice, rose from her spot on the couch.

"Sure," I said, glancing at her. If nothing else, I had backup if he attacked me.

Johan stood on my stoop without moving. He looked from me, toward where I'd glanced, but from his position, he couldn't see Vicki.

"Would it be all right if I stepped inside?"

I took another step back. He ducked his head once in thanks, and then stepped in, closing the door softly behind him.

And then we all just stood there. Johan looked like nothing in the world could bother him. No expression. No sense that he was angry or worried or about to whip out a gun and threaten me with it if I didn't back off. Vicki clutched at her popcorn bowl, and I knew she would smack Johan upside the head with it if he were to make an aggressive move. And then there was me, shifting from foot to foot, gnawing on my lower lip like Alleah had earlier that day.

"I'm not here to cause trouble." Johan said it casually, like he was asking for a stick of butter. "I would like to explain my actions to you before I go."

"To me?" I asked, happy that my voice didn't come out as a squeak. "Why not the police?"

His mouth twitched into a near smile. "Perhaps I will get the chance to do so soon enough, but for now, I'd like to talk to you. You're Rita's friend. You will understand."

I wasn't so sure about that, but I nodded for him to go on.

Johan looked pointedly at Vicki. He didn't say anything, but I got the gist.

"I'm not going anywhere, pal," she said.

"This is something I wish to speak of privately." Johan shifted, and I got the distinct impression he was considering leaving. If he had something important to say, something like, "Hey, I killed Glen," I didn't want him to walk away without telling me just because Vicki was standing there.

"It's all right," I said. "Go check on the cats. I'll be fine."

Vicki's eyes narrowed. "Are you sure?"

"I am." At least, I thought I was. I didn't know what I would do if Johan did admit to murder. The last time a killer was in my house, he'd just about pummeled me to death. I didn't think Johan would do the same, but with killers, you never knew.

Vicki set her bowl on the couch before walking slowly toward the hall. She didn't take her eyes off Johan until she vanished around the corner, and even then, I was pretty sure she kept her full attention on him, all the way into the bedroom.

Silence prevailed as Johan and I turned back to face one another. This was a man who'd rubbed me the wrong way since he'd started dating Rita. I didn't know what it was about him. The dead stare, the way he rarely showed emotion. I found him creepy, and it was looking more and more like my feelings were justified.

"I do not wish to hurt Rita in any way," Johan said, breaking the silence. "Nor do I wish any ill will toward you. I never have, despite what you might think."

I almost denied it but didn't. What would be the point?

"I know that I am . . . peculiar." That odd little smile appeared and then vanished. "I can't help it. It's simply the way that I am—have always been—and people take notice of that strangeness. It has led to somewhat of a lonely life."

Don't, Krissy. The guilt was starting to seep in. "I'm sorry about that," I said, and I meant it.

Johan bowed his head slightly before continuing. "None of that justifies what I have done. I have no justification other than it was easy and no one was hurt. Physically, anyway."

"Glen Moreau would disagree."

No expression shift. Not even a flinch or a lift of an eyebrow. "Glen was involved with us, but we were not involved in his death."

"Are you sure about that?"

"I am." Confident. "I did not kill him, nor did I want to. Neither did Alleah Trotter or Rod Maxwell."

"That's what Alleah told me." The longer he stood there without making an aggressive move, the more confident I became that he wouldn't. "I'm not so sure I believe her."

"It's true, regardless. We did not kill him, nor did we have him killed. We did not benefit from his death. In fact, Glen's demise has affected us greatly in a negative manner."

I thought back to the suitcases in Alleah's house. "You're running," I said.

Johan neither confirmed nor denied it. "The marathon was Rod's idea," he said instead. "His scheme."

A creak of a board told me Vicki was listening in, just out of sight. "A scheme? How so?"

He considered it a moment before speaking. "Alleah and Rod have been doing this sort of thing for years, but never in Pine Hills. They'd create an event, a charity drive, perhaps, and would obtain donations, claiming those donations would be given to the charity, but instead . . ." He shrugged, so I finished for him.

"They pocketed it."

"Some of it." He paused. "Most of it. I transported funds for the most part. Glen would do something similar, but not on the same scale. Rod had access to a building on Rosebud Avenue where he would leave instructions for us with an associate, one as oblivious to what we were doing as Glen once was. Glen and I would pick up those instructions and do whatever was required."

"Such as?"

Another shrug. It came off as indifferent. "I often handled the money. I'd bank it, take it to someone who needed to be paid off. Sometimes documents needed to be signed. Sometimes forged. Glen handled the easy stuff, the stuff that didn't require much explanation."

"Alleah said Glen didn't know what he was doing at first, but that he found out."

"He was more of a runner than someone who had any inside knowledge of what was going on. He was used so that the rest of us could avoid detection. If he was caught, he knew nothing of import."

"Until he did."

"Until he did," he agreed. "He poked around, discovered what we were doing, and decided he deserved a bigger cut of the profits."

"That seems to give Alleah and Rod a motive to kill him." I left Johan's name out on purpose. No sense agitating him, something I was learning was a good idea when dealing with criminals.

"Perhaps," he allowed. "But that is why we met that day. Glen was becoming more and more difficult. He'd started throwing threats around, warning that he would talk if he wasn't paid. And then he got paranoid, started claiming we were trying to kill him, though none of us were. It had gotten so bad, I decided I needed to speak with Alleah and Rod before I took care of other business."

I waited. If he was trying to make them appear innocent, he wasn't doing a very good job of it.

"We had no reason to harm Glen," Johan said, seeming to realize how his words were being taken. "We were going to pay him off and cut him loose. Alleah had already set things in motion, had checked to verify that Glen hadn't already spoken to some of his closest friends. The money we'd make from the marathon—"

Anger flashed through me, and I snapped out, "Money that was supposed to go to cancer research."

Once again, if he was offended or hurt by the insinuation, he didn't show it. "We were going to give him most of it. It's far easier to pay someone off than to cover up a murder. Glen goes away, we could move on. He dies, and then there's an investigation, which leads to . . . this."

"And everyone agreed to that?" I asked, though I was starting to believe him.

"It was what was for the best. Now that Glen is dead and the police are involved, we were forced to cease operations. Everything is gone, destroyed. I am tied to all of this, but I am not as involved as Rod and Alleah. They are the two with the most to lose." He paused, and for the first time, I saw sadness in his eyes. "Well, other than Rita. I . . ." He trailed off.

A new thought. "What about Jen Vousden?" She'd organized the marathon with Rod and Alleah, so she'd have to know something, wouldn't she?

"She was not involved." At my skeptical look, Johan went on. "She had the right connections to make the marathon happen. That's as far as her involvement went."

I wasn't sure I believed him, but that was something the police could figure out. "Could Rod have panicked after Glen threatened him at the marathon?" I asked. "It got pretty heated."

"No. He's not the type." Which was similar to what Alleah had said of him. "Once Glen's body was found, it took everything we had to calm him down. He was panicked, and he very nearly went to the police himself before Alleah managed to talk sense into him."

Likely at the Banyon Tree. It made me wonder how much of their conversation I'd missed. If I hadn't drawn attention to myself, would I have overheard all of this days ago? It would have saved me a lot of time and stress.

"If none of you killed Glen, do you have any idea who did?" I asked.

Johan shook his head. "I do not." The sadness flashed across his face again. "Please, do not hold what I've done against Rita. She knew nothing of what I was doing. I told her everything before you arrived earlier, explained myself more afterward. I failed her, and that is on me, and me alone."

"I won't," I said, not sure what else to say. This sounded an awful lot like a final confession. I didn't like it.

"I will make sure none of this comes back on Rita, even if I have to put myself in harm's way to do so."

"Johan," I said, my worry growing, "what are you going to do?"

Instead of answering, he turned toward the door.

A million thoughts went through my head then. Should I tackle him? Hold him for the police? Should I let him go? Beg him to turn himself in?

I knew the right thing would be to find a way to stop him and call Paul. He'd admitted to being a part of a fraudulent scheme that cheated charities out of money they desperately needed. He should be punished for that.

But at the same time, he'd been good to Rita, no matter what I thought about him. And, really, he wasn't the mastermind behind the scheme. He was just a cog in the machine—an important one, mind you—but it was Rod and Alleah who were the real culprits.

Johan opened the door and stepped outside. There, he paused, though he didn't turn back.

"You likely won't see me again," he said. "But I will keep you in my thoughts."

And then he walked toward a car of similar make and model as Rod's. He climbed inside and without a wave goodbye, Johan Morrison drove out of my—and Rita's—lives for good.

25

"Ah, crap."

Coffee sloshed out of my mug and onto the floor, causing me to raise the mug higher into the air, as if that would somehow stop it from spilling out. Another blob splashed out of my mug, onto my hand, with the sudden movement. That, of course, caused me to jerk back, which sent the rest of the contents of my mug flying. I ducked my head and scuttled across the room, out of harm's way. I avoided scalding myself further, but my kitchen floor was a mess.

I leaned against the counter, eyes closed, and just breathed. I was exhausted, both mentally and physically. At least my sunburn was mostly just peeling skin by now. Small victories.

Vicki had stayed long enough to watch an episode of a show that I couldn't remember because I didn't pay attention to it. I tried, I really did, but every time I attempted to focus, my mind went straight back to what Johan had told me.

Could Rod and Alleah truly be innocent of Glen's murder? If so, then who did that leave?

I grabbed a roll of paper towels and mopped up the mess. Misfit watched from the safety of the living room, making sure to keep well clear of me. He'd seen me bumbling around and knew better than to get underfoot.

Alleah didn't do it. Rod didn't do it. The murder had nothing to do with their schemes.

Coffee dripped from the paper towels as I tossed them into the trash. Another wad cleaned that up. I would need to mop at some point, or else the floor would get sticky. But right then, I didn't have the energy for it.

I rinsed off the outside of my mug, dried it, and filled it with coffee once again. The cookie I'd dropped into it was stuck to the bottom on the inside, so I didn't need to replace that. Once again, small victories.

This time, I made it to the island counter, where I sagged down to sip my coffee.

Let's say Johan was telling the truth. No one involved in the fraud scheme killed Glen. That left me with the ex-wife, the girlfriends, both current and exes. Maybe his son, Jase. Maybe Trevor, if what Calvin said about him wanting to confront Glen was true. That was still a lot of suspects.

And if Johan had lied to me? Well then, I'd have to add all three of them back into the pot.

One of these days, someone was going commit a

murder in Pine Hills, and they'd do it in full view of half the town, leaving me out of it.

I could call Paul, tell him what Johan had told me, and then leave it at that. They had the photos Skinny had given me. Once I unloaded the burden of Rita's (ex?) boyfriend, they'd have just as much information as I did. Maybe more, considering the ongoing investigation.

Still, the idea of going to the cops about Johan didn't sit well with me. He'd come to me because he trusted me in some capacity. If he was telling the truth, then what would narking on him accomplish?

There is *someone who likely knows more than they'd let on.*

One more visit. That's all I'd need. And then I could clean my hands of all of this and let the police finish the job. I mean, I'd gotten into all of this because of Johan. Now that he was cleared—in my mind, at least—did I really need to press further?

I took a large gulp of coffee, scraped out the cookie remains, and then rinsed out the mug before I grabbed my purse and keys.

It was time I got this over with, one way or the other.

The drive to A Woman's Place felt like it took forever. I kept second-guessing myself and very nearly turned around twice. Alleah was planning to flee town, as was Rod. Rod had threatened me. They'd been up to their eyeballs in criminal activity, activity that Glen had been a part of and was starting to demand a bigger slice of.

How could that not be a motive for murder?

But every time I thought about turning around,

I thought of Melanie's conversation with Jase, how she'd tried to pin everything on Ivy. Then there was Ellen, a woman who'd dated Glen and who had visited Melanie before Glen was killed and was there again afterward. A guilty conscience perhaps?

Melanie's PT Cruiser was sitting in her driveway all by its lonesome, telling me she was home. I parked next to her and climbed out of my Escape, but before I could reach the front door, it opened and Melanie hurried out, overloaded purse over one arm.

"Oh!" she said, coming up short when she saw me. "I didn't know anyone was here."

"Hi, Melanie." I put myself between her and her car. "Looking to skip town too?" I said it jokingly, but a part of me wondered if I might be right. She wasn't carrying a suitcase, nor did I see one in her car, but, boy, that purse sure did look suspicious.

"What?" Genuine confusion flashed across her face. "No. I . . ." She shook her head. "What's going on?"

"I think I should be the one asking you that."

More confusion. "What? I don't understand."

"I saw you with Jase," I said. "At the party. I talked to him once you went back inside. He was pretty adamant about Ivy not being involved with Glen."

"She . . ." Melanie floundered. "Jase is . . ." Her eyes closed, and her shoulders slumped. "All right, fine. Ivy didn't do it."

I blinked at her. That was easy. Too easy. "Didn't do what?"

"Kill Glen. She was with Jase at the time."

It took a moment for that to sink in. "Wait. *With* Jase? As in . . . ?"

Melanie nodded. "They're together."

It made a strange sort of sense when I thought back to what Jase had said. "But she was with Glen. His father. I . . . It . . ."

Melanie's laugh was bitter, void of amusement. "Tell me about it. Jase insists that Ivy and Glen didn't, you know, consummate their relationship. He says that she left him as soon as she realized he was already taken, and that their relationship grew out of some sort of bond formed over the betrayal. I don't know. It doesn't make sense to me."

Me either, but then again, since everyone seemed to be lying to me, I really didn't know what to think. "You don't approve of the relationship?"

"Of course, I don't! She's older than he is. And the history she had with his father, no matter how short it might have been? No. I can't. I just can't."

"That's why you pressed the Ivy angle so hard. You didn't truly believe she killed Glen. You just wanted Jase to leave her."

"I miss him." A tear formed in the corner of Melanie's eye. "Jase, not Glen. I try not to. He's a lot like his father, more than either of us would care to admit. But Glen did have a good side. He could be kind and gentle, and when you caught his eye, you became the most important thing in his world. That's what I want to see in my son. If I could see him."

I felt bad for her, I really did. Yet many of her problems with her son were her own fault. Even I could see that. "You've pushed him away."

"I know. I can't help it. Every time I see him, I

see Glen. In his posture, in his words. And then to know he's with Ivy, the woman Glen was cheating on me with, it's too much. The weight of all of this . . . It was breaking me."

I could see that. It made me wonder how Trisha could stand being around me, considering my history with Robert. Or Shannon because of Paul.

"What does Ellen have to do with this?"

Melanie pulled her purse close to her chest and then went completely still.

"I saw the two of you together and was told that you'd met before." I paused for dramatic effect. "Before Glen was murdered."

"Ellen isn't involved in any of this."

"Ivy claims Ellen was with Glen the day before his death, not her."

I could see the knee-jerk "No, Ivy did it" come to mind, but Melanie didn't stoop to that level. She licked her lips, looked past me, toward her PT Cruiser, as if she was thinking of making a run for it.

"Melanie," I pressed. "What does Ellen have to do with Glen? Was she seeing him? Could she have killed him?"

Melanie shook her head, but I couldn't tell if she was telling me that Ellen didn't kill Glen or if she was simply refusing to answer my question.

"I have to go," she said. "I can't talk about this now. So, please . . ." She tried to move past me, but I refused to let her.

"Ellen might be involved in your ex-husband's death." I spoke slowly, carefully, so that she understood the gravity of what I was saying. "I get that you want to help her, and that there's bitterness between you and Glen, but if she was involved in his murder, you can't keep it to yourself."

"What I discuss with the women who come to me is private," Melanie said, raising her chin in defiance, before sagging. "But . . ." She bit her lip hard. I could tell she was fighting with herself. "I'll give you her address. If she wants to tell you why she was here, then that's her business. I won't betray her trust otherwise."

"I understand." And I did. Besides, talking to Ellen in person would give me a better idea of who she was, and if she was capable of murder. I wasn't entirely sure I could trust whatever Melanie said, not after the Ivy fiasco.

"I will say this," Melanie went on. "Ellen isn't a bad person. No matter what you might think of her because of her choices. She's scared, and she came to me because she thought I might be able to help with her situation. That's it. I do good work here. I help people."

"I know you do."

She gave me a long, hard look, and then, apparently seeing that I was genuine, she told me Ellen's address.

"Be careful with her," she said. "She's barely holding on, and if you push too hard, she very well might break."

"I will." Though, if she'd killed Glen, I was the least of her worries.

We both climbed into our respective vehicles. In the back of my mind, I wondered if I was making a mistake in not keeping her there or forcing her to come with me. If Melanie had killed Glen—possibly because of something he'd done to Ellen or because of her own history with the man—then she could be joining Alleah, Rod, and Johan in skipping town.

But despite her evasiveness and attempt to frame another woman, a part of me still liked Melanie. She did help people, and that was commendable. No one was perfect, and as I'd proved time and time again, we all make mistakes.

It's just that some mistakes are far bigger and have much greater consequences than others.

Melanie backed out first. I hoped it wasn't the last time I would ever see her.

Ellen lived halfway across town, giving me time to prepare what I was going to say. I mean, what did I know about her? She may have dated Glen before his death. That wasn't a crime, nor was it a sure sign of guilt. She'd met with Melanie at least twice, which, once again, didn't indicate anything criminal.

I pulled into the paved driveway of a cute little house, complete with flower beds lining the front, a flagpole, its base likewise lined with flowers, and a large mat by the door, welcoming me to the home. I instantly noted the "our home" part of the mat and wondered if that meant Ellen was married or if she counted her pets as family, like I did.

Or I could be overanalyzing it.

Either way, I was about to find out.

I stepped up to the front door and noted how soft the welcome mat was. It was like stepping onto one of those memory foam mattresses, all squishy and comfy. It was almost a shame to dirty it up, and I had an urge to take a step back after I'd pressed the bell.

"Yes?" The blonde I'd seen with Melanie at the party answered almost immediately, as if she'd been waiting by the door. Up close, she was pretty, yet there were dark circles under her eyes, and frown lines were forming around her mouth. She looked both tired and wary.

"Ellen?"

Again, a simple, "Yes?"

"I'm Krissy Hancock." I considered holding out a hand to shake but didn't think she would take it. Ellen was clutching the inside door as if she were using it as a shield. The storm door was still closed, and I doubted she had any intention of opening it for me, to shake hands or otherwise.

I expected her to answer with another, "Yes?" but this time, all she said was, "Oh."

"I'd like to talk to you about Glen Moreau."

Her eyes darted past me and then to her watch. "I can't talk right now."

"It'll take just a minute."

"I really can't. My husband will be home soon."

Husband? My entire body started tingling. If Ellen had been sleeping with Glen and she was already married, that would give someone—namely, her husband—a pretty good motive for murder.

"Were you seeing Glen Moreau?" I asked before she could close the door in my face.

"Please." Ellen was looking frantic now. "Just go. You've got to leave before he gets here."

"Ellen . . ." I was growing worried. The woman was terrified. If her husband had killed Glen because she was cheating, could he be threatening her? Hurting her? "If you need help, I—"

"No. I'm fine. We're fine. He'll be home soon." She started to close the door, but I stopped her with a question.

"Who's your husband?" And then I had a flash of inspiration. Who wasn't able to be at home because he was currently sitting in jail? And who was going to be released that very morning, which meant, as Ellen had said, he would be home soon? "Is Calvin Davis your husband?"

Ellen started to open her mouth to answer but cut off with a squeak as her eyes went wide.

And from behind me, in a voice tinged with barely suppressed anger, Trevor Conway said, "No. I am."

26

Trevor had been the one to "discover" Glen's body. Trevor had wanted to confront Glen about something personal. Trevor was married to a woman who was allegedly sleeping with Glen before his death.

And now Trevor was towering over me, looking like a man ready to commit murder.

"You killed him." It slipped out before I could stop it. Trevor was wearing his knee braces and had a headband keeping sweat out of his eyes. He looked like he'd just returned from a pleasant summer walk, yet I still felt intimidated.

"No." His jaw worked soundlessly before he said. "We should discuss this inside."

Inside. Where I had nowhere to run.

"I think I'd like to stay out here."

Behind me, Ellen whimpered—actually *whimpered*—before she vanished inside.

"Let's go."

Trevor stepped forward, and on instinct, I stepped back, putting me within the threshold. There was a chance I could slip past him and make a run for it, but if Trevor grabbed me, I wasn't sure what I'd do. Scream, most likely.

"I'm not going to hurt you," he said, looking all the world like he was going to hurt me. "I just want to talk. Clear the air." He attempted a smile that was anything but friendly.

"The police know I'm here," I said, desperately wishing it was true. "So, if something happens to me . . ."

"It won't."

Trevor kept coming, so I retreated the rest of the way into the house. Fragile knickknacks sat on shelves by the door. There were fawns frolicking in fields, bunnies rolling together, locked in mid-play forever. The living room into which I was led was light and airy and, on any other day, would have been inviting.

Ellen sat on the couch, hands between her knees, eyes focused on the floor midway across the room. She looked terrified, which was no surprise. She had to have deduced the same thing I had. If she'd cheated on her husband with Glen, then said husband had a pretty darn good reason for murder.

"Sit," Trevor commanded with a point toward the couch.

I didn't want to comply, but Ellen scooted over, leaving a space for me. I sat down beside her, figuring we could give each other strength.

"I talked to Calvin," I said before Trevor could give me whatever spiel he had planned. "He told me that you were planning to confront Glen at the marathon, that it was personal." I glanced at Ellen out of the corner of my eye, but she didn't look up.

Trevor stared at me, jaw still working. "Tea?" he asked before striding out of the room without waiting for an answer.

In that moment, I could have run. But in doing so, I would be leaving Ellen alone with a man she was clearly frightened of. Could I do that to her, even if I could then call the police for help? A lot could happen in the precious minutes it would take them to get there.

"Ellen?" I whispered. "Are you okay? Has he hurt you?"

She refused to look at me when she shook her head. I wasn't sure which question she was answering, so I looked her over from head to foot. She didn't appear to be injured, just scared.

A bottle was shoved under my nose, causing me to jump. I took the iced tea, not because I wanted it, but because I was afraid Trevor might hit me with it if I refused. The seal was still intact, so unless he had a syringe filled with poison in the kitchen, it was safe to drink.

Trevor carried his own tea to a chair across the room. I noted he hadn't gotten one for his wife, which could mean anything. He sank down into his seat with a groan and a wince before rubbing at his left knee.

"I try to walk, to keep active, but this body of mine is bound and determined to break down on me. I guess that's why I'm not surprised things happened the way they did."

"Things" being murder, I assumed. "Tell me what happened." And to show him I trusted him, I cracked open the tea and took a sip. My throat instantly locked up, and it took all my self-control not to spit it across the room. A look at the bottle told me what I already knew.

The tea was unsweetened. Maybe he *was* trying to kill me.

Trevor chuckled and took a drink from his own bottle. "Gotta cut down on the sugar, though I suppose tea isn't the best thing for me." He smacked his lips, grimaced, and then replaced the cap. "What I wouldn't give for a good iced coffee."

Beside me, Ellen flinched.

"All right, here's the deal." Trevor started rubbing his other knee. "Glen, Calvin, and I had a plan; we were going to cheat at the marathon. Glen's idea, of course. Don't know why we decided to do it, but like most ideas of Glen's, it sounded good at the time."

"There was no prize money for the winner," I pointed out.

"I know that. Glen knew that too. He just . . ." Trevor frowned as he searched for the right words. "He liked to win, be on top of everything." His eyes shot to his wife, before returning to me. "If he wanted something, he took it. And he wanted to show everyone how, I don't know, in shape he was. Impress people."

"That's why he was on the wrong path."

"It was. There's an easy access point not far from the starting line. We could slip away without being noticed since it was pretty well hidden. I guess I decided to do it not because I cared about winning, but because I had something to say to Glen. We rarely were alone together in a place where I could talk to him about something personal, and well, I'd sat on it long enough. The marathon seemed like as good a time as any."

Beside me, Ellen flinched yet again, as if afraid her husband might launch himself at her every time he spoke.

"But Glen being Glen, he didn't wait for Calvin or me as we'd originally planned. He slunk off early, before the race started, leaving me to wonder if he already knew what I was going to say."

"If Calvin was there, how did you expect to get Glen alone?" I asked, genuinely curious.

Trevor considered his tea. "When I decided to do it, I wasn't thinking clearly. I guess I would have done it in front of him if he was there since we were all friends, but he wasn't. He got a call, and after that, I didn't see him, which served my purposes just fine."

Ellen's breathing had picked up. The more her husband talked, the worse she seemed to get.

"Since I knew where Glen most likely had gone," Trevor went on, "I hurried after him the moment I was able to slip from the pack. Wasn't too hard, considering my knees. No one expects a guy who struggles to walk without pain to finish a marathon, let alone keep up. I wasn't sure I'd be able to catch up to him, but what I found when I did . . ." He cleared his throat, and when he spoke again, there was a hitch in his voice. "When I got there, he was already dead."

I didn't say anything. I was looking for the lie, the sign that he was leading me on in an effort to shift blame to someone else. Ellen had the same incredulous look on her face I must have had.

"You don't believe me." Not a question, but a statement of fact. "I get it. If I'm honest, I'd say that if I'd gotten there first, I might have done it myself. I was angry, though I did a pretty darn good job of hiding it. And with how Glen was acting, the way he pretended he wasn't . . ." He sucked in an angry breath, blew it out. "By the time I went looking for him, I was fuming."

"It wasn't—" Ellen's whisper was but a puff of air.

"*Ellen* knows why I'm so angry," Trevor said, putting all his anger into her name.

"She cheated on you with Glen," I said, anticipating her flinch before it came. Sure enough, she recoiled like I'd punched her.

But there was something else there, something that told me I'd missed the mark.

Trevor's hand tightened on his tea bottle so hard, I expected the cap to hit the ceiling. "I found out because they were seen together at some café downtown. And with Glen's past and the way Ellen had been acting evasive lately, it wasn't difficult for me to put two and two together."

I couldn't help it, I turned to Ellen. "You were the one who was seen with Glen at Death by Coffee?"

She buried her face in her hands as she nodded. "He was helping me."

"Helping himself *to* you," Trevor all but snarled it.

"No." She sniffed, wiped her nose with her forearm. "It wasn't like that. Not with Glen."

Not with Glen. The words rang loudly in the quiet of the house.

"You weren't sleeping with Glen," I said as a

statement of fact. "But if not him, then who?" Because I couldn't imagine her acting like this if she hadn't been cheating on her husband with somebody.

"I . . . He . . ." She looked at Trevor, and then Ellen burst into body-wracking sobs.

"Wait." Trevor sounded confused as he looked at his wife. "What do you mean you weren't screwing around with Glen? You were seen with him, and with his history . . . It doesn't make sense."

My mind was spinning, going back over what I knew. Glen was seen talking to an upset Ellen at Death by Coffee. Ellen claims he was helping her, but how?

Glen had spent most of his life cheating on his wives and girlfriends. He was friends with Trevor, and in turn, likely was friendly with his wife. He knew what could happen once infidelity came out, how it could ruin more than just a single relationship. He'd lived it more than once.

Trevor finds out about the not-so-clandestine meeting, thinks he's put it all together, but he's wrong. He goes to confront his friend, not realizing that he has the wrong guy. However, he finds him already dead, strangled by someone else. In his anger, Trevor had probably said something to Ellen that clued her in to his intentions with Glen, made her think that he'd gone to the marathon to kill her lover.

But he was too late. Someone else got to Glen first. And, if I was right about everything else, that someone could very well have been the man who'd Ellen actually cheated on Trevor with.

The phone call.

"Calvin." His name slipped out as I realized what I'd been missing this entire time. No, not missing: minimalizing.

Ellen nodded without looking up. Her shoulders were heaving with sobs as she choked out, "It's all my fault. I c-c-called him when Mel-Mel-Melanie told me to. She was afraid Glen wa-was going to tell Tr-Trevor about us. I warned Calvin, just so he-he-he'd be prepared."

Trevor was frozen in his seat, eyes bulging from their sockets, mouth hanging open in his shock.

It all made sense now. Trevor was right that his wife was cheating, but he'd fingered the wrong man. Ellen knew that if Trevor confronted Glen, he'd discover the truth. So she called Calvin to warn him. Calvin, in turn, knew he had to do something or he'd lose not just his friends, but Ellen and his reputation. He knew where Glen was going to be, and like Glen, he'd slipped away early, to get in place so that he could confront Glen himself before anyone else got there.

I wasn't sure if he'd gone there to kill Glen, or if just to talk, but the result was the same.

Then Trevor found the body. Calvin knew he'd be there eventually, so he decided to frame him. He'd slipped me the bit about Trevor wanting to confront Glen about something personal, hinting that he might want to kill him. With both Glen and Trevor out of the way, Calvin could have kept Ellen all to himself.

I wasn't sure how that led to Calvin getting into a fight with Rod at Geraldo's, but he'd ended up behind bars nonetheless.

Or he had been. He was due to be released that very day.

"I've got to go." I shot to my feet and was to the door in a blink. No one else moved. Ellen and Trevor simply stared at one another in their shock.

I fumbled with my phone as I hurried to my Escape. I brought up Paul's name, hit CALL, and slid behind the wheel. A button press later, and I was backing out of the driveway at high speed . . .

And was almost hit by an oncoming car.

I yelped and dropped my phone as I put both hands on the wheel and jerked it to the side. The car whizzed by, horn blaring. My back tires were in Ellen and Trevor's yard, but otherwise, no one—or anything—was harmed. Heart pounding, I put the car in DRIVE and headed for the police station, without bothering to reach for my phone or the touch screen that it was paired with.

Besides, I could hear the muffled sound of Paul's voice mail, so it wasn't like I had anyone to talk to anyway.

I did my best not to speed as I drove to the police station. If Calvin had been released, he could be anywhere by now, even on his way to the Conways' to have a word with his friend. Or to steal Ellen away. I honestly had no idea what he would do if given the chance. One man was already dead, and a whole lot of people were on the run. I didn't want there to be another body. Or two more people hoofing it for the border.

"Please still be holding him. Please still be holding him." The mantra had my foot pressing down on the gas a little harder each time. I prayed Buchannan had decided to keep him a little longer, but I doubted it. As far as he knew, the worst thing Calvin had done was smack Paul in the face with his elbow.

The Pine Hills police station came into view. I pulled into the lot just as the door opened and Calvin Davis stepped out. Officer Garrison and Detective John Buchannan were trailing behind him. None of them looked happy. They were going to be even less so when they heard what I had to say.

I skidded to a stop, going far too fast in the small lot. Buchannan's hand actually moved toward his gun before he realized who the crazy driver was. I unbuckled, threw my door open, and all but fell out of my vehicle.

"Stop him!" I shouted. A clatter sounded, and I realized belatedly that I'd kicked my phone on my way out. There was a cracking sound, but right then my phone was of minor importance.

"Don't let him go. He killed Glen Moreau."

Calvin was a good couple of feet in front of the police officers and five times that distance from me. He looked toward the empty patrol cars and the other vehicles in the lot. I could see him weigh his options, and in that moment, I knew I was right.

Buchannan stood there, hand near his gun, looking at me like I'd gone completely off the rails, before he turned slowly to Calvin, who was being watched by a frowning Garrison. She was still two steps away and had made no move for him, despite my proclamation.

"It was you, wasn't it?" I took a step toward

Calvin, confidence propelling me forward. But, because it was me, I stepped right on my phone. The pressure of me stepping down with all my weight caused it to shoot out from underneath me with a horrible grind.

And I went sprawling onto the pavement on all fours, drawing every set of eyes but one.

As soon as Garrison and Buchannan looked away, Calvin sprang into motion.

But he didn't head for the road or one of the many parked cars, which would have been useless to him without keys.

Instead, he ran straight for my orange Escape, which was sitting there, door hanging open, engine running, as if in invitation.

My knees and hands were bleeding, and my entire body was a ball of pain, but I prepared myself to grab for Calvin.

But he never made it to me.

Officer Garrison might have been distracted by my fall, but the moment Calvin started running, instinct and training kicked in, and she reacted. She screamed at him to stop, but as most criminals do, he didn't acquiesce. She snarled, and in a blink of an eye, she'd closed the distance between them and tackled Calvin right in front of me. I was close enough to hear his teeth clack as his chin met the pavement.

For an instant, our eyes met. In them, I saw pure hatred and malice.

And then Garrison had him cuffed and back on his feet. She read him his rights as she led him right back into the police station.

"Well, that was something." Buchannan walked over and offered me a hand. "I assume you have proof?"

I winced as I was helped to my feet. My hands and knees were screaming, but I still smiled when I answered. "Have I ever been wrong before?"

Buchannan snorted. "Let's head on inside. Looks like we're going to spend the next few hours together finding out."

27

I tugged at the hem of my shorts in a vain attempt to make them longer. They were new and felt way, way too short. My knees were still healing and made me look like I spent most of my time crawling around driveways. Add to that my tank top, which left arms I usually kept covered exposed, and I was feeling rather naked. At home, I'd be okay. At Death by Coffee, and soon on the sidewalks of Pine Hills, I was far from it.

Yolanda was upstairs with Vicki and two other women, talking excitedly as they worked out the details for their board game group. They planned to use the coffee table upstairs since it was out of the way and could be used without displacing customers drinking coffees in the dining area. She'd thanked me at least ten times since she'd arrived, and I expected she'd do it another ten more if I let her.

"Hey, Krissy." I turned as Pooky waved on her

way past. I returned the gesture, feeling good about my contributions to her good mood. She was smiling, and when she turned back to work, she started whistling. Her brother had moved out with much apologizing, and her demeanor had changed overnight. Nary a spill or messed-up order since she'd reclaimed her home as her own.

"Come on," I muttered under my breath as I checked a brand-new fitness watch that had all the bells and whistles. I could respond to calls and texts without having to grab my phone, which was good, considering there was no way I was fitting my phone in the sorry excuse for pockets in my shorts.

The bell above the door jangled. I turned, but it wasn't who I was expecting.

"Lordy Lou, the pollen on that breeze is going to choke someone." Rita waved her hand in front of her face, saw me, and made a beeline to where I was standing. "I see you've finally decided to dress for the weather. I suppose it's better late than never, though it isn't nearly as hot out there as it has been."

"Hi, Rita," I said. "I've got plans to go for a walk, hence the clothing choice."

"Walking now, are we?" She looked me up and down before huffing. "You probably should have chosen a sports bra over that old thing. The straps are showing and, well . . ."

I absently tucked the admittedly well-worn strap under the edge of my tank; not that it would stay hidden for long. It *was* a bit loose and refused to stay in place, but it was all I had.

"Anyway, I just popped in for an iced coffee. I

plan on going shopping for a new outfit and need the fuel to keep me going." She gave me a teasing half smile. "I'll choose something a little more appealing, of course. Johan might be gone, but that doesn't mean I need to stop living my life."

Last I heard, Johan had vanished without a trace after he'd stopped by my place. I had yet to tell Paul about his visit, and I wasn't sure I ever would, at least for now. Maybe if he cropped up again or if Paul were to ask me directly, I'd tell him, but we'll see.

"I'm glad you're doing okay," I said. "I was worried."

"Oh, pah." She waved a hand at me. "There's nothing to worry about. I have it on good authority that he'll be back." A twinkle came into her eye then, one I didn't much care for. "Besides, I received an email just this morning from a certain author we both know. He promised to hand-deliver his next book, and well, that's why I'm shopping today. I was thinking the lingerie store will be my first stop." She winked.

Before I could make a gagging sound, she laughed and spun toward the counter for her iced coffee.

I still had a shocked, slightly horrified look on my face when the door opened again and Paul Dalton walked through.

"Something else happen?" he asked. "You look ill."

"I'm fine." Though I vowed not to close my eyes for the foreseeable future because I was afraid I'd see Rita in skimpy underwear serenading my shirtless father. I mean, just . . . no. "Only a bad thought about something I most definitely don't want to be thinking about."

Paul looked me over, and a slow grin spread across his face. "You look comfortable."

I immediately tugged at the leg of my shorts again and pushed my bra strap back where it couldn't be seen. It lasted all of three seconds there before slipping back into view.

"I'm going for a walk."

The shocked expression on Paul's face would have been funny if it wasn't close to being insulting.

"Hey! I told you I planned on exercising more."

"You did. About twenty times over the last, what? Two, three years?"

"Yeah, yeah." I couldn't help but smile. He wasn't lying. "I'm not quite ready to start running, but I figure the walk will do me good. Work into it."

"That's probably a good idea." His smile turned into something that made sweat bead my brow. "And if you pull a muscle, just let me know. I'll work it out for you."

My breath caught, which meant I couldn't say anything when Rita headed for the door, iced coffee in hand.

"See you later, dear. Tell James I'll be waiting for him when you talk to him next."

I stared after her, torn between horror and the pleasing image of Paul rubbing the soreness out of my legs.

"How's she doing?" he asked, watching as Rita left Death by Coffee, strolled down the sidewalk, and out of view.

"Good. I think an email from my dad helped."

"An email I'm sure you had nothing to do with."

I merely shrugged. So what if I'd told Dad about Rita's recent issues with Johan. He knew as well as I did how she felt about him—my dad, not Johan—and I knew he'd know what to do to make her feel better.

Of course, now I was afraid it had worked *too* well.

"We're not sure where Mr. Morrison has gone," Paul said. "And, honestly, I'm not sure what to think about him. Alleah Trotter and Rod Maxwell are both in custody. There's enough evidence to convict both without him, so we don't need him for that, but there are still some unanswered questions that only he can answer."

"I wish I knew where he'd gone," I said, which was true.

"Me too." Paul sighed. "We found quite the collection of documents in the back of Mr. Maxwell's car. Let's just say Ms. Trotter wasn't too thrilled to hear it, considering she thought those documents were ash."

I'd heard through the grapevine that Rod had been just outside of town when his car had broken down. When he'd called for a tow, it was the police who'd showed up instead of the tow truck. I'm not sure how that had happened, but I was guessing Buchannan had something to do with it.

"That's good." And to veer the topic away from Johan, I asked, "What about Glen's murder?"

"We lucked out in that regard, too. Mr. Davis copped to the crime almost as soon as John got him alone. From what I gather, it had been eating at him since Glen was his friend, so it was something of a relief for him to get it out. He'd tried to frame Rod Maxwell for the murder, but he couldn't quite pin him down the way he'd hoped."

"By fighting with him in Geraldo's?"

"That, and with a Facebook post he created that made it appear as if the tension between Glen and Rod was far worse than it really was."

I'd wondered about that. I supposed it made sense that Calvin would want to frame someone, though I'd thought Trevor was the obvious choice. Maybe he wanted to remain friends with him, despite sleeping with his wife, and it wasn't until he was in jail for hitting Paul that he'd changed his mind. People are weird sometimes.

"Poor Glen," I said. "All he'd tried to do was help his friend's wife, and he ended up dead. He didn't deserve that."

"Most people don't." Paul gently rubbed at his eye. The bruise was fading, but it appeared to still be tender. "Davis is hoping to cut a deal, claiming he's got information on Maxwell and Trotter. Says he found out about their fraud and that was why he was with Maxwell at Geraldo's." And likely why they fought.

"Think he'll get that deal?"

"Doubt it. We've already got enough on those two. But you never know." His face brightened. "I'm not sure if anyone told you, but the money from the marathon should get to where it was supposed to go. Jen Vousden took control of everything once the others were taken into custody."

"Will she actually do the right thing?" Call me cynical, but I was having a hard time believing in anyone tied to the marathon at this point.

Paul shrugged. "I hope so."

"Why can't people just be honest?" I wondered out loud. How many people's lives were turned upside down, all because a few bad apples decided to lie and cheat their way through life?

Paul cleared his throat, "I was thinking." Another throat clear. "We never did get to talk—"

The bell above the door jangled once again as Cassie Wise entered, wearing a similar outfit as mine, though she looked far better in it.

"Sorry I'm late," she said, hurrying over to where I stood with Paul. "I hope you haven't been waiting for long."

"I haven't. Cassie, you've met Paul?" I couldn't remember if they'd actually been introduced or not. My memory of the marathon was still hazy, and a part of me hoped it would fade completely away. I was tired of thinking about murder.

The two greeted one another before Paul turned to me. "I'll let you go. We can talk later." He tipped his hat to Cassie, then to me, and then sauntered out of Death by Coffee.

"I'd say you were lucky, but I think you already know that," Cassie said.

"I do." Boy, did I ever.

"Are you ready for this?" Cassie asked, bending over to touch the floor with her palms. Her legs were straight, and my hamstrings screamed for hers.

My gaze traveled out the plate-glass window to

the town beyond. The sun was shining, and a cool breeze blew through Pine Hills. It was a good day for a walk with my new friend, the first of what I hoped would be many.

"As ready as I'll ever be."

And with the sun beating down upon us, we walked, and I couldn't have been happier.

Visit our website at
KensingtonBooks.com
to sign up for our newsletters, read
more from your favorite authors, see
books by series, view reading group
guides, and more!

Become a Part of Our
Between the Chapters Book Club
Community and Join the Conversation

Betweenthechapters.net